W9-CCL-380

Becoming
Ellen

ALSO BY SHARI SHATTUCK

Invisible Ellen

Becoming
Ellen

SHARI SHATTUCK

G. P. PUTNAM'S SONS

New York

G. P. PUTNAM'S SONS
Publishers Since 1838
An imprint of Penguin Random House LLC
375 Hudson Street
New York, New York 10014, USA

Library of Congress Cataloging-in-Publication Data

Shattuck, Shari.
Becoming Ellen / Shari Shattuck.
p.   cm.
ISBN 978-0-399-16762-1
I. Title.
PS3619.H3575B43   2015   2014049769
813'.6—dc23

Printed in the United States of America
1   3   5   7   9   10   8   6   4   2

BOOK DESIGN BY NICOLE LAROCHE

For my siblings, Dwayne, Stephanie, and Shawna.

What a wonderful journey life is with you three beside me.

Becoming
Ellen

1

Ellen Homes was feeling jaunty, which was interesting, because until recently she'd never found any use for the word *jaunty*. Sure, she'd read it, but with her particular brand of detached living, which excluded most conversations—or human interaction, if at all possible—she'd never had a chance to try it out. Jaunty, Ellen decided, felt like a sunny day with a thrilling breeze, though right now it was dark, only a couple of hours before dawn. She looked out the window of the bus at the deserted, gray, early-a.m. sidewalks and suppressed a smile.

Not that anyone would see the fleeting expression. It wasn't difficult for Ellen to fall naturally into her old state of invisibility, not for someone with as much practice as she had. For more than twenty years, Ellen had developed the knack of being absent. It had begun simply, with seeking shadows and silence, because the alternative was *notice*, which had never been a good thing for Ellen. Concentrating hard on withdrawing from the physical world, she would *will* herself to not be a part of it. Her diligence, coupled with the fact that nobody in her life had ever *wanted* to see her, had finally, and happily, resulted in the ability to virtually move through life invisibly.

At least it had until she'd run into Temerity—or, to be more accurate, until the blind girl had run into her. Without vision, Temerity had "seen" Ellen in a way that Ellen was unprepared for, a way that lacked the judgment of physical appearance, because for Temerity *appearance had no meaning.*

The bus shushed and roared in its bizarre syncopated way as it followed its familiar route. There was another word that Ellen had learned from Temerity, who was a musician—*syncopate.* "Oh, it means that the backbeat, the weaker rhythm, changes and becomes stronger than the primary beat," the violinist explained when Ellen had asked.

Syncopate, the weak becoming stronger. Ellen liked that. She wasn't sure why exactly. It might have been the way the word felt as it came out of her mouth with a rhythm of its own, in three short, distinctive bursts. *Sync-o-pate.* But she suspected the more likely reason was that she just loved words. She had spent so much of her childhood hidden in closets and attics, with only the characters of books to keep her company, that vocabulary and phrases had become her friends.

But Ellen was most fascinated by honest human interaction. Observing and noting those exchanges had tethered her to the world, but loosely, anchoring her at a safe distance. To her, strangers weren't just curiosities, they were *riveting.* Ellen studied their minute behaviors and recorded their exchanges with each other in her lined notebooks. Life's little snapshots, she called them. Turning from the window, she directed her attention to the other passengers and took out her current notebook.

Almost directly across from Ellen, a woman and a child were

slumped in their seats. They had the exhausted, malnourished look that Ellen recognized from her own neglected childhood. The girl was playing with a small plastic toy, but she looked up at the bus advertisements and pointed to an elaborate doll. Her mother glanced up and then shook her head wearily. The girl pleaded, clinging to her mother's arm, until her mother shoved her and told her to stop being stupid.

Frowning, Ellen wrote the exchange down in her notebook. But then she noticed something else. The mother's tired gaze shifted again and again to the ad, and her own eyes filled with tears, which she wiped away angrily, and then she kissed the top of the girl's head, and Ellen wrote, *Mother feels badly.*

As the bus pulled up to the next stop, the doors opened and a very large white man, ruddy, and so big that he almost filled the aisle, lumbered up the steps, where he stood, aggressively scanning the other riders. Ellen slipped farther down in her seat, and the man's erratic, drug-altered gaze slid past her without so much as a pause— as usual when she encountered people. He rubbed his fingers against his thumbs rapidly and licked his lips. Ellen could see that he was extremely unstable, either under the influence of some strong drug or mentally ill. A young, thin black man wearing jeans and a zipped-up leather jacket slipped around him and took a seat in the back.

The threatening stranger swayed slightly as the bus pulled away. Then he leaned down until his face was inches from an elderly passenger's. He spat, "Hey, geezer, give me a dollar."

The senior whimpered with fear and shook his head. "I don't have any money. Please leave me alone."

Ellen checked to see what the driver would do. She could see him watching furtively in the huge rearview mirror, but he maintained his neutrality.

In the center of the slightly raised row of seats along the back of the bus, Ellen noticed the young man in the leather jacket watching the bully with a blank face. It was the *lack* of expression that was notable—the absence of fear.

"What are you looking at?" the large man shouted down the bus at him.

"Nothing," the man in the leather jacket responded. "Less than nothing."

Ellen decided she liked him.

The bully started toward him. "You want some of this?" He pounded his chest with his fists.

"No," the other man responded lazily, suppressing a yawn. "I don't want none of that."

The driver finally spoke up. "Sir, I need you to take a seat," he called out.

For a few seconds—Ellen counted to twelve slowly—nothing happened. The disturbed man's eyes shifted right and left several times. It appeared he was trying to digest this information, and there was clearly a glitch in the processing. Then he took another step toward the back.

"Sit down, sir!" the driver called out with more force.

With surprising speed, the big man spun and ran at the driver with an apelike roar, his arms outstretched, his fingers curled into claws.

The driver saw him coming and slammed on the brakes. Ellen and the other passengers were flung forward. Ellen managed to stop her face from hitting the seat in front of her only because she already had her hands braced up against it. The young man from the back flew forward but landed on his feet at a run and kept running toward the attacker, who had his hands around the driver's neck. The bus went into a slide.

The bus's wheels hit the curb as the vehicle flipped and landed on its side. Ellen's shoulder slammed hard against the window to her immediate right. She felt a hard thump as something landed on her left hip, but everything was a mess of sounds and motion. It was hard to separate the screaming from the screech of metal on concrete and the smashing of glass from the whining of the bus's engine.

The bus rocked twice, and then found its sideways balance. Ellen raised her head and looked around.

The man in the leather jacket had grabbed the back of the emergency seats on the left and was dangling a couple of feet over the facing seats. As she watched, he let himself drop and moved immediately to the attacker, who was lying in a heap on the ground. She watched him seize the man's arms, twist them behind him, and produce handcuffs. The bus driver dangled by his seat belt, blood dripping from his forehead.

Ellen became aware that something was digging into her side. Twisting awkwardly, she looked down. The little girl who had been sitting across from her was lying on top of Ellen, her mouth open in silent shock. *Well,* Ellen thought philosophically, *at least she landed on something soft.*

"Are you okay?" Ellen asked as gently as she could. Speaking to children under any circumstances was alien to Ellen, and this wasn't just any circumstance. The girl stared at Ellen as if surprised to find that there was someone underneath her. Trying to avoid the glass shards around them, Ellen worked her fanny onto what had been the wall of the bus below the window, the glass of which was now replaced by exposed cement. Putting one arm around the girl's tiny waist, she shifted her so as not to sit on her, which, Ellen was sure, would crush the little fledgling. "Are you . . . uh . . . okay?" Ellen repeated.

The little girl looked into Ellen's eyes, said, "I think so," in a mewing voice, and then threw herself against Ellen. Ellen's whole body went rigid, but she resisted the instinct to shove her away and sat frozen, patting the child's back with an open palm.

Where was her mom? But before she could look, Ellen smelled something that disturbed her more than the moans and cries that were oozing up around her . . . smoke.

"All right, then," she said to the little girl. "We need to get out. Come on." The child didn't so much as blink. Ellen tried to think of some way to motivate her. From the depths of her past she remembered something someone had said to her when she was entering yet another unwelcoming foster home. It hadn't made the home any better, but it had helped Ellen walk through the door. So she said it now. "Be brave. Okay?" She got to her feet and pulled the girl up. The child wrapped her arms around Ellen's thigh, but she moved with Ellen as they made their way toward the window, now above them, with the words EMERGENCY EXIT in gleaming red.

Glancing back, Ellen saw that the big man in handcuffs had rocked himself onto his knees, and his crazed eyes were fixed with hard, insane hatred on the man in the leather jacket who was trying to free the driver.

"Wait here, just one second, I'll be back," Ellen said, unwinding the girl's arms from her leg. The girl allowed it, but watched Ellen's face with dazed anxiety.

Halfway to the front, Ellen was stopped by the sight of something wedged between two seats. It was the girl's mother, completely still, with her face twisted strangely against her chest. Beyond her, the bully growled and planted one foot in preparation to stand.

Without even thinking, Ellen put one foot on his chest and shoved hard. He went over backward, his weight pinning his arms underneath him. Then she took up a position beside the man struggling to release the driver's seat belt. He looked startled at her sudden appearance but he smiled, a little desperately. Bracing herself on the center divider, Ellen reached both hands up over her head and pushed up on the driver's hip with all her might. "Okay," she forced out. "Now."

With the weight somewhat eased, they were able to unfasten the seat belt, then break the driver's fall.

"Okay, I've got him, you get out!" the man in the jacket commanded.

When Ellen reached the emergency exit, the little girl attached herself to her again. The window was open, and a man was reaching down.

"Hurry!" he told Ellen as she lifted the small girl, who barely weighed more than her obese cat, up and through the exit. Then it was Ellen's turn, though she was not so eager to trust her considerable weight to other arms.

But she had no choice. So she allowed herself to be hoisted up until she flopped out onto the side of the bus and then was helped to the street before scuttling out of the way.

She was sitting on the curb, panting, when someone put the little girl in her lap. "Here's your mommy," the man said, patting the child's head.

Ellen opened her mouth to say, "She's not my . . ." and then she thought of the real mother still inside the bus, the unnatural angle of her neck, and she said nothing.

With a siren's scream of relief, the first emergency vehicle pulled up, scattering Good Samaritans and spectators alike.

Suddenly the soft brown eyes of the young man appeared in front of hers. "You guys doing okay?" As he leaned down and his jacket fell open, Ellen saw something shiny clipped to his belt over his faded black jeans and white T-shirt. A badge.

Not used to being seen, much less spoken to, Ellen just nodded and kept her gaze down.

"Thanks for your help." Ellen felt pressure on her shoulder and looked at it. Her whole body seemed to pulse and writhe, seeking escape, but he turned and called out to the paramedics, "Let's get someone to take a look at these two."

"No," Ellen objected, her heartbeat fluttering up from its already accelerated pace into a flurry of constant thrumming. "No. Please. I'm fine."

But as she said it, she saw a figure strapped tightly to a backboard being lifted down from the bus. Ellen reached out and pulled the little girl's birdlike body against her, instinctively trying to prevent the child from seeing.

When she looked down, she saw that the girl had already registered the image that Ellen knew she could never erase of her mother—helpless, unconscious, and clearly broken. Then Ellen noticed a large red bump was beginning to rise on the child's forehead.

Every instinct in Ellen was screaming *Hide! Find cover!* but for the first time in her life she did not want to listen. She needed to stay present, to help, to watch over, to be . . . was it possible? *Responsible* for someone else. Ellen's pulse steadied, settling into a furious but determined drumroll. "Yes, please, right away."

In the ER, the child was put in an individual room, her tiny figure dwarfed by the adult-size gurney. Ellen pulled up the room's single hard-plastic chair to the side of the bed farther from the door and slumped, keeping her head low and the girl's small hand in hers, marveling at the soft fragility of the bones in the tiny fingers, like slim weeds in the crack of a sidewalk, dried brittle in the sun.

The admitting nurse approached them. "What's your daughter's name?" she asked, readying a clipboard to receive the information.

"I don't know," Ellen said.

Using their linked fingers, the girl pulled herself close to Ellen's ear and whispered, barely audibly, "My name is Lydia."

"Lydia," Ellen told the woman without making eye contact. "I'm not her mom, she's . . . she's in the next room. There." Ellen pointed.

The nurse glanced up, brow furrowed, but smiled grimly. "Are you in pain, Lydia?"

Lydia twisted to look up at Ellen, who thought, *In her world, she's been told not to say anything to strangers.* Ellen nodded once to the girl, granting permission, and Lydia responded to the query with a quick shake of her head.

At that moment, two policemen entered the small room. Ellen reached up with her free hand and wrapped it tightly around her upper left arm. The spidery scars there itched as though they were freshly scabbed instead of years old. She wasn't even sure why, only that whenever she saw police in uniform, Ellen had flashes of one of her early foster homes, of a policeman with a drinking problem and a cruel streak, and she remembered the startled look of pity on the face of the teacher who had noticed the multiple scabs scratched into Ellen's arm, prompting yet another change of foster homes. Ellen shook it off now, like raindrops from an umbrella.

The first officer in scanned the room twice before he spotted Ellen. "We need to get some information and a statement from you, ma'am."

Ellen took a shaky breath and tried to think of how to tell them with the least amount of words and notice. "A guy, big, white, probably on drugs, got on the bus and attacked the driver. It crashed." She was rubbing her arm furiously.

"Are you all right?" the officer asked.

Ellen stopped the rubbing and held her fisted hand firmly in her lap, though the sensation on her arm grew into a burning so strong she imagined she could hear it sizzling. "I'm fine," she said quietly.

"Ms. . . . Homes, could I speak to you outside for a moment?"

A gale force terror struck Ellen and she squeezed her eyes shut to block the wind of it, momentarily rendered incapable of movement. Then she rose stiffly and pried Lydia's hand from hers. "I'll be right back," she told the girl.

"Don't leave." The girl spoke simply, almost inaudibly. Yet the two words crushed Ellen.

"I won't," Ellen said, then she thought, *Don't lie to her!* So she added, "Not yet." As Ellen followed the officer out, his partner sat down next to the bed. Lydia ignored him and kept her eyes riveted on Ellen on the other side of the glass.

"So, you wouldn't have any idea who we could contact to pick this child up, would you?"

Ellen's heart leapt from her chest, slammed against the wall, and slid to the floor, shriveled and bruised. She stood motionless until it flopped its way back into her chest. This was too much like her own story, no one to come for her. It was one of many chapters of her life too painful to be relived. She had survived it precisely because she did not relive it—ever.

Ellen shrugged off the shadow of her own debilitating scenario and managed a single word. "No."

The officer shook his head. "Child services is on their way, and they can place her for the night at least."

Ellen thought of the mother's battered body being carried from the bus and understood that one night would almost certainly become a hundred, then a thousand. The memories of her own mother's desertion that ambushed her now were so painful that, out of desperation, she began to shut down. The Novocain of denial, of a lifetime of conditioning herself not to feel, to look only forward, never back, began in her gut and spread. The addictive response was a hit of saturated numbness.

"Can I go?" Ellen asked the officer.

"I'm not going to keep you."

Without waiting, Ellen gratefully turned away from him and back toward the room. She would go in and tell Lydia that she had to go but that she, Lydia, would be all right. Though the only thing Ellen knew for certain was that the girl was about to become a ward of the state. Through the glass, Lydia was watching her with her strange, round eyes. She raised her hands and held them out toward Ellen.

Ellen felt something just above her stomach splinter, like thin ice fracturing, and it crumpled her. She put one hand against the window to steady herself. She tried to force her body to turn toward the doorway and go back in, but at that moment a woman in tan slacks and a tight bun walked briskly through the emergency room doors. Ellen knew what she was even before the woman took up her position in Lydia's doorway. She'd seen this same person a dozen times before, and each time they had been different ages, had different hair, skin color, were a different sex, even had different accents, but they'd all been the same person to Ellen. Not even a person really, more like a force, an *institution*.

"Lydia Carson?" the woman called out, advancing on the girl like an animal she'd struck with a car and that was bleeding on the side of the road. Through the open door, Ellen could hear her say, "My name is Serena and I'm here to help you. There's no reason to be afraid."

Ellen could not enter while the generic face of so many of her nightmares occupied that space. *What a stupid thing to say,* she thought bitterly. *Of course she's afraid, of course she has reason. Why pretend to a child who knows fear so much better than you?* She remembered hearing the same banal words, the same promises of safety and care that were never delivered. She stood, wondering if anyone could see that she was inside out and praying that they couldn't see her at all. Struggling to fend off the panic, Ellen began to take sharp, shallow gulps of air as the woman's expression, a fixed smile that did not extend to her eyes, stimulated a flurry of ugly images for Ellen. Before she fell spinning into that dark, gaping void of emotions she could not control, Ellen fled.

She reached the corner of the hallway and powered on around it, so targeted on the anonymity that would hide her beyond the exit that she did not see the man directly in her path. Ellen tried to alter the direction of her momentum—not an easy shift when her one hundred and eighty pounds were fully committed elsewhere.

"I'm glad you're okay. Are you leaving?" It was the undercover police officer from the bus.

She looked up in both surprise and relief. Somehow this capable cop in jeans didn't frighten her the way the uniforms did. The harshly lit hallway revealed that he was much older than he first appeared, closer to midthirties, she thought.

"Uh, yeah," Ellen managed.

"I'm glad I ran into you. I wanted to give you this." He pulled out a card and handed it to Ellen. She looked down at it to avoid the naked feeling of his eyes on her. It read DETECTIVE LIONEL BARCLAY. Beneath that were his precinct and phone number.

Ellen mumbled, "Sure," and pocketed the card.

"How's the little girl?" Detective Lionel Barclay asked.

"I don't know." She hesitated. For some reason she felt compelled to share something with this man. The sensation was alien, yet not as threatening as she would have thought. So she ventured, "I don't suppose she's doing very well, do you?"

Lionel Barclay sighed. "No, I don't suppose she is. I think it really helped that you were there. You seem to be good with kids."

If the detective had pulled out his gun and shot her, Ellen could not have been more startled. *Good with kids?* Kids had made her own childhood a living hell. She had been *good* at avoiding them, but that was the extent of it.

"I, uh, don't really know any kids," was all she said.

The detective laughed. "Well, let me know how you're doing. I'm really grateful to you. If there's anything you need, please let me know."

Ellen nodded shallowly and got going more carefully this time, but picking up speed as her need to be invisible grew to an aching necessity. The hospital doors opened and Ellen felt the chilly early-morning air rush over her, soothing her tattered nerves.

But the name Lydia Carson repeated itself over and over with a steady, constant beat in her brain. The mantra grew from weak to strong, forcing back the paralyzing memories.

Lydia Carson, Lydia Carson. Over and over, Ellen repeated the feeble syllables of the name in a syncopated rhythm until they steadied and grew stronger. *Lydia CARson, Lydia CARson, Lydia CARson,* like a new heartbeat born of intent.

2

"Are you sure this is coffee? It smells like something BP scraped up off the Gulf of Mexico," Temerity was exclaiming loudly to Justice as Ellen opened the door to the loft. The blind girl sniffed at the green mug and wrinkled her nose. Her brother looked beseechingly across the expanse of floor at Ellen and shook his head.

"Just add some hot water if you think it's too strong," he told his sister.

"It doesn't matter how much you dilute battery acid, it's still acid."

"You're a bit acidic yourself this morning," he countered, slurping his coffee audibly to let her know he was enjoying it.

"Which gives me an idea for this Drano." Temerity found the sink with her free hand and poured the contents of her cup down the drain. Then she set about making herself a fresh pot of coffee in what Ellen now knew was a "French press." Even after knowing Temerity for a year, Ellen was still fascinated by the way she could navigate the kitchen, not to mention the rest of the world, with nothing more than her "antennae," as she called her hands.

"You have an overdeveloped sense of taste and smell," Justice told her. "There's nothing wrong with my coffee."

"Not if you're using it to remove paint." Temerity laughed. "Hey, Ellen!" she called out before Ellen had even closed the door.

Blind people, Ellen had learned, have an overdeveloped sense of hearing, too.

"Hi," Ellen responded. She didn't know how she had come to be comfortable around these two people out of the mass of humanity she so invariably distrusted, but it had been that way from almost the moment she had met them. They were different from anyone else she'd ever met or observed. Ellen suspected that they always had been. She put the mail, which she picked up every morning on her way in, on the table.

"If you want some *drinkable* coffee, it'll be ready in five minutes," Temerity called out.

"My coffee is *fine*," Justice retorted as he ducked down to pull something from the cabinets. "I put your mug out, Ellen."

"If you value your stomach lining, you'll wait," Temerity warned.

Since she already had the shakes, Ellen thanked them both but refused. She made it halfway across the open space before Runt, the twins' big shaggy mutt, bounded up to her and ran in clumsy circles around her legs until she patted his head. On the sofa in the seating area, her cat, Mouse, raised his huge head, shook his tattered ear and a half, and stretched before tucking his butterball body back into sleep position. Runt galumphed over to Mouse and sniffed him. The cat made a low noise and placed a paw on the dog's nose.

Justice pulled out a frying pan and set it on the burner. "Eggs and toast?" he offered as Ellen reached the bickering sibs.

"Yes, please."

"You're late, young buttface," Justice said, fixing his gray eyes on her with a mock look of disapproval.

Temerity threw one hand onto a hip. "Oh no, you did *not* just call her buttface."

"Did they not take skin from Ellen's backside to repair her scar?" Justice asked with a wink at Ellen, who actually liked the familiarity, though affectionate teasing was taking some getting used to. "So, I get to call her buttface."

"It doesn't surprise me you don't know the difference between a butt and a thigh," Temerity proclaimed.

"Well, I can't call her 'thigh-face.' That's not nearly as much fun," Justice objected. Then he turned to Ellen like the big brother he'd become to her. "If you're this late again, I'm giving you a time-out."

"There was an . . . accident," Ellen said, feeling the unusual compulsion to tell them.

Temerity was measuring coffee into the pot by scooping up the grounds, then running a finger over the top to level them off, but she froze. "What happened?" she asked, her pretty brow creasing in concern. Justice, too, had suspended his task. In that moment it wasn't only their dark hair and similar body types that made them look like twins, it was also their matching expressions of deep concern.

"Uh, the bus kind of, well, crashed."

"*What?*" Temerity dropped the scoop and hurried around the counter that separated the kitchen from the open living space. She found Ellen with two exploratory sweeps of her arms and took hold of her shoulder. Ellen could tell Temerity was holding herself back from enveloping her in a hug, with which she knew Ellen was not comfortable.

"Some drugged-out guy got on the bus and attacked the driver. It turned over sideways, but luckily toward my side, so I didn't fall, just got bruised a bit." She rubbed at her left hip where she had taken Lydia's weight.

"Oh my God! It flipped over?" Temerity spun in her brother's general direction. "Why didn't you tell me about this?"

Justice just raised his arms before letting them flop to his sides. "Because . . . I'm not psychic?" He performed an exasperated roll of his eyes for Ellen's sole benefit, and then immediately became serious. "Are you all right? Were you injured?"

"No," Ellen said, though in truth she could already feel herself stiffening up into one large ache, and the gnawing in her stomach was beginning to actually hurt. "I'm hungry, though."

"I'll bet you are," Justice said emphatically. "Four eggs and toast coming right up!" He turned back with renewed purpose to the stovetop. "You want cheese on that?"

For some reason, the offer of cheese made Ellen want to cry. Normally, Justice discouraged cheese, though mostly by suggesting a healthier alternative, but he understood that calories were the pillow that cushioned Ellen from the pointy bits of life. "Yes, please," she said. She swallowed hard, and Temerity sensed the movement. She began to rub Ellen's back between her shoulder blades with the flat of her hand, a gesture that the two of them had settled on. Though Ellen was still hyperconscious of the touch, she had braced herself not to fear or resent it.

"Okay, spill," Temerity said, and climbed up on one of the stools at the counter, patting the one next to her with her free hand. "Up," she ordered.

Ellen set down her bag and obeyed. She told them about the accident, using considerably more words than she had with the police, and before she was finished, Justice had set a steaming plate of scrambled eggs smothered in cheddar cheese, with four pieces of buttered wheat toast, a fork, and a jar of jam, in front of her. Ellen picked up the fork and pushed the eggs onto some toast, then took a big mouthful. The taste and the heft of the food insulated her like a heavy jacket in a blizzard. As the result of her facial surgery nine months ago (which had made chewing difficult), she had lost close to eighty pounds. Adopting some of the twins' healthier eating habits had helped her to lose even more, but today required food, substantial and caloric. Her inner shivers subsided.

Temerity and Justice were both silent for a few moments, and then Justice said, "Adventures do seem to find you, don't they?"

"It's not my fault that guy picked my bus," Ellen objected, reaching for the giant glass of orange juice Justice set down near her plate.

Justice, who was now officially a doctor—of anthropology, it was true—had spent two years in medical school before switching majors, and that made him the resident expert on all things physical. He measured out three ibuprofen into his palm and held them out for Ellen to take. "Okay, you need to get into a very hot bath. When you are in an accident, you seize up and it's the equivalent of pulling almost every muscle in your body. Amanda is coming by tonight after her shift at the hospital, and we'll have her give you a once-over."

"But I was already at the hospital," Ellen objected.

Justice fixed her with a steady, stern look, and Temerity slapped a palm on the countertop. "Ellen, now be honest. Were you examined?"

Ellen swallowed. "Well, no," she admitted, continuing on rapidly to distract them from that line of questioning. "But there's nothing wrong with me. I was only there because of the little girl."

There was a slightly charged silence during which the siblings *would* have exchanged a look, if Temerity had vision, but the pause on its own sufficed for their version of a knowing glance. Temerity stood up. "This is going to require coffee," she said. She moved around the counter, poured the water, which had boiled moments before, into the press, put the top on, and gave it a swirl. Then she crossed her arms and faced the counter, where Ellen was seated. "What girl?" she asked.

"Of course," Justice said without enthusiasm. "There's more."

"There was a girl, on the bus, with her mother, and when the bus went over, well, the little girl, Lydia, landed on me, but her mom . . ." Ellen's voice faded out as the image of Lydia's mom jammed between the seats came back to her, and she tried to mentally swipe it away.

Justice put one hand to his forehead and shook his head slowly. "She's dead?" he asked.

"No, I don't think so," Ellen said. "But her neck was twisted really funny."

Temerity gasped a little and Ellen saw that her hands were balled into anxious fists. She still didn't understand how Temerity could feel so much for people she didn't even know, but she did. "How horrible. We have to help that little girl!" Temerity exclaimed.

"Whoa, hold on, at least let Ellen finish telling us about it before you form a posse and gallop off in a cloud of dust," cautioned Justice.

"So," Ellen went on, "I sort of stayed with Lydia until . . . someone came to get her."

"Oh." Temerity calmed down. "Thank goodness she has family."

Ellen shook her head. "Not family. Someone from social services," she mumbled, wanting to spit after the hated words had slithered from her mouth.

Justice reached across the countertop and put one hand over Ellen's. She resisted the instinct to pull away, though it was still an effort. "Ellen, I know that you had very bad experiences in foster care, worse than bad, horrible even. But not everyone does. I'm not saying it's ideal. No matter what, it must be lonely, scary, and a thousand other difficult things, but it can be the best—sometimes the *only*—choice for kids with no options."

Ellen couldn't look up at him. She knew that he was right, she'd heard stories of loving foster families, but her own experiences had taught her what it was to live in a place where your very presence was treated as some kind of repellent infection.

She did, however, have hope for Lydia that she hadn't had for herself. Lydia had one huge advantage. "Well, there's one thing that *is* different for her," Ellen said matter-of-factly. "She's a *cute* little girl. That might help. Maybe someone will want her around more than they did me because . . . you know." She dropped her eyes and her left hand went up to pull her hair down over her scar before she remembered it wasn't there, but the motion was too well memorized to stop it. "I mean, I don't know." She forced her hand down and sat on it. That would teach it.

Temerity turned away too quickly and busied herself pouring the coffee, but Ellen could see her friend's shoulders quivering slightly, the way someone does when they are crying but trying to hide it. Concerned, Ellen looked to Justice. He was shaking his head silently at her to not mention it. Ellen was glad to comply. She never knew how to identify and handle emotions, especially other people's, having had very little practical experience. Justice said, "All right. Before you two saddle up, I'm going to call Amanda and see if we can find out how the mom is doing. Maybe we're worrying for nothing, maybe she'll be all right, or some other relative has shown up."

Amanda and Justice had been dating for a few months, and she was finishing her residency at the hospital. "What do you think, Tem?"

But the slim, dark-haired girl was standing still now. Her graceful hands resting on the counter and her body leaning over it, with her head cocked. "Listen," she said in a whisper.

Ellen strained to hear what her friend could, a feat that was not always easy or even possible. In a moment, she realized that strains of piano music were seeping in through the kitchen vent. The music was exotic and enticing, all the more so because of its mysterious origin.

Temerity listened for a minute, swaying slightly. "Oh, that's nice! I've never heard it before. But I like it."

"I wonder who it is," Justice said. "You know somebody is subletting the Dlugoleckis' place while they're in Europe for a year. I think she said it was a cousin or something. Maybe it's them. Or could the Rogerses be playing the stereo?"

"No," Temerity stated firmly. "Someone is playing. Actually, I think they might be composing." Even as she said it, they heard a discordant note, and the player repeated the musical phrase, switching the notes to a more harmonious progression. And Temerity whispered, "The change to minor, yes."

Justice was gazing at his sister wistfully and it surprised Ellen. She had never seen him pity his sister, because of course that would be both unwelcome and absurd. Temerity was one of the most capable, remarkable people Ellen had ever seen, but Justice's gaze as he watched her now—swaying, a look of longing on her face—seemed somehow sad. Then the cloudiness cleared away and he turned to Ellen. "Right. Now, young lady, you go get into a hot bath and then to bed. Doctor's orders!"

The counterweight of a full stomach steadied Ellen's rocking anxiety so that now exhaustion had its chance at her. She was grateful for both the advice and the excuse to be alone. Rubbing her heavy eyes, she thanked them for breakfast, picked up her bag, crossed the huge open room, and went through the door into the hallway.

Off of that, a smaller door, barely wider than Ellen's short and stocky shape, opened onto an equally narrow stairway that had probably, before the building's conversion into lofts, been an attic access. Ellen climbed the stairs and retreated gratefully into her compact bedroom. The bed, luxurious in its queen-size comfort, beckoned her, but Ellen went first to the window.

There was only one, but it was all that was needed. It was round, Ellen's favorite shape, and at least as large in diameter as Ellen was tall, five foot four. It dominated the wall on the street side of the long, thin room. Best of all, it offered what for Ellen amounted to a panoramic view of the street below and the apartment house across the way, which had much more conservatively sized units than the co-op lofts in this one. The facing building offered one- and two-bedroom apartments, Ellen knew from the occasional FOR RENT signs out front, as well as her glimpses inside those apartments from her vantage point.

She took the prescribed hot bath, reveling as always in the treat, though this time, as she climbed into the huge tub, deep enough for even her to sink in up to her neck, she noticed large, darkening areas on both her right thigh and upper arm. *That's going to be colorful,* Ellen thought. She mused on the fact that physical bruises were often obvious, Technicolor even, but emotional wounds were either invisible or dark gray. She imagined them dark gray, anyway, like ashes. Maybe some people saw their emotional scars as burning red or dark blue, but Ellen's were so shadowy that they had no real color.

But then maybe, she thought, as she let her head rest against the porcelain rim of the tub, just maybe that was because she couldn't, ever, let them out into the light.

3

Even after nine months, Ellen still found herself mildly surprised to wake up in this bed upstairs from two people with whom she actually *willingly* cohabited. In truth, she spent most of her time alone in her small bedroom, which she thought of as her aerie. Ellen preferred it that way. She often wondered why the twins allowed her, encouraged her even, to stay here, but when she had finally steeled herself to inquire, Justice had sighed with exaggerated and uncommon impatience. "Really?" he had asked, giving her a look that said *Use your brain.* "You saved my sister's life—twice—and you wonder why we like to have you around?" He fixed her with an exasperated stare. "Oh," Ellen had exclaimed, embarrassed, "I thought it was because I was amusing." She gave him a half smile to let him know she was joking, but it hadn't been necessary. Justice had laughed outright. "That's just a perk!" he told her, and that had been the end of it.

She paid rent, of course, but Temerity and Justice had insisted on working it out on a square-footage basis, and her cozy room, compared to the loft, which took up an entire floor of the building, came to no more than her old studio apartment in the downtrodden neigh-borhood of Morningside.

She still found "relating" difficult, even with Temerity or Justice, but when she thought about it, it amazed her how she'd *accepted* sharing the loft with them, and how she had tolerated being *seen* in the process. But she was doubly surprised to find that, today, when she awoke to a gentle tap on her door, she experienced neither of her two preprogrammed, wake-up responses—fear and exhaustion. Instead, she felt calm, peaceful, and rested. Before she'd come to live with the twins, being jolted awake repeatedly to shouts, sirens, dis-turbances, relentless traffic, gunshots even, had been a daily occur-rence. Because it had been easier than going out in the world, Ellen's former life had consisted of about twelve hours of broken sleep a day. Though *rest* always eluded her.

But here, in a comfort and safety previously alien to her, she had eased into the habit of sleeping for several hours at a time. When she opened her eyes to see that the wall clock read five o'clock, she actu-ally felt ready to get up. Until she moved.

"Ellen?" Temerity called from the top of the stairs outside the small room. "I just wanted to check on you. How are you feeling?"

"Uh . . ." Ellen sat up and grimaced. Even that hurt. All of her hurt. "I'm . . . a little sore. Come in."

Temerity came through the door and trailed one hand along the wall to lead herself. When she was fully in, she called out, "You still in bed?"

"Yes," Ellen told her, sliding her legs off the edge of the mattress, which pushed the bottom of her pajama pants up to a bunch around her knees. "Ouch," she said.

"Sore?"

"Only everywhere." Ellen tried a cautious stretch. *"Ouch,"* she said again, more emphatically this time. Ellen got carefully to her feet, immediately realized that she was not ready for such an ambitious physical undertaking, and sat down again. "Any news from Dr. Amanda?" she asked as her pain brought back the memory of the night before.

Temerity needed only that. "Yes!" She took up a position, looking like she'd been called upon to recite a poem in school, with feet evenly spaced and one hand raised. "Justice talked to Amanda, and as far as we know, the mom—she can't tell us her name—is still alive, but she's in extremely critical condition, severe spinal stuff. That's all she could say without violating patient confidentiality, but she *could* say that much, because it's in the paper. Amanda couldn't tell us anything about Lydia except she's not at the hospital." Temerity's dark eyes—so dark that the pupils were almost absorbed into the irises—dimmed with frustration. "Some kind of legal-issue thingy-bob. Stupid laws."

Ellen had expected as much. "I didn't think she would be." More cautiously this time, Ellen got to her feet and tried a few hesitant steps to the chair where she'd dropped her clothes before going to bed. She picked up the drawstring pants and the big pullover sweatshirt with the intention of putting them in the laundry basket. Out of habit, she checked the pockets and found a small, stiff rectangle of paper.

It was Detective Barclay's card.

"There must be *some* way to find out if Lydia is okay and maybe help," Temerity said wistfully. She had turned to bask her face in the warmish sunlight from the window.

Ellen stared at the card. She knew that the force that was Temerity would not rest if there was a source for information. Barclay had said, *If there's anything I can do for you.* But contacting him would mean showing herself again, and she flinched at the thought of inviting another onslaught of participation when she was already drained from the last battle. She slipped the card onto her dresser and dropped the clothes into the basket, closing the lid.

As was her custom, Ellen showed up forty-five minutes early for work. The Costco night-shift cleaning crew, of which Ellen was a distinctly silent member, began at ten p.m., when the store was closed to the public. Ellen had long ago found that it was easier to avoid potential contact with the other employees if she showed up by nine fifteen to put her stuff in her locker and collect her personal smock and gloves. Then she checked the work assignment posted in the co-ed break room and went to the storage room to get her cart and replenish her cleaning supplies, thus avoiding the traffic to and from the locker rooms over the shift change.

As a secondary precaution, she entered through the loading docks instead of the employee entrance. The dock was alternately deserted or so busy that she could sneak through without much fear of revealing herself with an accidental bump or noise. She slunk up one of the access stairs to the dock and moved between two high rows of stacked crates, but found her route to the floor blocked by two men. Slipping into a narrow space between the crates, she stood waiting for them to leave. Leaning around so that she could see, Ellen recognized one of the dock managers and a worker. The manager was a very tall white man with long blond hair, which he wore pulled back in a thin ponytail. His name, Ellen knew from hearing other people use it, was Eric. She had noticed him because he stood out from most of the dockworkers, who were almost uniformly either Hispanic, of stocky build, or both. Eric, by contrast, was thin, blue-eyed, and his skin was pale, despite being often suntanned.

The other man, Daniel, was shorter, stockier, and darker.

"Listen up," Eric was saying in a harsh, warning tone. "I made sure that Thelma will take the blame for the ruined crates of fruit." He glared down at Daniel. "But it's the last time I cover for you. If you get caught using, I won't know squat about it. Understand?"

"Sure, sure, I know."

This acquiescence seemed to restore Eric to good humor, and he punched the smaller man's arm playfully. "Back to work, buddy, and be cool!" The two men moved on, leaving clear Ellen's way into the break room.

She was pleased with the job list for the night. She had the paper goods section, one of the more remote and isolated aisles. *Excellent.* She left the locker room, went quickly through the thankfully empty break room, and moved on down a long hallway to the large supply room, where all the cleaners' carts and products were stored.

Since she was there first, she picked one of the few carts that rolled straight when she pushed it. It was going to be a good night.

Then she went back out into the hall. This was a tricky bit of the evening for remaining unseen, as there was nowhere to blend in if she came across anyone else, though over the years she'd developed a strategy. *Whenever possible, have a plan* was one of Ellen's most basic rules of survival. Before rounding the corner of the L-shaped hallway, she snuck a look around it and spotted a form moving toward her from the far end of the hall. It was an extremely compact man with the redundant, and unwelcome, nickname of Squirt. Pushing her cart near the wall, Ellen stooped down behind it and pretended to busy herself looking for something.

Between the cart's wheels, Ellen watched the man's work boots go by and thought that they could easily be mistaken for a child's. He went on around the corner, and Ellen emerged again, nudging the cart along more quickly toward the open floor of the warehouse. But she still had almost twenty-five minutes before the store closed and her shift began, so she found her favorite hideout, a seldom-used broom closet, in which she had stashed a folding chair, a paperback, and a few snacks. Pulling a plastic bucket from a high shelf, she selected a pack of peanut butter crackers from her stash of snacks and settled back to wait out the stream of other employees preparing either for work or departure.

The book, recommended by Justice as a "classic," was charming, though its theme of finding husbands for five sisters mystified Ellen. She had never even imagined wanting a husband, much less *having* to get one, but she was enjoying the words and the story when she heard loud voices outside the closet. Ellen closed the book and pressed her ear against the crack between the door and the wall.

In the hallway outside, Ellen could make out the distinctly throaty voice of Thelma, the produce manager. Thelma kept to herself and out of everyone else's business, unlike many of her other coworkers, who had a great deal to say about Thelma and her "wife." Though Ellen didn't care for the mean-hearted talk, she found it impossible to avoid hearing it, especially on the docks. It was one of the downsides—or benefits, depending—of being unnoticed. The other voice she identified as Eric's. They were having a heated argument about some exotic fruit spoiling because it had been left out in the weather. Ellen assumed that it was the same ruined stock she had already overheard Eric tell Daniel he had falsely blamed on Thelma.

"You know those crates were marked 'Perishable,'" Thelma was saying forcefully, though she was clearly in control of herself. "Don't try to make it sound like I just forgot to stock it, you never moved it to refrigeration. It was on the asphalt for God's sake!"

"It's your responsibility to get the perishables onto the floor," Eric shouted at her with genuine indignation.

It was always interesting when this happened, thought Ellen. She had learned over the years that people got the most aggressively defensive when they were lying. She assumed that was because their carefully formulated story was being challenged. Clearly, Eric had put some work into his version.

"Lower your voice," Thelma snapped at him. "I'm not here for you to yell at. This is *your* screwup, and *you're* going to fix it."

"Nope, not my problem. I already explained to the general manager that I told you it was there and you just ignored me."

Thelma took in a breath so sharply that it hissed. "That is a lie, and Billy knows me better than that. And even if you did tell me, it's not my job to forklift crates up off the pavement outside the loading dock."

Ellen heard the taunting note enter Eric's next comment. "Well, that's not where they found it, is it?"

"You moved it *after* it spoiled! You know you did. When I found it this morning it was in the same spot I just cleared and shelved last night!"

"Aw, too bad, wittle baby." The insulting smugness turned Ellen's stomach. "Well, that's not the way the powers that be see it, so suck it."

"Listen to me," Thelma said in a low, composed voice. "If you don't go to Billy and tell him what really happened, I'll—"

"You'll what?" Eric sneered. He used the baby voice again to say, "Hit me? Tell your girlfwend on me? Ooh, I'm so scared."

Ellen reached up and flipped the closet's light switch off, then she turned the knob and pulled the door open a millimeter. Thelma's back was to her, but she could see Eric's face over the top of Thelma's head. Though the produce manager was much shorter than Eric, she was a strong woman and she did not seem intimidated, and that, it appeared, Eric had not anticipated.

"I'll report you to corporate," Thelma said, pausing while he laughed. Then she went on. "And not just for this. I'll let the 'powers that be' know all about the rumors that you and your buddies are doing drugs at work and faking your time cards. All of that will go in my report, too." She turned and started away. Ellen could see the determined set of her face.

Behind her, Eric blanched and his whole body went slack, but his brief lapse into weakness appeared to only fuel his anger, and he pulled himself together. "It's my word against yours!" he shouted. "I'll say you're making it all up because you're afraid of men. It's not like *that's* a big secret."

Thelma froze and spun back. "What did you say?"

"What? Aren't you supposed to be all proud and equal rights and crap? You decided to be a dyke." He sniggered, but the sound choked off in his throat as Thelma reversed direction and strode fearlessly back to him.

She crossed the few feet in a beeline to Eric, not stopping until she was inches away from him. A thin sheen of sweat appeared on the dock manager's face and reflected the ugly fluorescent lights overhead. It gave him a nauseous, puce tinge. Thelma gazed steadily up at Eric, her fists balled and her body rigid with controlled fury. "I am *gay*," she pronounced emphatically. "But straight or gay, I will never be afraid of a bigoted idiot like you."

Clearly unsure of how to deal with this woman he couldn't bully, Eric muttered something inaudible and backed away, beating a hasty retreat.

When he was gone, Thelma stood looking after him for a moment, head high and perfectly still. Noble, really, Ellen thought. Then Thelma checked to make sure she was alone, and burst into tears.

Startled at the reaction, Ellen silently closed the tiny gap that had given her a view into Thelma's world and took out her notebook. She recorded the conversation, Thelma's reaction, and then added a comment—*Frightened bullies can be dangerous.*

She packed her book away, switched off the light, checked to make sure the hallway was clear, and went to collect her cart, which she'd left outside the break room. But she stopped a few yards away when she saw that she was not alone.

Standing near the break room door with their own carts were two of the other night-shift cleaners, whom Ellen had nicknamed the Crows because of their habit of sticking their beaky noses into everyone else's business. Gossip was the Crows' religion, as far as Ellen could tell, and church was in session. Ellen took her cart and moved away quickly.

Just inside the dock doors that led to the sales floor, Ellen could see Squirt preparing to climb onto the large floor polisher. One of the dockworkers shouted at him, "Hey, buddy, need a leg up?" He and his friends laughed meanly. Squirt ignored him, but encouraged by the amusement, the worker shouted out again. "Hey, Squirt! They call you that because if you don't have a step stool for the urinal you squirt all over the floor?"

The small man froze, and turned. He said quietly, "My name is not Squirt. And just back off, Ed."

There was a low muttering from Ed's buddies. Challenged, he

moved forward with his chest thrust out and planted himself right in front of the smaller man, blocking his way to the machine. "Lighten up, munchkin, or I'll send you back to Oz."

"Get out of my way," the smaller man said, and stepped forward.

But Ed didn't move. Instead, he reached out and shoved Squirt, who lost his balance, then recovered and came back swinging.

"Stop it! Right now!" The sharp voice belonged to Billy, the general manager. "Ed, gather your stuff and meet me in my office."

"What?" Ed shouted indignantly. "He tried to hit *me*."

"No, sir." Billy was shaking his head. "I saw you push him and I heard you try to provoke him. That kind of physical intimidation is illegal, not to mention just plain mean. I have to fire you, and you know it. Get your stuff."

Ellen felt a little rustle and a rush of pleasure in her chest like the reverberation of a crowd cheering, and moved on. It was so seldom that the good guys won.

Later that night, when her break usually took Ellen either back to the closet or to one of the restroom stalls to enjoy her coffee and snacks in private, she chose instead to pay another visit to the docks.

As she passed through the produce section on her way there, she saw Thelma stacking an orange fruit that Ellen didn't recognize. Slowing her step, Ellen watched Thelma for signs of her earlier outburst, but instead she saw only a determined focus on the woman's face, and her lips were moving as though she might be singing. Ellen couldn't hear anything because Squirt was coming near with the floor polisher. As he passed, he called out, "Evening, Thelma!"

The produce manager stopped, turned, and shouted above the machine's whirring brushes, "Hey, Johnson!" and the two slapped a high five as he passed her, his normally scowling, defensive face opening into a friendly grin during the fleeting exchange.

Johnson. So that's Squirt's real name, Ellen thought. As she went on her way, she wondered at the difference that small amount of respect had made to the man, and it had cost Thelma nothing.

The crated merchandise on the docks offered multiple nooks in which to lurk unseen during her break. Ellen found a spot in the shadow of some tall boxes with a clear vantage point to the edge of the truck-loading platform and set her coffee and notebook on one box and herself on a lower one.

For a while, she drank her coffee and munched her snacks in relative peace, as there was nothing to see, but it wasn't long before there was something to write. The distinct, earthy smell of marijuana came drifting to Ellen's nostrils. Dutifully, she recorded the wafting misdemeanor.

Ellen had never tried the drug, but the twins had. Justice had told her that "some restrictions apply." Both marijuana and liquor, Justice had explained to Ellen, impaired the ability to operate any kind of machinery, so driving under the influence of either was taboo. Temerity said that was fine by her, as *her* ability to drive was somewhat impaired anyway, due to the fact that she couldn't read the road signs, or find the car.

So when Ellen saw Eric and Daniel emerge from the men's restroom looking distinctly red-eyed, she wondered if it was a good idea when Daniel climbed onto a forklift.

Eric stood with his back to the dock office door, counting out some bills. He stuffed them in his pocket, then went in.

Just as Ellen was putting her notebook away to return to work, she heard a shout and looked up. On the forklift, Daniel had miscalculated. Instead of inserting the teeth of the lift into the flat beneath a huge box marked KETCHUP, 50 ONE-GALLON SIZE, he came in too high and punctured the box. There was a crunch, a spurt, and the smell of sweetened tomato sauce wafted across the open space. It made Ellen want a hot dog.

Alerted by the sound of the impact to a loss of inventory, Eric came out of the office and stood with one hand on his hip as he stroked his blond hair nervously with the other. Ellen wrote down the incident, included the time, packed up her notebook and pen, and went back to finish her shift, *after* she microwaved a wiener.

Ellen rode home on the bus with her fingers clenched on the back of the seat ahead of her, watching with suspicion every passenger who boarded, but the ride was uneventful, and she allowed herself a deep sigh of relief when she reached her stop.

Once she was on her way down the deserted sidewalk to the alley that led to the loft's door, Ellen's thoughts returned to Eric and his behavior. It had nothing to do with her, of course, and a few months ago she would have noted it in one of her books, been diverted by the "snapshot," and forgotten it. But now . . .

The problem, of course, was that Ellen wasn't a tattletale. First of all, being invisible required that she never, ever draw attention to herself. Second, revealing anyone's bad behavior would have been suicide in her unprotected childhood world *if* she had ever been able to stand up in front of "authority" and speak the truth.

But she couldn't. Authority hadn't been reliable or even very fair, and it definitely had never offered her protection from the very things and people she might have ratted out. Her life worked best when she went unnoticed. Nonetheless, it made Ellen squirm to think that doing a dangerous job on drugs could seriously hurt someone.

Still, facing or calling on *authority* was not in the game plan. Though Ellen knew she had made decisions, had acted on things that had changed her life and, on reflection, others' lives as well, they had been last-second decisions, spontaneous and unplanned. *Fate.* And Ellen knew that without Temerity, those split-second instincts would have been the beginning and the end of her involvement. That was just the way it was for her.

Yet, she thought as she turned the key in the huge door and went to check the mailbox, *maybe there's another way.*

A different way.

4

When Ellen reached the fourth-floor landing, Temerity was coming out of the apartment with Runt on a leash. Overcome with enthusiasm, as usual, the dog panted and barked. It began with a throaty growl then rose to a shrill high note on the end. The sharp sound echoed painfully in the stairwell.

"Runt, hush! Hi, Ellen," Temerity said. "I'm taking Runt out to the dog park, want to come? We could pick up some muffins at Tami's and eat them there."

Ellen considered the stairs, thought about the oversize muffins Temerity often brought home from the organic bakery on the corner, and her mouth watered. As much as Ellen had enjoyed the cellophane-wrapped cousins of those muffins over the years, when Temerity had brought her a freshly baked one, still warm, it had been a food revelation.

It was chilly out this morning, with a gray sky and air roiling with mist, and the thought of a scalding-hot cup of coffee and a muffin straight from the oven was irresistible. Plus, she didn't like Temerity to take Runt out alone, he was not the brightest of his species. Temerity liked to say that if he was a child, he would be in remedial math.

"Sure, let me set my bag inside." Ellen did so, left the mail on the table, and then came back out, closing the door behind her. "Where's Justice?" He was usually the one who took Runt for his daily constitutionals.

Temerity made a huffing noise. "Didn't come home. Again. He left me a message asking me to do his doggy duty." The palm side of a long-fingered hand shot out toward Ellen's face. "I know. I set you up. Don't even go there."

Ellen asked, "Dr. Amanda?"

"The one, the only, Dr. Amanda!" Temerity said, though it seemed to Ellen that there was a shiver of dislike or . . . no, that wasn't it . . . more like annoyance in the flippant comment. Temerity unfolded her white, red-tipped stick, took it in one hand and the leash firmly in the other. "Please don't kill me," she said to Runt as they started down the stairs.

On the second-floor landing, a young man was going into the apartment. He was holding a stack of mail and wearing only pajama bottoms and slide-on slippers. He was tall, and his face had an intelligent look about it, the kind that really took in the world around him. So few people lived in this building that Ellen had seldom encountered anyone on these stairs, and to judge from the way this person half hid himself behind the door, he hadn't expected to meet anyone, either. Ellen slipped in behind Temerity but peered curiously at the man's face as he turned to regard the trio. Runt, sensing a stranger, broke into a frenzy of barking. "Hush, Runt!" Temerity called above the din as the man said at the same time, "Settle down, boy."

Temerity tilted her head to listen, and shushed Runt again, who looked up at her, then settled into an enthusiastic panting. Temerity called out, "Sorry! He's a very gregarious puppy. Just likes to hear himself."

"I've got a brother like that. See you, Runt." The man smiled at her. "Sorry for my state of undress. Didn't know anyone would be coming down."

Temerity waved a hand. "Oh please, wander around naked, it makes no difference to me."

"Well . . . that's sort of disappointing." The deep voice was riddled with humor. "Thanks for the invitation, though." He closed the door, his eyes tracking Temerity as she turned away with a grin of approval.

Temerity patted Runt's head and sniffed. "I like his scent," she said. "Like fresh pine and . . . something spicy . . . black pepper, that's it." Ellen smiled. Temerity had told her that everyone had a unique smell, which, to her, was as distinct as a face was to someone who could see.

They got to the street and walked along together for a few minutes, with frequent stops as Runt paused to pee on each and every lamppost he encountered, while Ellen thought about what could be tainting Temerity's mood. Ellen was still confused by her friend's earlier sarcasm about Amanda; it gave her the constant sensation of a missed step. Finally, she said softly, "I thought you liked her."

"Who?" Temerity turned her pretty face halfway to Ellen, indicating that she was listening.

"Dr. Amanda."

Temerity looked surprised. "I do. She's great, smart, funny, devoted to helping people, and she's crazy about Justice. I couldn't really ask for more." She sighed quietly and added under her breath, "For him." Then, as the sound of a bus approached from behind them, she took a firmer grip on the leash. Runt was well known for his fanatical pursuit of buses. Somewhere in his shallow canine brain those big, noisy, rolling boxes needed to be captured and brought down a notch or two. Conversely, he was afraid of squirrels. He growled and bristled as the bus passed, but Temerity kept a firm pressure on the leash and intoned to him hypnotically, "Don't do it. Don't look at it. Don't chase it. Don't try to bite it."

Runt turned a hopeful face up to his human and made a noise like squeaky brakes as the bus went past. Ellen translated this noise as *Then can I just lick it?*

They resumed their stroll. "So . . ." Ellen faltered. She was lost again, unable to translate into something coherent this foreign language called human relations. Temerity had said she liked Amanda. Ellen liked Amanda, too. The young doctor had overseen her recovery from surgery, after calling in favors to get the surgery done in the first place.

"So . . . what?" Temerity asked after a few seconds.

"Uhm . . . Why don't you seem happy? I mean, about her."

They had reached the crosswalk and Temerity felt for the crossing signal. When it cleared for them, the flashing WALK sign was accompanied by a tweeting beep—not unlike birdsong, but too uniform—that meant *go* to the visually impaired in the neighborhood. Temerity still paused to listen carefully that the traffic had stopped in both directions before she started out into the street.

Temerity's brow had furrowed and her lips tightened a little as they crossed. She didn't speak until they got to the bakery, where she handed over the leash and told Ellen she'd be right back. "The usual?" she asked brightly.

"Yes, please," Ellen answered softly, glancing self-consciously at the other pedestrians, though no one paid the least amount of attention to her, as usual. She whispered, "And a coffee with—"

"Extra cream," Temerity finished for her, barely mouthing the words. Then she leaned over to pet Runt's head and muttered out of the side of her mouth to Ellen, "Sorry, I didn't see that you were invisible today." She giggled.

Ellen shifted her feet. She told Temerity, "It's been kind of a weird week."

Temerity shook her head. She whispered to Ellen, "I know. Sorry. Sometimes I don't see the forest for the trees." She barked out a laugh and went in to be enveloped in the sweet scent of baking, while Ellen waited outside, envious, but also grateful that her friend had the courage to go where she did not.

To avoid the increasing stream of pedestrians going to work, Ellen led Runt down the side of the bakery and stood against the brick wall. A window, the glass of which was opaque and laced with wire, was partially open, and through the small space wafted the smell of contentment. Standing on her toes, Ellen could see into the kitchen. The gleaming stainless-steel work surfaces were scattered with flour and dough, and two bakers, both plump and dressed loosely in white, worked with silent satisfaction. A small radio played jazz piano. It was a stark, yet beautiful, paradise.

Ellen was so enthralled by the surfeit of intriguing scents and sights overwhelming her senses that she forgot to watch for Temerity. Looking up quickly, she saw her friend turning in a slow circle and whispering to thin air. Ellen hurried back to her and took the paper bag—emanating wisps of that specific dreamland—and one of the cups of coffee so that Temerity could work her stick. They walked the remaining three blocks to the dog park and let Runt off his leash. He gamboled off to investigate the other two dogs. When one greeted him with a playful bounce, Runt took off like a shot for the far side of the run.

The two women sat next to each other on their usual bench and wrapped their scarves tightly up around their necks while they sipped the coffee and ate the muffins. Temerity tore her food into bite-size pieces and placed the measured portions into her mouth. It was really quite graceful, which was the opposite of what Ellen had imagined it would be like to watch a blind person eat.

Temerity said suddenly, "I suppose it's because I know things will change."

Ellen looked around. But except for a couple of other dog owners on the far side of the park, they were alone in the misty a.m. "Wh-what?" she stuttered.

"Amanda and Justice. I suppose I am sort of sad—even though I'm really happy for *him*—because, you know, it won't be *us* anymore." She hummed as she placed another morsel of muffin in her bow-shaped mouth. "Selfish, I know."

But Ellen didn't know. She'd never had a sibling, much less a twin, or even a parent, so it was impossible for her to find a comparison. "But what about you?" Ellen asked, suddenly fearful. "What if *you* find somebody else?"

Temerity frowned. "Oh, I don't think there's much fear of that," she said. "Not a huge market for blind chicks."

Ellen twisted to try to relieve the tightness in her torso. "Have you ever, uh, you know, had a boyfriend?" Her face flushed hot.

To Ellen's amazement, Temerity wrinkled her nose. "I've dated. But the only guy I felt serious about . . ." She hesitated. "Well, let's just say it didn't work out."

"Why not?" Ellen couldn't stop herself. The thought of Temerity moving on and not being around anymore opened a rent from the base of her throat to her midchest.

"He was fooling around, right in front of my useless eyes," Temerity answered quietly.

Ellen shifted, sliding an inch closer to her friend.

"It sucked," Temerity continued. "But Justice would have to be blinder than me not to see that Amanda's worth keeping!"

"Oh," Ellen said. A sense of churning, open space came into existence below her but she didn't want to look down because she was afraid of what might be there. "Is Justice leaving?" Her throat had suddenly constricted and the last word came out in a breathy wheeze.

Temerity threw her head back and laughed with her whole body. "God, I hope so!" she half shouted. Then, before Ellen could find her balance, Temerity wrapped an arm around Ellen's thickly jacketed shoulders and said, "Look, it's normal, natural, for him to find someone and get his own life. That's what he's supposed to do. That's all good. It's just that, I suppose it doesn't make it any easier to let go, because . . . well, I'm jealous, if you want me to go ahead and expose my most sordid thoughts. God, listen to me. Pathetic. Who knows? Right?" She stood up. "Maybe Mr. Right is out there somewhere." She took three steps and called out loudly, "Prince Charming? Charming? Yo! P.C., I'm waiting!" She sighed and turned back to Ellen. "I don't hear any hoofbeats." She cocked an ear as if listening. Across the park, Runt, unable to distinguish canine from equine, perked up his ears. "I'm just not holding my breath."

"Me neither," Ellen said. "I hear it causes brain damage," she joked.

Temerity snorted. "So do relationships, so breathe away!" She sat back down.

Relaxing back, Ellen looked up at the depthless sky and just let herself fall up into it, relishing the unavoidable cold. She liked the gray morning, the dogs chasing one another, the warm cup in her hand, and Temerity's laugh. Most of all, she loved Temerity's laugh. It was the one fearless thing she knew.

"All right, tell me about work, any drama?" Temerity asked, effortlessly switching gears and moods. Change was one of the many things that Temerity, unlike Ellen, was good at.

So Ellen did. She told her about Eric doing and probably selling drugs and his fight with Thelma, and who said what. Last, she told her how Thelma had burst into tears when she thought she was alone. "She always seems so, you know, in control," Ellen said. "I don't know why she would cry like that."

Temerity was shaking her head. "Because she was *hurt.* It's hard to be different, as you and I well know, and when people mock you for it, or pretend that you are less than them, it's really hard to keep your head up."

Well, that was as true as anything Ellen knew, which, she thought, wasn't much.

"I hate mean people." Temerity, riled now, got to her feet again. "I'd like to teach him a lesson!" She raised her hands in mock attack mode. "We could just sneak up behind him and . . ." She took a step away from the bench and flipped right over Runt, who had slunk silently back across the damp grass.

Ellen said, "Yeah, he'll never see us coming."

Temerity hooted with laughter and turned onto her back on the chilly ground to enjoy it. Runt put both front paws on her chest and stood on her, panting with happiness. As she struggled to untangle herself from the dog's shaggy form, Temerity called out, "Ouch! Runt, get off!" He didn't. *This,* he seemed to be thinking, *is the right idea. Everybody down on the grass!*

Ellen got up and pulled Runt away. Temerity lay there for a minute more, inhaling deeply and angling her face upward. "The sky feels nice today."

Ellen looked up and around, thinking that Temerity didn't need to look at things to see them. Yes, the sky did feel nice today, cold and bracing. Temerity liked things like that.

Ellen fastened Runt's leash to his collar and they made their way back home. As Temerity was unlocking the door in the alley, she suddenly stopped and turned her head sharply to the right. Runt, confused by the lack of the door opening, tilted his head up at her and whined.

"Shush," Temerity said to him so sharply that he actually did, turning to look over his own back.

And then Ellen heard it, too. A scraping, grating sound. "What is that?" Temerity whispered to her. But Ellen couldn't see anything. For a few seconds, her eyes scanned the seemingly empty alley. Then, without warning, Runt bolted, yanking Ellen along by the leash wrapped around her wrist. She almost went down, then recovered her step and pulled back hard. But Runt dragged her, resisting, over to a grating about two feet square set just above the concrete that Ellen assumed was some kind of vent from the basement of the building. The dog stopped abruptly and the sudden loss of tension dropped Ellen backward onto her bottom. She landed with a bump, sitting on the sidewalk, facing the grate.

Ellen found herself looking at something behind the grate in that murky darkness, something so shiny and blue that it startled her. It was shocking that such a dank place could produce such vibrant color. The bright pair of eyes stared at Runt until the dog thrust his shaggy muzzle up against the metal and barked. The eyes blinked in alarm and disappeared.

"Ellen? What is it?" Temerity called after her.

"I'm not sure," Ellen said. "But I think it's a person. Maybe somebody lives down there."

"In the basement? But that's not an apartment, it's a . . . Oh."

There was no need to say any more. The space behind the grating, the best Ellen could make out, was an unfriendly one. It had no heat and very little light—a dismal, damp, and moldy place.

But that didn't mean that someone didn't live there.

5

When Ellen woke up around four thirty that afternoon, she came downstairs to find Temerity rehearsing with Rupert. Temerity played the violin in the city's symphony orchestra, and Rupert played the cello. Occasionally they got together for some extra rehearsal.

When Ellen came in, Rupert, a very large and shy man, stood up and offered his embarrassed hello to Ellen, fumbling even those few words. Ellen understood that the cellist was very private and not very social, traits she shared, to say the least, which was the reason she had been able to allow him to see and converse with her.

"Sorry," Ellen said, "I didn't mean to interrupt. I'm going to make something to eat."

"What are you making?" Temerity asked, looking hopeful.

Completely unsure of either what she had or what she *could* make out of whatever it was, Ellen said, "I don't know yet." She opened the fridge and leaned in to see what was there. "But . . . it will definitely involve bacon."

"I'm in!" Temerity said. "Ooh, actually, there's some heirloom tomatoes I bought and some really good sourdough bread. How about a BLT?"

"And . . . what else goes on that?" Ellen asked.

"What else is on a bacon, lettuce, and tomato sandwich?" Temerity said wryly. "If only there was some clue." She tapped her bow against her cheek, leaving rosin marks.

"Mayo?" Ellen tried to cover her ignorance.

"Sure, if you want. I'll have mine with mustard. Rupert?"

His round, naturally splotchy face reddened, an automatic accompaniment to speaking. "I'll have mayonnaise, please."

Even though Ellen had helped Justice and Temerity prepare meals many times now, she was unfamiliar with preparing food for other people by herself. Her experience with cooking before she came here had almost exclusively been microwaving frozen foods, but had included the use of the stovetop to make bacon. True, she'd mastered boiling water, and recently learned that it could be used to make pasta, as long as she used jarred sauce. She could also now make a salad and even the occasional bowl of rice. She steeled herself to put the BLT ingredients together, unsure if she should toast the bread first. She decided yes. After years of toaster strudel or frozen waffles as a part of at least one meal every day, she could handle a toaster. *Uncooked bread, beware!* she thought. Then, *No, wait, that's not right. Bread is already cooked.* For a blissful moment, the smell and the freshly-baked-to-golden-perfection loaves through the window at the bakery rushed her senses. Ellen thought of the bakers, and she envied those wizards who had mastered the magic to produce something so excellent from . . . well, she wasn't exactly sure what all went into bread. Still, she was in awe.

From the end of the room, under the huge bank of windows

gracefully draped with their sheer white curtains, came the magnificent sound of the musicians playing. The melody created a moving picture in Ellen's mind of a sunny country road, or at least that's how Ellen imagined it, though she'd never been to the country, or even out of the city.

While she was frying the thickly sliced bacon, her favorite kind, Mouse came and purred at her ankles until she gave him his share, a nice fat slice, which disappeared quickly into his pillowing folds of furry tummy. The music rolled on through Ellen's imagination as the two instruments each lent their own unique sound to create a new, more glorious one. The piece ended as she was slicing the sandwiches.

She sighed as the last of the vibrations faded away into the open space. Symphonies were stories, they took her places, places Ellen knew she would otherwise never dare to go, and she was grateful for the journey.

They sat at the counter and ate their sandwiches. "This is delicious," Rupert said as he washed down a huge bite with half a glass of milk.

Ellen agreed, pleased that Rupert shared her love of food, especially bacon.

Temerity finished off her sandwich and announced, "I've got to go get dressed. Talk to you at rehearsal tomorrow, Rupert. Thanks for coming over here."

Rupert muttered something inaudible, turning so red that his splotches took on a quilted effect against the remaining areas of pale skin.

To Ellen's surprise, though, Rupert did not immediately hurry to put away his instrument and leave as he normally did. Instead, he sat shifting on his stool, which made it creak and groan a bit. He cleared his throat several times but said nothing. Ellen got up and put the dishes in the dishwasher, an amazing luxury that had been yet another adjustment for her. Albeit a good one.

"Uhm, Ellen?" Rupert said, his voice squeaking slightly.

Ellen looked up at him, but he was twisting his calloused fingers into knots and studying them with intense interest.

"Do you like movies?" he asked.

Ellen wasn't sure how to respond, she didn't really care for movies or TV. Rupert was still fascinated by his fingers.

"Movies?" Ellen said, confused. "Uh, yeah, I guess. I mean, I don't watch many, just the ones I get on my little TV. I mostly like the older ones. You know, the black-and-white ones." She turned away again, and then remembered that Temerity had told her it was polite to ask someone about themselves if they asked about you. So she added, "Do you?"

"Yes." Rupert nodded enthusiastically, still without looking at her. "There is a theater not far from here that plays those kinds of old movies. Maybe you've been there, the Royal. I thought . . ." He trailed off.

"I don't go to theaters," Ellen explained quickly. "It's because of, well, you know, I don't really like to be around people if I don't *have* to be . . ." She trailed off as well. Rupert knew some things about her, but she wasn't sure he knew how she was when it came to sliding through public unseen, or avoiding it altogether.

"Oh, I see. Okay. Well, I guess I should go." He climbed clumsily off the stool and made his way over to where he'd left his cello with his unique, rolling walk, which Ellen found charming, and began the loving process of wiping it down with a soft cloth before he laid it gently in its case. Ellen liked the way he did that. When he was all set, he went to the door of the loft. "Bye," he said. He opened the door and then stopped. "Ellen, I just thought I would tell you that there's always a great old comedy at the Royal every Tuesday night, and there's never very many people, and you could go in once it's dark. I was thinking . . . Well, I just thought you might like to know." Having got this out, he went through the door as fast as he could and pulled it shut behind him.

Temerity reemerged from the hallway door, dressed now in brown jeans, an orange top, and blue boots. "Was that Rupert leaving?" she asked, smiling a little like a cat as she came to the counter.

"Yes."

"How did it go?" Temerity said in a growly voice, raising her eyebrows twice.

Ellen studied her. "Uh, okay, I guess." Temerity was still grinning like a kid with a hidden candy stash. Ellen didn't get it. So she asked, "Why?"

"Oh, no reason." Temerity rubbed her palms together and climbed onto a stool, placing her elbows on the counter.

Confused, Ellen finished putting away the dishes. "He said something about a place nearby that plays old movies. Then he got all . . . *Rupert* . . . you know, and he went."

Temerity let her head fall to the countertop with a thump. "Ellen," she groaned from between her arms flopped around her face, "did you say 'No'?"

"To what?" Ellen was completely befuddled now.

Slowly, Temerity's face rose toward her. "Ellen Homes. Please do not tell me that Rupert finally got up the nerve to ask you out and you turned him down."

The floor heaved, and the walls spun. Ellen reached out and grabbed the countertop to steady her environment. "But . . ." she sputtered. "He . . . he just . . . he didn't ask me *that*. He just said I might like the comedies they play on Tuesdays, and that it would be in the dark and not crowded and . . ." Her voice died as she realized how very difficult it must have been for Rupert to ask her to go, and she, Ellen—who had never been asked to go anywhere—had missed it entirely.

Temerity was nodding. "Exactly."

Ellen was terrified. What did this mean? But even stronger than her own fear of being asked to participate was her mortification that she might have hurt Rupert's feelings. His was a fragile soul. "I didn't know," she said lamely.

"Well . . ." Temerity brightened and slid to her feet with a small jump. "Now you do. Okay, time to find out what we can about Lydia's mom. We'll deal with the Rupert situation later. Let's go spying!"

Spying was good. There was no interaction in spying. The very idea of being present without being known calmed Ellen. She went to get her coat.

Still, the whole walk to the hospital, which was only a few blocks away, Ellen was jittery and uncomfortable. It felt like she had swallowed a large egg that had hatched and something reptilian was thrashing around in her stomach, trying to crawl out. *Rupert had asked her to a movie. A movie. Rupert. A grown man had asked her to do something. Out.* No, no matter how hard she tried, she could find no way to still the squirming, many-tentacled sea creature that had nested in her gut. There just wasn't any place to put it, or the confusion that it introduced.

When they went through the hospital's lobby to the guard station, the woman with a braid thicker than Temerity's arm said hello to Temerity and told her to go on through. Temerity had become familiar to most of the security staff when she came in with Ellen so often during her rehabilitation. Ellen had tried hard to stay invisible, but it had been next to impossible with so many visits and sign-ins. The exposure to doctors and staff had been a nightmare for Ellen, and even now she winced and placed her left hand against the side of her face. For the thousandth time, she was startled to find it smooth.

They first went to the waiting area outside ICU, but after about twenty minutes they had not seen or heard anything useful. The sea beast was now doing flip-flops in her gut so Ellen proposed a trip to the cafeteria to feed it, since that usually helped. Temerity agreed, and they made their way back to the first floor.

They chose snacks and sat at a table by the window. Then Temerity reviewed their situation.

"All right, all we have is a last name, Carson. I'm assuming that she and Lydia share a last name."

"I'll bet they do," Ellen said. "They didn't look to me like there was a father, if you know what I mean." She wasn't sure if Temerity would, but Ellen had spent so many years watching and observing people that she had learned to draw certain conclusions. Ninety percent of the kids she had crossed paths with in the foster system had never even known their fathers, and no father had appeared at the hospital, so it wasn't too far-fetched to assume that Lydia Carson shared her mom's last name.

"And we know that she had a spinal injury. What we need," Temerity said after a brief, thoughtful break, "is a patient list."

"Uh, that's confidential?" Ellen suggested, but hesitantly, since Temerity seldom paid much attention to that sort of thing.

"Or *is* it?" the blind girl said. Her mouth curled into a sly smile. "I have a very cunning plan."

Ellen was familiar with Temerity's plans, and the cunning part usually involved her, Ellen, doing something far outside her comfort zone. She ate faster, hurrying to finish her tuna pasta salad.

Temerity stood up. "Dr. Amanda Bendon, please," she said to Ellen, as if giving an address to a cabdriver.

Her office, Ellen knew how to find. She'd spent too much time in that tiny space, where Amanda had allowed her to wait so that she could avoid the waiting room and its smattering of people. Many of the interning doctors had small offices, not much bigger than the broom closet where Ellen enjoyed so much fine literature and packaged snacks. With a slight chill of anticipation, or the possibility of unpleasantness, Ellen led the way.

"What are you going to say?" Ellen whispered as they arrived.

"Oh, I'll think of something," Temerity practically sang. She tapped her chest. "Famous for that," she added, and knocked on the door. Then, almost as an afterthought, she asked, "You know how to type, right?"

Before Ellen had time to set Temerity straight on that, the door opened and Amanda exclaimed, "Oh my God, Temerity! And Ellen," she added as she leaned around to see Ellen half hidden behind the doorjamb. "Well, hello, ladies, what brings you down here?" The room was so small that she hadn't even risen from her chair to open the door.

Dr. Amanda looked frazzled. Her naturally wavy hair was sticking out in different places from the knot she'd tried to contain it with, especially over her right ear, where not one, but two pens were stuck in it. Several opened files were stacked on her lap and the computer screen was emitting its hazy light.

"Actually, I wanted to talk to you about something," Temerity told her.

"Oh. Uh . . ." Amanda's eyes cut from the pile of work on the tiny desk to the computer, and then back to her visitors. "Justice asked me to come to dinner tonight."

"I know," Temerity said. "But I wanted to talk without him, if you know what I mean. He's such a pain in the . . . I mean, boys, you know. All they talk about are sports and cars."

"Sports and cars? Justice?" Amanda seemed bemused.

"Well, not Justice specifically, but boys in general. Anyway, is it a bad time?"

Amanda seemed to come to a decision. "You know what? No. I was just about to go grab a cup of coffee. Want to join me?"

"I do!" Temerity enthused. "But Ellen probably doesn't. Do you, Ellen? Can she just stay here, maybe, and wait for us?"

This might have been an unusual request for anyone else, but having known Ellen for nine months, Amanda didn't even blink. "Sure, that's fine. Do you want us to bring you something, Ellen?"

"No, thanks."

Amanda got up and changed places with Ellen, who sat down in her seat and wished fervently that Temerity could see her panic. But of course, it was wasted wishing.

"We'll be right back, Ellen. Maybe you can find something informative to read on the hospital website," Temerity said. "You were just asking me about vitamin supplements, weren't you?"

Amanda turned back. "Wait, let me sign in for you." She leaned across Ellen, who shrank away, and punched in a few numbers. "There, click on nutritional information, or . . . Ooh! There's going to be a farmers' market in the parking lot on Thursdays now. You can check that out."

Temerity took Amanda's arm, and as they started away she fluttered her other hand behind her back, as though she were punching something with her fingers.

As she watched them go, Ellen thought sadly, *She wants me to hack into the patient register.*

Ellen's lack of knowledge about how to use a computer was almost complete. Justice had tried to show her some basics, but it was all so overwhelming and just seemed so *unnecessary.* Especially since Ellen didn't own a computer of her own, and didn't want one. When Justice had tried to interest her in social networks, she had reminded him that she didn't know anyone. So after explaining to her how to research a topic she might be interested in, he had let it go.

Ellen looked at the screen in front of her. Up on the right was a little oblong space next to the word *Search.* She recognized that. Painstakingly, finding one letter at a time, Ellen typed in *p-a-t-i-e-n-t l-i-s-t.*

To her absolute amazement, the screen changed. Now a little box asked her for a patient name.

Ellen typed *c-a-r-s-o-n.*

The machine flitted, and then offered her three choices. Armin A. Carson, Jeffery Clark Carson, and Madeline Carson. Ellen clicked on the last one and a file appeared.

The first thing on the file was the name and a number. L-346. Ellen began to scan below it. There appeared to be lists of drugs, treatments, times and dates of personnel who had worked on this patient, and then Ellen saw a few sentences that didn't seem to be in Arabic. It was a report written by a doctor.

The patient was admitted with extreme spinal trauma with damage to the (a whole bunch of words that Ellen assumed described parts of

Madeline Carson's body or spine) *she was unresponsive, but her vital signs were strong. She was sent to surgery where Smith and Valripieri performed a* (more technical stuff) *and was sent to the spinal wing to await recovery. As of 1-16 at 9:15 p.m. there has been very little discernable nerve response and the patient has not recovered full consciousness. Prognosis, partial paralysis of the* (mumbo jumbo) *and permanent nerve damage. Patient has no medical coverage. Recommendation, transfer to a state facility.*

Ellen sat back and stared at the evil words.

Partial paralysis. Nerve damage. And worst of all, *state facility.*

She hit the home button and was infinitely relieved to see the screen that Amanda had been looking at when they came in.

She heard Temerity talking loudly in the hall, more loudly than was necessary. "So, in conclusion," Temerity said as they came to a stop and she reached out to feel for the doorway, "I'm offering a swift kick in the butt, if you feel you require assistance."

Amanda laughed. "He worries about leaving you alone."

"Crazy, right? Who could be more capable than me? Why, just this morning I made a citizen's arrest of a carjacker. Though in retrospect, it might have been *her* car, based on the fact that she had the keys and I heard the kid in the back call her Mommy. Let's go, Ellen."

They said good-bye and started for the elevator banks. "Did you find it?" Temerity hissed.

Ellen wanted to say no, to say that she hadn't found anything. More than that, she wanted to have *not* found anything, but it was too late for that.

"Yes. I found it."

"She's here?"

Ellen looked at Temerity's happy face. She hated crushing that hope. But there was only one answer she could give. She exhaled forcibly and said, "Yes, she's here."

"*Great!*"

"But not for long."

"Great," Temerity repeated. It sounded like a completely different word.

6

The "wing" turned out to be a detached building. Ellen and Temerity went up to the third floor and found a kind of covered walkway that took them right over the busy street below. There was no separate security for the spinal wing from this entry, the logic being, Ellen supposed, that you'd already passed muster if you made it this far.

L-346 was on the same floor. They found the ward quickly and quietly because the halls were mostly deserted but well marked. There was no door that closed off the large ward from the hallway, only a wide opening. As they came to a stop in it, Ellen could feel her friend's hand tighten on her shoulder in anticipation. "What do we have here?" Temerity asked in a low voice.

"There are two rows of beds," Ellen whispered. "Five on each side, and lots of . . . machinery."

Temerity blew air through her pursed lips, in an obvious effort at staying calm. "Life support. Some of them anyway, I'm guessing. Others may just be monitors. Is anyone else here?"

"No hospital staff, if that's what you mean."

"Okay, let's go, bwana."

"Let's go . . . what?" Ellen was confused. Temerity often used words she didn't know, but she suspected that she'd made this one up.

"Bwana. It means 'boss,' or something like that. I read it in a Tarzan book. In this case I'm using it because you're the guide, like on safari."

That made Ellen think she should have some kind of rifle or at least a machete. They started down the right side. The beds were separated by curtains on tracks, pulled closed on the sides for privacy, but left open to the center of the ward. As they went along, Ellen read the names on the charts hung on the foot of each of the beds. She stopped at the fifth and final bed.

"This is her," she said, staring fixedly at the chart because she didn't want to look up. The memory of the woman jammed between the seats on the bus had been hard enough to see. A second, unerasable imprint of the result of those injuries Ellen preferred to avoid, if at all possible.

Temerity let go of Ellen and slipped in along the right side of the bed. She was able to avoid the machines that beeped and whirred by their sounds and a careful exploration with her hands. Ellen slid along the left side of the bed until she was partially concealed by the curtain, which was drawn to shade the bed from weak sunlight coming from the windowed wall next to it. Feeling somewhat safer, she finally raised her eyes to find that Temerity was holding the woman's limp and bruised hand. Ellen waited to see what would happen, if the woman would wake up and say something. Or not.

Speaking softly, Temerity said, "Hi, I'm not sure if you can hear me, but my name is Temerity and I'm here with my friend Ellen. She helped your little girl when the bus crashed. We wanted to come and see how you are doing."

The only response was the humming and clicking of machines. Ellen whispered, "I don't think she can hear you."

Temerity sighed and said, "Maybe. We don't know. How does she look?"

Ellen scanned the bed, the monitors, the tubing that led into the Carson woman's throat. Ellen didn't know anything about all this equipment, but the rising and falling of the blue accordion-like shape in the clear-plastic cylinder matched the same motion in the woman's breast.

"Not good."

Temerity sighed again. She asked Ellen, "What's her name?"

"Madeline."

"Madeline," Temerity repeated, first to herself and then to the inert form. "Madeline," she called out softly. "No, you wouldn't go by that would you? Maybe . . . Maddy. Hi, Maddy, nice to meet you. Wish it was under better circumstances."

To Ellen's consternation, but not really surprise, Temerity groped around until she found the single visitor's chair and pulled it up to the bed. "So, Maddy. We came because we wanted to find out how you are doing, and we don't think our answer is a very good one. So here's the thing."

Ellen stood watching in awe as, even though her voice was clear and never wavered, a tear trailed down Temerity's cheek. "We know that you're worried about Lydia, and we want you to know she's okay. She wasn't hurt at all, and we think she went to stay with another family for a while until you get stronger."

For an instant, when Temerity said the name Lydia, Ellen thought she saw Maddy's eyelids flutter, but it may have only been a trick of the blinking monitors.

"As soon as we know more, we're going to come back and tell you. We think you'll feel better if you know what's going on and that Lydia is okay."

There it was again, Ellen was more certain this time. Just a flicker of movement when Temerity said the name. Ellen was so startled that she actually said, "Did you see that?" to Temerity.

Her friend's response was a roll of her head in Ellen's direction. "I'm sorry," she said dryly. "Were you speaking to me? I don't believe we've met. My name is Temerity and I'm blind."

"No, I mean, I know, but she . . . that is, I think . . . Say the kid's name again."

"Lydia? Oh!" Temerity exclaimed, and her mouth dropped open. "Oh my goodness, I think her hand twitched. Maybe it was a muscle spasm." Temerity stood up now and leaned closer over Maddy Carson's chest, missing the head by a good bit, but who could fault her? "Maddy? I want you to know that we're going to find out where Lydia is and make sure she's okay. Do you understand?"

But as hard as Ellen focused, and as tightly as Temerity held the hand, there didn't seem to be any response. They were both so intent on the patient in the bed that they were completely startled when someone spoke sharply behind them. "Can I help you?"

Ellen dropped, disappearing behind the curtain and bed. Temerity turned in her chair and let go of Maddy's hand. From the doorway of the ward, a nurse was regarding her sternly.

Temerity answered. "Oh, no, thank you. I just came to visit a friend."

"Did you sign in?" the nurse asked, and Ellen could hear her coming closer. Then there were two sets of footsteps. Someone was with her.

"No, I didn't see anyone." Temerity pointed to her eyes. "I'm sorry. I'll go now."

Through a tiny slit between the curtains, Ellen watched the nurse—who was wearing scrubs in a shade of purple that could only be described as *blatant*—as she arrived at the bed. Behind the nurse was the social worker Ellen had seen with Lydia in the emergency room. Serena, she had said her name was.

Serena stepped efficiently up to Temerity. "Ma'am, do you know this woman?"

"You mean Maddy?" Temerity asked.

The social worker squinted at Temerity. "So you do know her."

"We've just been introduced." Temerity was looking amused. Ellen knew she was pleased she had guessed the nickname correctly.

Suspicion deepened Serena's permanent frown. "Then how do you know she's called Maddy?"

"Well, I assumed, actually. Madeline is kind of a mouthful. How do *you* know? Has she woken up?" Temerity asked so hopefully that Serena's restrictive nature seemed temporarily disarmed and she actually answered.

"No. Her daughter told me."

"I'm Temerity Bauer. My roommate, uh, knew her. Well, to be more accurate, she was on the bus with her when the accident occurred. She's the one who helped her daughter, Lydia, and so, naturally, we were curious to know how her mom was doing. And *you* are?" Temerity leaned forward slightly and canted her head. "Sorry, but I'm not very good with faces." Temerity's mouth slanted to match her head, in a sarcastic line.

63

"Serena Hoffman, I'm the social worker assigned to this case. I'm asking if you knew Ms. Carson because, as yet, we've been unable to locate any family members or close friends who might be willing to assume custody of her daughter."

Well, thought Ellen, *at least she doesn't beat around the bush.*

But why was it that *efficient* was so often synonymous with *cold*?

Temerity answered, "I wish I could, but I can't help you with that. How is Lydia? Where is she?"

The suspicion slipped back in. "She's fine. I'm sorry, but if you aren't family I can't discuss her case with you. I hope you understand."

Temerity straightened her head and nodded. "I think I do."

The nurse's mouth was pursed tightly in disapproval as she watched this exchange. "Well," she said perfunctorily, turning to Serena Hoffman. "If this young lady will kindly allow you to have her seat, I'll close the curtains and you can have a minute to write your report."

Nurse Purple waited for Temerity to get up and unfold her stick. But instead of leaving immediately, Temerity paused. "Ms. Hoffman?"

"Yes?"

"Could you tell me, what is the process? I mean, if a person wanted to foster a child."

Through a tiny opening in the hospital curtain, Ellen saw humanity in the face of social services. It broke through, and for the briefest of moments, all the weight of the world swam in those brown eyes. And then it sank away, replaced by the thin metallic shield of efficiency. Cold, but Ellen understood more now. "I'm sorry, if you mean yourself, you wouldn't qualify."

Temerity nodded sadly. "I didn't really think I would. But maybe my family might, so . . ."

The woman reached into her pocket and pulled out a card. "Here, the website is on there." She touched Temerity's hand with the card, and Temerity found and took it. "If someone is interested, all the basic information can be found there. Requirements, government subsidies, most things they would need to know."

"Thank you," Temerity said. She turned and walked in the general direction of the doorway, though she was angling too far to the right. The nurse pointedly pulled the curtains all the way closed, sealing both herself and Serena inside with the patient.

Trapped between the bed and the wall, Ellen moved carefully along the curtain to the end of the bed and was about to bolt, to intercept Temerity before she ran into one of the opposite beds, when two things happened. Temerity touched a leg of a bed with her stick, corrected herself, and walked confidently out of the ward, the sound of her clicking stick fading as she turned into the hallway, while at the same time, the nurse asked, "So where is the kid?"

Hardly daring to breathe, Ellen stayed her forward rush. The social worker sighed and though now Ellen couldn't see her, she could feel the hopeless detachment in her voice. *That* was something she understood.

"I placed her with a family called the Rushes in Highland Park. First-time foster family, actually, an older couple with a kid in college. Empty-nest syndrome is my guess, but they do have a history of supporting social causes. And, for a change, they don't look like they're doing it for the monthly government check, like so many." There was a brief pause, and then she added, "Too many."

There was a collective sigh of frustration. Then Serena Hoffman accelerated back to her professional speed by asking, "Do you know if there were any drugs or alcohol in her system when they brought her in? No? Okay, well, that would be a good sign as far as returning the kid to her eventually, but I don't suppose it will make much difference here. When will the doctors make their rounds? I need to get one of them to sign off on this report. I've got six more visits before I can even get back to the office. Sometimes, I . . ." She trailed off, exhausted.

The nurse's sharp voice responded to the unfinished thought, though now there was a catch in it that betrayed a knick in the razor-edge. "I know," she said. And Ellen could tell that she did.

It was time for Ellen to go. Sidestepping until she was clear of the bed, she moved for the exit as quickly as she could. She tried to be as noiseless as possible, but in that constant stream of humming, beeping, and whooshing, the sound of her rubber-soled boots on the linoleum was little more than passing insect wings.

Ellen intercepted Temerity at the entrance to the glass bridge. Ellen could tell from her stiffness that she was barely containing her anger and sadness, and they hustled out of there.

They didn't speak until they were free of the antiseptic hospital smell and sucking in big breaths of fresh, misty air on the street.

Revived to speech, Temerity said, "See? I told you it was Maddy."

7

B y the time they had returned to the loft, Ellen had told Temerity everything. Temerity was full of plans to find Lydia
the next day, but tonight she had a concert, so she rushed to
change into her long black velvet dress and grab her violin. Justice
and Amanda were cooking dinner and invited Ellen to join them.
She refused. She required time alone, and it was just too awkward,
they were so . . . *touchy*, it made her feel electrocuted by low voltage
every time they kissed.

Though it was Ellen's night off, she had never found it possible to
change her sleeping schedule for a day, or rather, for a night. So after
a bath and a chapter of her book, she got dressed in broken-in jeans,
a sweet find at the thrift store, and a voluminous navy blue sweater.
Recently, Ellen had expanded her color choices from black to in-
clude other night colors, deepest blues and grays, shades that suited
her covert lifestyle.

It was after nine thirty when Ellen snuck past Justice and Amanda,
who were curled up together on the sofa, and slipped out the door.

She went down the stairs and out into the liberating chill of the night. She turned right, then stopped.

Slowly, Ellen turned and went to the grating just above the sidewalk. A faint glow was emanating from inside, the light not strong enough to cast even the feeblest shadow of the metal grate's pattern onto the pale cement of the sidewalk.

But looking straight at it, the grating itself was silhouetted from the inside. As carefully as only someone who has spent an invisible lifetime could, Ellen leaned down and peered in. At first she could see nothing, and then, a few yards away, she made out the source of the light.

It seemed to be a single bulb, dangling from a mass of wires and ducting. The light it spewed was feeble, enough to illuminate a single chair, of the discarded, armchair variety, in fact one of its legs was gone and had been replaced with a precarious stack of bricks. A few feet away, on what seemed to be a piece of plywood supported by cinder blocks, was a dirty sleeping bag and a few blankets.

Ellen caught her breath. Something, no, *someone*, stirred in the chair. What Ellen had taken to be a discarded blanket had moved. And now Ellen could see that, curled up under that rag, was a boy. Ellen guessed he was maybe twelve, but it was hard to tell. In the insufficient light, his face was slack and sallow.

Ellen watched for a few minutes almost impassively. Lost, destitute, and unwanted people were a reality common to her. An overpass in her old neighborhood had offered insufficient shelter for a fair number of homeless people, many of them families with children. Sharing the sidewalk with them as she passed to and from her home had made it impossible to simply look away and pretend they didn't exist, as most people chose to do. She had also personally known three young boys and one girl who had run away from foster homes and of the abuse they had suffered during their time there. Though she had only discovered what became of one of them, she had always suspected the other two had found a fate similar to this, possibly worse.

Backing up a few steps, Ellen dug in her bag. It had long been a precaution of hers to never be without snacks, and today she had brought a banana, a package of Rice Krispies Treats, and a granola bar. They were all wrapped in a plastic grocery bag. Very carefully, Ellen tested the grating. She slid both her little fingers in opposite corners and tugged gently. It moved, swinging hinge-like toward her. Pulling it open as noiselessly as she could manage, she laid the bag just on the inside, and pushed the grate closed, so that the top of the bag was caught between the metal and the brickwork. The offering dangled just beyond the pattern of metal.

Silently, Ellen backed up and went on her way. Emerging onto the avenue, she glanced up at the round window of her room and smiled. *Mine,* she thought. This word was new and risky for her. Possession had always made her vulnerable because she had never had much she could call her own, and what she did could be taken from her in an instant. But now she was beginning to trust, cautiously, a feeling of permanence, though with an understanding that only those who have truly had nothing can know. Everything in life was borrowed, really. And she was all right with that.

She crossed the wide street at the pedestrian crosswalk and continued down the main avenue. It was one of her favorite kind of nights, not quite raining, but the mist had added a silvery black-and-white luster to the world, like an old-time photograph. Ellen loved these nights that glowed softly.

Turning left onto a street lined with commercial shops and restaurants, she walked along, staying as far from the light of the shop signs and windows as possible. The shops were closed and deserted at this hour. On the corner was a funky neighborhood café. It was the kind of place Ellen thought she would have liked if it wasn't for the fact that people were there. The café sold sandwiches and pastries, had shelves filled with books and knickknacks for sale—mostly used—overstuffed armchairs in dark corners, and very few customers. She would have enjoyed sinking into one of those chairs, the size of which would have welcomed, and even enveloped, her. She would have delighted in browsing through the books and picking out a new world, a new voice to speak to her as she read the chapters inside. She loved dog-eared, well-read books the best. The idea that others had been there before her made her feel a sense of kinship.

Drawn to the very notion of the place, Ellen found herself floating toward the store's display window.

Cookbooks. They might interest someone who could actually cook, but Ellen liked stories, and here there were none. She was turning away when a title caught her eye. *Best Baking for Beginners.* Ellen liked Bs, they were round and soft, the overstuffed sofas of the alphabet, and felt good when you said them quickly in a row. *Buhbuh-buhbuh.* Below those friendly Bs was a picture of cupcakes, stacked on a three-tiered glass cake stand.

Ellen felt in her pocket. She had come out with some cash, as she always did, just because, well, you never knew when you might need an emergency snack. She fingered the ten-dollar bill and looked at the price tag on the well-worn, secondhand book; three dollars.

Slipping sideways until she was at the edge of the next window, through which she could see into the coffee shop, she saw the only person there was a small woman behind the counter.

Ellen listened to her heart pound for thirty seconds. Then slunk to the corner, where the door opened at an angle, and slipped inside.

She went to the counter and stood, uncertain. The woman, who was cleaning the coffee machine, took no notice of her. Gathering her nerve around her like clear armor, Ellen focused hard on the counter and spoke without looking up. "Uh, excuse me." In her peripheral vision, Ellen watched the woman turn and lift her head with a swift jerk that told Ellen she had not been detected until she had used her voice. Though this reaction was familiar to Ellen, it still left her feeling naked and unprotected.

"Oh, you startled me!" the woman exclaimed. "Sorry. Good evening, what can I get you?"

Out of a lifetime of habit, Ellen kept the left side of her face angled away from this unknown human. "Uh, I want to buy that baking book in the window."

"Okay, you can go ahead and grab it, and I'll ring it up for you."

Relieved to turn her back, Ellen retrieved the book and returned to the counter. She laid the ten on the counter with the book. The woman rang it up, and then stood there, holding out the change. Ellen wished that she would just set it on the counter where her eyes were fixed. But the woman seemed to be waiting for something.

Hesitantly, Ellen looked up. The woman *was* waiting, and what she was waiting for, Ellen realized with a jolt, was eye contact. "Here you go, have a nice night. Enjoy!" Her eyes, warm and eloquent, said much more than the simple words. She handed over the change. Ellen fumbled it into her pocket, picked up the book, then retreated, resisting the impulse to run.

As she hurried down the street, Ellen thought about the stranger's determination to acknowledge her. It was unlike what Ellen had come to expect. Fleetingly, she wondered if her face had still been the scarred image of a year ago if the woman would have reacted with the repellence Ellen had come to anticipate. Somehow she thought not; that woman's gaze had been unflinching. It had been . . . *brave*. But bravery was rare—Ellen knew because she paid attention—there were very few truly courageous people in the world. And that fact had made it necessary for her to move unseen and unnoticed through life.

It was an enigma that puzzled Ellen until she entered the park and was swallowed by the solitude and the darkness. She made her way to a bench surrounded by a favorite stand of trees. In that spot, light from the streetlamps filtered through the bare branches. Resting the cookbook on her knees, Ellen ran a hand across the glossy cover.

She opened the book to a random page, and there, on her lap, was a recipe for cinnamon buns with a full-page photo across from it showing the delectable treat still hot and steaming from the oven. Ellen's chest twitched with longing. The image moved her to joy. She did not consciously recall the moment, ever, but a package of cinnamon rolls—tossed to her when she was five years old and starving—had been a turning point in her life. It had been sustenance, relief, and the most delicious thing she had ever eaten. Even now the sight of sweet pastry wrapped in cellophane sent its unconscious message to her. *Eat me and you will be safe.*

And here was something *beyond* that message. Something that said, *Make me and you will be happy.* On the next page, a further series of pictures illustrated the preparation, which included kneading the dough—which Ellen imagined to be like wet, soft fabric—and shaping the buns. She felt a craving to try it.

The enticing pictures made her hungry, and the fact that she had given away all of her emergency food formed a thin sheet of panic crust on Ellen's rib cage. Closing the book, she placed it carefully in her bag and headed for home, though she decided to take another route.

It did not take long to cross to the opposite side of the park, past the baseball diamond, along the fence of the deserted dog run, and emerge on the street that ran parallel to the one from which she had entered the park. Three blocks later, she was on the sidewalk outside of Tami's bakery.

It was closed, being almost midnight, but bakers worked at night, and Ellen knew from being employed on the night shift herself that the delivery trucks made their rounds a couple of hours before dawn. She knew from her "borrowing" that the bread was best then, the warmth of the oven still lingering on their paper wrappers.

The front of the store was dark, the sign inside the window said SORRY, WE'RE CLOSED. But down the street, Ellen could see light coming from the back windows. She made her way toward them. Unlike earlier in the day, the windows were shut. Placing one hand on the opaque glass, she was surprised to find that it was not cold, as she had expected, but radiating heat from inside. On impulse, she pressed an ear against the smooth warmth.

She could hear the whir of a machine, a mixer maybe, then a rapid clinking, like a spoon against a metal bowl. The savory, enticing scent was present, too. Ellen moved farther down the side of the building, hoping for a glimpse into that magical world where sugar and carbohydrates were transformed into delicacies. There was a word for that, Ellen thought, a word she had heard or more likely read that described what went on in there. As she reached the corner, it came to her, *alchemy*—that was it. This was the closest thing she knew to turning base metal into gold. Halting, she leaned forward so that she could see into the alley behind the bakery. She was not surprised to find a back door giving easy access for loading in supplies, or bringing trash out to the two huge dumpsters looming in the shadows of the far wall. What she had not expected was to find it propped open.

She stared at the door in some confusion. She could not see into the kitchen from this angle, but if she positioned herself so that she could, she would open herself to detection. Still, she wanted very much to watch those wizards at work again. As she hesitated, someone came out, opening a second metal-grated security door, and Ellen shrank back. It was one of the bakers, and he was carrying a tray on which were a few crescent-shaped pastries.

"Okay, guys, croissants are up," the man called out. And Ellen was surprised to see two men with straggly beards and skin so long unwashed it was black in the light from the doorway, emerge from where they had waited motionless in the shadows of the dumpsters. They shuffled, anxious and apologetic, toward the offering, mumbling humble thanks as the baker balanced the tray on a trash can, wrapped three of the treats for each of them in paper, and handed them over. The surplus humanity barely raised their eyes to the baker. Then they hurried away, clutching their treasures.

The baker watched them go. As he turned back toward the kitchen and the light fell across his face, Ellen could see the sadness on it. He went in, the security door locking with a click behind him.

After a moment, Ellen crept forward and stood, watching through the metal mesh for a long time. There were three bakers tonight, two women and the man. They moved around one another and the equipment with easy grace. Speaking quietly, laughing occasionally, they went about their work. Everywhere around them were the divine smell of baking bread and, Ellen felt sure, the certainty that what they did brought happiness—the bonus prizes of their profession, the invisible benefits. Ellen felt a small shiver of envy.

Perhaps, thought Ellen, *this is what people mean when they say they've found their place in life.* Ellen liked her job okay, she guessed, because it was solitary for the most part and she could be independent while remaining invisible. It was what she had found that suited her, had protected her from welfare or homelessness, but equally important, it was employment that would have *her,* and she'd never really considered, or aspired to, anything more. But now Ellen watched the bakers and felt her heart longing.

This, she decided, was what it looked like when you were given that magical gift of doing what you loved. Joyful work that turned simple basics into something complex and beautiful.

Alchemy.

8

When Ellen reached her own alley, she checked the grating. No light came from the basement inside, but the bag had disappeared. *Good,* she thought. *He ate tonight.* Ellen climbed the stairs to find Temerity still up. She'd stayed late after the concert for a birthday celebration. She was standing at a window that she had cracked open. Her face was flushed.

"Isn't it a great night?" she enthused. "So moist and fluffy."

"Speaking of which," Ellen said quietly as she moved toward the window, "I was wondering about something."

Temerity rocked a bit and a huge, silly smile cracked her pretty face. "Shh. Just a second. Listen." Ellen turned her head and, sure enough, she could make out the piano music floating up from the loft below over the quieter nighttime street noises. The melody was sad yet lovely. It made Ellen think of someone crying with a smile on their face, as if remembering another time or person, long gone, but recalled with fondness. The music ended, and Temerity held her hands out the window and began to applaud. When she stopped, a voice came up. "Thank you! I'll be here Thursdays and Fridays. Don't forget to tip your waitress!"

Temerity laughed with delight, turned to Ellen, and said, "You gotta love a musician with a sense of humor!"

The pleasure on her friend's face gave Ellen such a warm sensation in her chest that she thought, *I already do.*

"Anyway, wondering is always good." Temerity pointed a finger accusingly at the air. "People should do it more." She crossed to the sofa and sat down, letting her head fall back where it rested on Mouse, who was curled on the top of the cushions. He made an annoyed sound but didn't move. "Ouch," Temerity said. "You think you'd be softer with all that flab."

"Uh, yeah, I guess," Ellen responded.

Temerity snorted a laugh. "I meant the cat."

"Actually, we're both pretty squishy," Ellen said, having no illusions, about that anyway. "But I meant I guess more people should wonder. But I don't really know that many people."

"You know more *about* people than anyone else I know," Temerity said. "Most people are so involved with themselves they don't see anything else. Anyway, what were you wondering about?"

"Can you teach me how to use the oven?"

Temerity reached around behind her, picked up the big cat, and set him in her lap. She cocked her head to one side, thinking. "It depends on what you want to use it *for.* I mean, I can show you how to set the temperature. It talks, you know, for my benefit. Just turn the dial and it will tell you what degree you've set it on. What do you want to make?"

Fixing her gaze on the big windows across the room, gilded by the lights of the city outside, Ellen said, "Gold."

"Excuse me?"

"I mean, uh, cupcakes, maybe, and . . . stuff."

"Sweet! And I mean that both literally and metaphorically. It's a little late to start baking tonight, what brought this on?"

"I bought a book," Ellen said, holding it up for absolutely no reason, since Temerity couldn't see it. "I'll get the ingredients tomorrow night at work."

"Or, we can pick them up tomorrow day while we're out in the burbs."

"The . . . what?" Ellen was confused.

"The suburbs. I found an address for the Rushes in Highland Park, and we're going to check on Lydia. Remember we promised?"

Ellen distinctly remembered *Temerity* promising, but she didn't say so.

"Shall we go in the afternoon? Say around three?" Temerity suggested. "Will that give you enough time to sleep?"

"Okay," Ellen said. Though the very thought of going somewhere unfamiliar made her insides feel like they were being whisked with a rusty eggbeater, she knew Temerity would not be deterred.

Temerity stood up, grunting with the effort of lifting the eighteen-pound Mouse, who hung limp in her arms, making a sound like an idling motorboat. "Here." She handed the huge cat over to Ellen. "I know he likes to sleep on your feet."

Ellen grinned. It was true. Temerity said good night and made her way to the hall doorway, singing and zigzagging a bit as she went. Ellen looked down at Mouse. He was watching Temerity go with something like annoyance. She set him down and he pretended to groom himself and not care.

Ellen made a peanut butter and grape jelly sandwich and put it on a plate with a few cookies. She poured a glass of milk and headed

upstairs, pausing at the door for Mouse to take his sweet time saun-
tering through. When she was in her room, she pulled her chair over
in front of the window and watched the different apartments as she
ate her snack.

One particular woman, Ellen had noticed, was often awake at this
time. She was standing in her open window, looking out, but she
never looked at Ellen, which was usual. Ellen recorded this and everything she'd seen tonight—the baker's generosity, the woman at
the coffee shop, the child in the cheerless basement. When she was
done, she began to close the book but paused. The pen did not want
to leave her hand. Ellen turned to a clean page and sat looking at it.
There was nothing more to report, but somehow, Ellen felt, there
was more to *say*.

And so, she began to say it. For the very first time, Ellen not only
recorded what she had seen and the possible reasons for it, but she
allowed herself to envision what *might* be. Having learned long
ago that if she expected nothing she was far less likely to be disappointed, projecting had always been a restricted activity.

It was odd, this transfer from fact to supposition, and it did not
come easily. After a very few phrases, a complete sentence or two,
and eventually two full pages, Ellen stopped. She read it back as she
finished off the last cookies. It surprised her.

Ellen brushed her teeth and climbed into bed. Mouse settled into
his usual spot between her calves, effectively pinning her legs down.
If she moved or shifted, he *rrrawed* at the air in annoyance, raising
one paw and placing it on her calf with the claws extended. Ellen
patted his huge head with an awkward open palm, which he seemed
to like, leaning into it until she scratched harder than she thought
he could bear. When she left off, he was clearly put out, but he nestled his huge head on his paws and fell noisily asleep.

Usually when she lay down to sleep, the thoughts of the day stalked busily through her brain until they made camp and finally fell quiet. But this morning Ellen had already watched that parade, and, having transferred all the thoughts onto the lined pages of the notebook, she dropped right off.

When she woke in the afternoon, the first thing Ellen did was check her notebook. She'd written that she'd like to be a baker. *Weird,* she thought. *I didn't even know I wanted that.*

Temerity was waiting for her downstairs. She'd made Ellen an egg sandwich and a big cup of coffee, and she tapped her foot in an impatient tattoo as Ellen ate. Runt's furious barking at the door told them both that Justice was home. He came in as Ellen was putting the plate in the dishwasher.

"Hello, ladies!" he called out across the loft as he hung up his coat on the row of hooks by the door. "How's tricks?" He wandered over to the table as he searched through the mail he'd retrieved, since Ellen hadn't been out that morning. "Here's the mail. There's one for you, Ellen."

Ellen sighed. It would be a credit card offer. "Just leave it there, I'll throw it out later," she said.

Justice laughed, but then he said, "I think you might want to open this one. It looks kind of official."

Curious now, and afraid—nothing "official" had ever meant good news to Ellen—she took the envelope from Justice as he came around the counter into the kitchen area. On the top left was the name and address of social services. At first she assumed it was some kind of form letter or questionnaire, which she occasionally received, but then she noticed that her name was handwritten.

"Oh," said Ellen, feeling numb. She didn't want to open it, to give them any further power over her. Maybe if she just ignored the letter, it, and all its bad associations, would go away. "I'll open it later. We were just leaving." She left the unpleasant thing on the table.

"Where are you two off to?" Justice asked, his eyes narrowing.

His sister piped in. "I'm taking Ellen to the suburbs. She was curious about landscaping."

Justice's eyes had thinned to slits. "Uh-huh," he said suspiciously. "Sure she was. Do me a favor?"

"What?" asked his sister, starting for the door.

"Try not to get involved in any"—Justice counted on his fingers as he reeled off his list—"murders, knifings, shootings, robberies, rebellions, or general mayhem."

Temerity's long-suffering sigh took a full four seconds. "Well, we'll try, but you know how it is."

Justice turned pleading eyes on Ellen. "Not really. It's a mystery to me how much trouble you two can find."

"Got a date tonight?" Temerity asked in a thinly veiled attempt to change the subject.

"No. Amanda's working, again."

"How's things at the Institute for Saving the World?" Temerity asked.

"The Institute of *Educational and Behavioral Research* is fine, thank you. I've got a ton of archived information to go over. We've been asked to prepare a list of possible suggestions for teachers to integrate into their classrooms. Bullying in schools is a huge problem now."

Ellen leaned over to pick up her bag. "Not just *now*," she was surprised to hear herself say under her breath.

Justice heard her. "Too true, as usual, my intuitive friend. Sadly, it seems that problems must become desperate epidemics before anyone pays attention to them. Until then, people pretty much just suffer or look away, depending on whether they are the bullied, the bullies, or the 'afraid to get involveds.'"

Ellen thought, *I used to be the first one, now I'm the last.* But she sensed that wasn't *exactly* true.

"What about political upheavals, revolts, and mutinies?" Temerity challenged. "Aren't those examples of people getting involved and saying 'No' to bullies?"

Justice clapped his hands together. "My point exactly. Generally, a well-fed and fairly treated populace doesn't start guillotining the aristocracy. It's usually a *really* hungry, angry mob that takes on the well-armed powers that be, even if that's just a big kid stealing lunches on the playground. Anyway, the institute wants an overview by the end of next week so that we can prepare a list of suggested inclusions in the curriculum."

"So . . . you're supposed to isolate the cause of ignorance and cruelty, fire up some Bunsen burners, and come up with a vaccine?" Temerity asked.

Justice's face went all starry for a second and he said, "Wouldn't that be great? A society where you could send a kid to the school nurse for an injection of kindness. Or a power-crazed egomaniac could be injected by court order, for that matter. Of course, we'll need a shot for apathy, too." He made a thoughtful humming sound, as though it might not actually be impossible, which impressed Ellen. Always, Justice's positive, yet realistic, attitude impressed Ellen.

He turned to her. "You two be careful out there. Are you taking the bus?" Ellen nodded. "Well, call me if you need a ride back, I'll be home."

They gathered their things, Temerity her shoulder bag and stick, Ellen her medium duffel bag with her work clothes, and they set out.

The ride took over an hour. They switched buses twice, each

change lowered the size of the apartment and office buildings through which they snaked, until the third bus made its way out of them altogether, into neighborhoods that had strip malls with parking lots, then individual homes. Ellen, who had spent her entire life in the city's urban or industrial areas, shrank farther and farther down in her seat. It wasn't that she hadn't been in big open spaces, she loved the city parks, some of which were large enough to get lost in. But this wasn't a park, just . . . space. Finally, they got off and Ellen looked around.

She and Temerity were the only people actually standing or walking on the wide sidewalk. The bus stop consisted of a covered shelter with a bench and a large map of the bus system. Just that—there were no ads, no trash in the gutters, no graffiti.

And then even the reassuring presence of the bus abandoned her as it pulled away, and Ellen found herself standing in a strange new world.

9

"All righty, then," Temerity said as they stood stranded on a sidewalk with nothing edging it but grass and trees. Ellen felt marooned, lost, and utterly forsaken, except for Temerity. *Temerity,* she thought, *isn't afraid of having no boundaries.* She felt the shiver of jealous fear.

"We have to walk from here." Temerity unfolded her stick. "What do the directions say?"

"It says go south on Winston and take the second left on Florita," Ellen told her, swallowing her dismay. She turned in a circle. In the city you could tell which way was south by the street numbers getting bigger or smaller, but there were no street numbers anywhere in sight and the next road sign was too far away to make it out. "How do we know which way is south?"

Temerity pointed up. "It's winter, late afternoon, the sun sets in the west. So . . ." She turned until the weak warmth of the sun fell full on her face, then pointed a finger to her left. "That way!" she announced.

They went south. Ellen realized very quickly that there were no such things as "blocks" in the suburbs. She felt like they'd been hiking for miles when they finally turned left into a community of homes. Ellen stared at the similar brick houses, all two-story, with lots of windows. Of course Ellen had seen this kind of suburb on television and in photos, but this was her first actual visit, and it was like a cartoon come to life. Everything seemed so . . . endless. Most of the houses actually had their own *trees*. Full grown, glorious *trees*. It had never occurred to Ellen before that individuals would own trees. Plants of course you could buy, lots of people had plants or small potted trees even, they carried those at Costco, but something thirty feet tall? She wondered why Costco didn't sell them; they sold everything else. She would have enjoyed having a big oak tree in the store, though dusting it would be a challenge.

"How are you doing?" Temerity asked as they took a right onto a curving street called Lilac Road.

"Uh . . . Okay. It's really far away from . . . everything." Ellen was fighting down her open-space panic. It was easier to hide when you weren't the only one.

"Have you ever been out here before?" Temerity asked.

"No. I've never actually been out of the city. It smells nice, I guess." Ellen would have felt safer if she could crawl under something.

Temerity giggled. "Yeah, that it does. Okay, we should be getting close. What's the address, 3250 Lilac, right?"

A glance at the sheet in her hand confirmed this and Ellen thought to ask, "What are we going to do when we get there?"

"Scope it out, of course," Temerity said.

In a few minutes they had come to the house, which was the last one on the dead-end street. After she had taken a look at it, Ellen said, "There are trees all behind and beside the house. I think that if we hide there, we'll be able to see into the windows on the side of the house."

Walking past the house and driveway, they took a sharp left into the trees at the end of the street. Pushing through a bit of light shrubbery, they positioned themselves beneath the canopy of leaves and pine needles, where they were shielded from anyone inside the house. It smelled even better here, though Ellen thought a whiff of truck exhaust might have gone a good ways toward calming her nerves, every one of which had split ends. The trees edged a narrow strip of lawn, maybe ten feet wide, that separated the house's property from the woods.

"I hope they don't spot us. Although it's not likely anyone will think I'm a Peeping Tom." Temerity laughed out loud at the idea. "But they might think I'm the Wicked Witch of the Woods. Justice used to scare the bejesus out of me with that one." She raised her stick and cackled, "Fear me or face my monkeys!"

"Your . . . what?" asked Ellen.

The blind girl turned toward her. "Do *not* tell me that you have never seen *The Wizard of Oz.*"

Ellen couldn't help it. "Do *not* tell me that you *have.*"

Temerity threw her head back and laughed until she was doubled over. "Oh my God," she wheezed as she wiped a tear out of her eye. "Sometimes I forget that you have almost no iconic childhood images. *Cinderella?*"

"What about her?" Ellen asked.

"Did you see that?"

"I saw part of it on TV once." Ellen didn't mention that she had related only to the drudgery in the fairy-tale character's life. It had seemed completely normal to Ellen that the stepmother and sisters had treated Cinderella so badly. The whole ball-gown/rescued-by-a-prince thing seemed, frankly, absurd. Talk about setting yourself up. What she mostly recalled about *Cinderella* on TV was being caught watching from the hallway by the real son of the household. He had shouted at her and harangued her for being an ugly freak until she retreated to her bare mattress where she slept in a thin sleeping bag. There had been no princes in Ellen's childhood, and believing in them would only have made getting through each day more difficult. "How do *you* know what's in those movies?" she asked her friend, to banish the stinging, sticky feeling churned up by the memory.

"I listened to them. And by the way, they were both books first and I *can* read."

Looking at the house from the side, Ellen could see into a large open kitchen that opened onto a porch with stairs down to a backyard that had both a trampoline and a pool.

A pool. Ellen hadn't ever been in a pool. In fact, she'd never been swimming, but she'd stood outside the fences of public pools, wishing she could have one to herself. The idea of being able to soak in cool water on a hot day Ellen found enchanting, and far more magical than a pair of glass slippers, which struck her as uncomfortable and impractical, not to mention downright dangerous. *Glass* slippers?

The daylight was fading, which made it easier to see into the large kitchen. Ellen leaned forward and studied the interior intently. At first she saw no one, and then a woman came in. Even from this distance, Ellen thought her face looked kind.

Ellen leaned around the base of a large pine tree, until, with a little thrill of discovery, she saw Lydia. She was dressed in a pink turtleneck with a red sweater. Her dark hair was neatly brushed and held in place by a pink band with a sparkly green flower. The girl was writing in what looked like a workbook. As Ellen watched, the older woman poured a glass of milk and brought it over to the girl. Then she sat down next to Lydia and took up a pencil. Heads together, the two of them worked on something until Lydia held up the page with a shy smile. The woman clapped her hands together and then put an arm around the girl's shoulders for an easy hug. Lydia did not pull away. Ellen couldn't help a small gasp.

"What? What do you see?" Temerity asked impatiently.

The two of them stood together for another fifteen minutes, while the air grew chillier and Ellen related the scene before her, saying out loud to Temerity what she would have written in her notebook. The table was cleared, Lydia helped set the table for three. The woman brought a large steaming bowl to the table and a man joined them. He patted Lydia on the head and gestured to the table before he sat, nodding his head and smiling as if he were deeply impressed. Lydia smiled down at her shoes before climbing up into her chair and being served a steaming bowl of rich-looking stew and biscuits from a napkin-covered basket.

At this point, Temerity touched Ellen's shoulder and said gently, "I think we're done here."

But Ellen didn't want to leave. In all her experience with foster care, with group homes for the truly unwanted, with her own barely remembered monster of a mother, she had never imagined finding anything like this. Lydia, it seemed, had hit the jackpot. Ellen knew you couldn't always tell from a first impression how safe a new home was, but to see the little girl, who had been terrified to speak to a stranger, smiling with this couple, told a deeper story.

"Wait," Ellen said, unwilling to leave.

"We'll come back," Temerity said, squeezing Ellen's shoulder kindly. "We'll check again, but so far, I'd say we have something good to report."

Good? thought Ellen as they turned away and started the long walk back to the bus stop. This was better than good. It was a fairy tale *that had actually come true.*

Ellen was quiet for the long bus ride home. Temerity seemed to understand, and so she sat humming quietly to herself and occasionally patting Ellen's knee, probably to reassure herself that her friend was still there. *Or maybe,* thought Ellen, *it's the other way around.*

When the bus pulled up in front of their building, Temerity stood and said, "Okay, bye. Don't forget your baking stuff."

"I won't," Ellen told her. She watched Temerity make her way down the bus aisle with her stick extended. Some people shifted uncomfortably away, as though blindness might be contagious. A few stared openly, even looked pityingly. Ellen just smiled. They had no idea of the confidence that was Temerity. There was nothing to be pitied—quite the opposite.

Ellen arrived at work, early as usual. She was climbing the dock stairs when she noticed Eric going out to meet a small van, the side of which read FRANCO'S HANDMADE TORTILLAS.

Ellen was intrigued, because Costco generally took in only very large shipments of goods and this truck was better suited to a family-restaurant delivery. She watched as both driver and Eric checked around carefully before they moved to the back of the van. Ellen slid in behind the huge, retracted, vertical plastic strips that could be pulled closed across the loading ledge either completely or partially in bad weather. She waited.

A few boxes were unloaded onto a handcart that Eric himself had brought down. That in itself was unusual, but when Eric pulled out a fat manila envelope and handed it over, the driver quickly buried it under his jacket. With a quick fist bump, the driver climbed back into the van and backed away. Eric wheeled the handcart up a ramp, but instead of stacking the boxes in the inventory area, he turned toward her. Squeezing her backside firmly against the cement block of the warehouse wall, Ellen waited as he passed. Eric looked around, and then deposited the four toaster-size boxes behind high stacks of boxes marked PAPER NAPKINS, 500 COUNT.

Harsh, tinny rock and roll music sounded, and Eric fished a phone from his pocket. He looked at the caller ID, checked around, then held it to his ear. He snapped, "I told you not to call me at work, Mom! I'll have to call you back."

"Eric?" a voice called out, and Eric jumped, literally rising an inch or two off the ground. Twisting, he seemed to calm when he realized that he was out of sight of whoever was calling his name, and with a fearful glance back at the boxes, he hurried away.

Ellen followed him, or rather she paralleled him between rows of stacked cardboard waiting to go into the recycle bins.

The general manager was waiting for Eric outside the dock office. Billy, the GM, was, or had been, a redhead, but there was little left to show of his hair now except for a ring that stretched from ear to ear around a bald spot. Eric approached him with what Ellen knew was an affected ease. "Billy, hey man, what's up?" he said to the GM.

Billy was holding a purchase order, and with a grim shake of his head he said, "I see here that we had another accident last night, lost a couple crates of ketchup. And it was Daniel again. This is the fourth or fifth time he's damaged merchandise."

"Well"—Eric held out his hands like he was checking for rainfall—"stuff happens sometimes."

"Yeah, I know, but here's the thing . . ." The timbre of the general manager's voice dropped. "It seems to be happening almost entirely on your watch."

Eric stepped back like he'd been slapped, and his mouth fell open.

"Are you holding me responsible? That's not cool, man." He did some headshaking of his own. "I can't control everything." He rubbed his eyes, and Ellen thought she could detect a quaver in his voice as he added, "It's been hard since my mom passed, but I've really made an extra effort to get in here and help out."

Billy put a hand on the other man's shoulder. "I'm so sorry, I didn't know your mom died. That's tough. I'm sorry. Maybe you need to take some vacation time?"

"No." Eric wiped at his face and made a show of straightening his spine. "Thanks, but it's better if I, you know, stay busy."

Billy nodded. "All right, try to stay on top of things, and if you do need some time off, you let me know."

"Thanks, man, I really appreciate it."

"We need to go over the time sheets," Billy said, opening the door to the office.

As soon as the door closed behind Eric, Ellen went back to the boxes that he had hidden and read the labels. GOURMET FOOD ITEMS.

From her fanny pack, Ellen pulled out a box cutter and some packing tape that she used to open and repair packages from which she wanted to "borrow." She flipped a box upside down and slit the tape open. Inside she found shredded paper, and nestled in that, three fist-size plastic baggies filled with whitish powder.

Interesting, she thought. She wasn't sure what the bags of powder were exactly. "Gourmet" they might be, but food they were not.

Ellen resealed the box with her packing tape, and then hurried back into the shadows. Eric reappeared, now wearing a jacket with large pockets he must have put on in the office. As Ellen watched, he slit open each of the boxes and she could see a glimpse of the baggies as they were furtively stuffed into the pockets. As soon as all the boxes had been emptied, Eric hurried to the restrooms. As he got to the men's room and reached for the handle, the door opened suddenly. Squirt was coming out, and Eric jumped so sharply that, for a second, Ellen thought the handle of the door had electrified him.

"Watch where you're going, you gnome," Eric snapped at him, then waved a dismissive hand and went in.

Ellen watched Johnson seethe for a moment, until finally he swore quietly and went on his way.

In another minute, Eric emerged, still wearing the coat, but when he crossed to the now empty boxes, he took it off, draping it over the handcart. Then he quickly broke down the four small GOURMET FOOD ITEMS boxes and carried them to the box crusher.

As quickly as she could move, Ellen scooted out of her hiding place and checked the pockets of the jacket. They were empty.

Ellen retreated, taking a shortcut by way of the management offices, a long hallway flanked on one side by small glassed-in cubicles, and headed to the floor.

The lights in the long hallway were on their night setting. Only one fluorescent out of six or eight was lit. The solitary tubes flickered feebly, inadequate wattage for the high, wide hallway, reflecting a watery, algae-colored light in the glass of the office partitions. About halfway down the hall, a sole office was brightly lit, and the door was partially open. As Ellen passed it, the contrast of the darkened hallway and the illuminated cubicle made the office's interior look like a department store's show window. Staying in the deepest of the shadows, Ellen went on past a few feet and then paused when she heard crying. She realized that this was not the night manager, as she had expected, but Thelma.

Hugging the far wall, Ellen looked in. Thelma was leaning over a woman in a chair with an arm around her shoulders. The woman was wearing green scrubs and Ellen wondered if she was a nurse, or a doctor even.

"It's okay, honey," Thelma was saying. "We knew this was a possibility."

"I know," said the seated woman. She raised her head and dabbed at her eyes with a crumpled tissue. "It's just hard to hear."

Tenderly, Thelma brushed the woman's bangs out of her eyes. "Look at me, Beth." Beth turned her tear-streaked face up to Thelma, who placed a gentle palm on Beth's cheek and smiled down at her. "Listen, this isn't the end of the world. Do you trust me?"

Beth smiled sadly and two big plump tears ran down her flushed cheeks. "You know I do. I'm just sad."

"I know. So tell me exactly what Dr. Patterson said." Thelma sat on the edge of the desk, facing Beth.

"She said that the fibroid tumors would pretty much make it impossible for me to keep a pregnancy." Beth showed her strength of character by smiling through her tears. "Bad luck."

"I know. But I have you, and you have me. I call that pretty lucky," Thelma said. "You know what? That's gotten us through a lot, and we are going to get through this, too."

Beth was beaming up at Thelma even though the pain in her expression was still evident. It was like layers, the love being the deeper base color, and the pain, a wash of tint over it. "I love you," Beth said, and standing up, the two women embraced, rocking each other for mutual comfort.

Ellen hurried on down the hallway. She did not like dwelling on the unfairness and misery that were so prevalent in the world. In fact, she diligently avoided them, which was the only way to move among the chaos without being crushed by it. But her life was changing, opening up, and she began not only to observe and consider, but to *question*, the injustice she observed. The shell of detachment she had worked so hard to construct around her was beginning to show cracks. This had a petrifying effect on Ellen that threatened to incapacitate her. *Caring*—in Ellen's world—had led only to a sucking whirlpool of despair and loss. Disconnecting from emotional response was the key, and the secret, to her survival.

Or it had been. Ellen thought about Temerity patting her back when she was worried about her and Justice telling her not to forget her umbrella when rain was impending. She was no longer completely alone, and somehow that offset the crunchier bits of nastiness. It insulated her, the way only food had once done, from the meanness of life.

She collected her cart and spent the next three hours cleaning furiously, scrubbing and wiping and sweating the hulking mass of wrong from her conscious brain. In between her assault on grime and greasy fingerprints, she found the items she had listed for her recipe—brown sugar, baking soda, and cinnamon. With each acquisition, she felt a tiny bit safer. Carefully noting the cost, she did some quick math for how much overtime she would work off-the-clock to "pay" for her borrowing. It came to roughly twenty-five minutes, but she'd give it a half hour, just to be fair.

At six a.m., Ellen punched her time card and then went back to work for the promised thirty minutes. As she mopped a particularly sticky portion of the sea of sealed concrete floor, she thought about the boy in the basement. If the boy thought someone was watching him, he might very well leave. He hadn't chosen to live in that moldy place for any good reason, and she could easily guess what the bad reason might be. She knew Temerity would want to help him, to get him home. But Ellen wasn't sure that Temerity knew that "home," for some children, could be worse than the street.

No one raised on love and fairy tales could fathom the depths of fear in which too many kids lived, suffered, and sometimes died. Ellen personally had known three children in her foster homes who had not made it through. One, a teenager, had taken his own life, and two younger children had died, one from beatings, and the other of neglect when he'd been ill.

As she pushed the heavy mop, Ellen also pushed away these thoughts, replacing them with the burn in her shoulders, the mind-numbing comfort of manual labor, and the quieting effect of repetitive movement. The thick, dried-up stain of what had possibly been syrup resisted her attack, but she persisted, thinking, *I will wash you away. You will not defeat me.*

10

As Ellen rounded the last corner for home at about seven a.m., she caught a movement at the end of the alley in her highly developed peripheral vision. Stopping in her tracks and shifting backward in a single, programmed response, she held her breath and peered around the brick.

At first she saw nothing. But if she listened intently, she could hear coughing. And then she noticed that the lid to the dumpster was open. As she watched, a head covered in a dark stocking cap bobbed up, and then a bag came flying out, and the someone in the dumpster climbed out after it.

He was smaller than he had looked through the grating, sleeping under the dirty blanket. So thin that he might have been ten years old or even fifteen, but it was impossible to tell. Before he opened the loosely knotted grocery bag and began rooting inside, the boy scanned the alley once more. He gave no indication of sighting Ellen, who had blended seamlessly into the shadow of the city-smudged building.

The boy rummaged in the bag and pulled something out. He

sniffed at it, and then held it up almost triumphantly. It was an un-opened can, Ellen could make that out, but she couldn't see of what. Next came a loaf of bread and then a bottle of juice. They all looked unopened.

She waited patiently as the boy placed the whole bag in a flimsy backpack, then climbed up on the side of the bin and with a shove let the heavy rubber lid fall closed with a whoosh and a thud. With another furtive glance to be sure the sound had not attracted atten-tion, he started in Ellen's direction.

She turned her back, walked a few steps to a sheltered doorway, and slipped into the slight recess. When the boy passed in front of her, his body was shaken with a throaty cough. It was so powerful that it brought him to a stop, and he doubled over, coughing phleg-matically until tears streamed down his cheeks, and he spit out some greenish mucus onto the sidewalk. He rested with his hands on his knees for half a minute, gasping for air. Ellen could hear the wheeze of his labored attempts to draw air into his soggy lungs.

In a moment he had recovered, and, wiping his mouth with the back of his jacket sleeves, which were too short for his gangly arms, he straightened up and went on his way, his blue eyes darting left to right with the practiced, nonchalant posturing of unwilling prey. Ellen knew the need for that facade as well as she knew anything.

Show weakness—be eaten.

She kept her eyes on him until he crossed the street and disap-peared down the next alley, on his way, no doubt, to the next un-locked dumpster.

Slowly, she turned back to the alley and her own door. After she collected the mail from the box, it was a long climb to the fourth floor, but Ellen hardly noticed it this time. She was thinking.

She went in the apartment and carried her bag with its bounty of baking supplies over to the kitchen area. As she set the mail down on the counter, she noticed an envelope with no address, only the handwritten words *Runt owner.*

Ellen picked it up again, perplexed, and flipped it over. It wasn't even sealed. Temerity came into the room, rubbing her palms briskly against each other. "So . . . did you get the baking stuff?"

"Uh, yeah," Ellen said, tearing her eyes away from the curious communication. "I think this is for you," she said. "It's addressed to 'Runt owner.'" Ellen put the envelope in Temerity's hands. Temerity flipped it, feeling the unsealed flap. She removed the single sheet of paper, unfolded it, and then handed it back to Ellen.

"What is it?" she asked.

Ellen looked at the few lines, neatly handwritten, and the signature at the bottom. "It's a note."

"No way," Temerity drawled, "a note! I would never have guessed from its flatness." She looked thoughtful for a moment and then added, "I don't suppose you'd like to use your ability to process light and read it to me, just for giggles."

So Ellen read.

> "*Dear Runt owner, I hope you don't mind the*
> *presumption, but I believe that it is the mellifluous*
> *strains of your instrument that I hear stealing through*
> *my kitchen vent. I was wondering if sometime you might*
> *like to meet on the landing for a chat, or a sonata or two.*
> *Right now, only 22 stairs separate us. If we both brave*
> *11, we can meet in the middle. If not, I will continue to*
> *savor the sound of your playing and my curiosity for the*
> *handsome lady behind the music.*
>
> "*Harmoniously yours, Piano guy, two floors down.*"

Ellen's face flushed as she read, but she made herself finish, though she felt as if she'd stumbled into a private moment that did not belong to her. The irony of this struck her, since, of course, for her whole life that had been the extent of her contact with others.

When she did look up, Temerity was chewing her lower lip, her brow slightly creased. "Nicely written," she said, but beyond that she did not comment. Though Ellen could tell that she was pleased.

"It must be that guy who we saw on the stairs the other day." Ellen didn't know what else to say.

"No, he's the guy *you* saw on the stairs," Temerity corrected her. "I just heard him. He seemed nice enough. But obviously he didn't notice *this*." She pointed to her eyes and shook her head.

"Why do you think he didn't?" Ellen asked. Temerity's blindness was so second nature to Ellen that she couldn't imagine anyone minding it.

"Because . . . he apologized for how he looked?" Temerity suggested.

"What was he supposed to do?" Ellen asked. She put the note in Temerity's hands again. "By the way, he looked pretty good." Ellen flushed, thinking of his shirtless chest, but that wasn't what she'd meant. "I mean, he looked like he was . . . you know . . . a good person." She bit her lip, unclear of how to explain that the way he had watched Temerity—admiring, but with respect—had reminded Ellen of the way Justice looked at Amanda.

"Well, whatever, it doesn't matter." Temerity began to busy herself around the kitchen, though Ellen didn't think there was any purpose in the action, and she saw Temerity slip the note into her pocket. It was the first time she had seen her friend look flustered, and it was as if someone had painted the loft a garish color that was just wrong.

"'Mellifluous' is a nice word," Ellen said. "You could just talk to him."

"I could." Temerity frowned. "But why disappoint us both?"

Ellen couldn't fathom this. Who would be disappointed in Temerity? "Well, at least you could play some music together," she suggested.

"Yeah, I've heard *that* tune before," Temerity joked. "There's a bassoonist who apparently bathes in aftershave who is always inviting me to 'make music.' He's slept with every woman in the orchestra who will have him. And he's really hairy."

In spite of her embarrassment at this proclamation, Ellen couldn't help asking, "How do you know he's hairy?"

"I've been warned," Temerity said, grinning.

"Do, uh, lots of your friends 'sleep with' someone, just once?"

"Don't go thinking they have one-night stands. Think of it this way: This guy has had multiple 'auditions' and never made the cut, if you know what I'm saying."

Ellen didn't, exactly, but all she said was "Oh."

"Okay," Temerity said, "back to reality. I have to tell you that I'm not much of a baker. An enthusiastic eater of bakery goods . . . yes. A baker . . . no. But I do know someone who's really good at it and can help you learn the basics. They'll be here later this afternoon, when you get up."

The shock of this announcement hit Ellen like an air-raid siren. She stuttered, "Wh-what? B-but I don't want to . . . I mean, uh . . ." What had Temerity done? Ellen didn't want to learn about baking from someone new, she didn't want to *meet* someone new. It was too much. Her panicked brain hurled itself into conniption fits, trying to find a way out. "It's . . . no. I mean . . . uh, it's nice of you, but it's, well, not something I can . . . it's not what I . . . it's . . ."

"It's *Rupert*," said Temerity. "He's an excellent baker, makes cakes for everybody's birthdays in the orchestra. He loves it. You going to make some breakfast?"

Breakfast? Ellen almost laughed out loud. After that fright, she could eat two breakfasts *and* dinner.

"Sure," she said, catching her breath. "In a minute. I want to change first." What she really wanted was for her heart to stop pounding out a military march.

Ellen was already at the door to the hallway when she remembered with a lesser—but also traumatic—spasm what Temerity had told her about Rupert and his last visit. The blaring alarm immediately resumed. "But wait," Ellen said, turning back. "What about him, uh, asking me . . . you know."

"Oh, right." Temerity paused, standing in the open refrigerator door. "The vaguely possible date." She pretended to consider. Ellen could tell she was pretending because she was grinning. Temerity sometimes had trouble faking expressions, which was understandable. She raised one finger and her eyebrows as though struck with a revolutionary thought. "Here's an idea. Don't worry about it. It's *you and Rupert*," she pronounced emphatically. "For the two of you, an afternoon mixer—by which I mean the electric one with beaters—and a hot hour or two—by which I mean the oven—is highly unlikely to end at the Happily Ever After wedding chapel in Niagara Falls."

With a burst of giggles that she tried to disguise as a cough, Temerity ducked down and pretended to forage in the refrigerator, her laughter following Ellen. As she reached the bottom of the stairs up to her room, Ellen heard Temerity break into song.

She couldn't make out all the words, but it sounded like "Love is in the air . . . every sight and every sound. Love is . . ." Temerity went on, half humming, half singing. Ellen went through and closed the door.

Hours later, Ellen walked downstairs to find that the big open room was empty. She went into the kitchen area and began to pull out the ingredients she had put in a cabinet under the sink until she had time to label them.

When you live in a house with a blind person, a certain order needs to be maintained. Everything in the cabinets, for example, was put away as neatly as possible, and marked with a Braille label maker. There was no other way for Temerity to know the difference between, say, cayenne pepper and paprika, except for smelling it, and a nose full of hot red pepper would be a costly way to find out.

So the first thing Ellen did was take the label maker from the drawer and punch in the names of the ingredients. Letting her fingertips trail lightly over the Braille bumps on the keys, which were printed with letters and numbers as well, Ellen typed in *c-i-n-n-a-m-o-n*. She pushed the print button and the little device spit out the series of bumps that meant those letters. She peeled off the paper to expose the adhesive, and stuck it to the side of the jar. She followed this procedure for the other ingredients.

Once she had finished, Ellen began lining up the things she needed for her cinnamon muffins on the counter. That was when she spotted the letter from social services that she had discarded on the table and tried to forget.

It lay in the midst of a sea of warm wood, rigid and pale as a dead fish on a dock. Unable to ignore it, Ellen went to pick it up, hoping she might have been wrong, that the address read some other name, one close to hers, but just enough different to not *be* her.

But the lettering, handwritten, was clear. *Ellen Homes*.

There was a noise in Ellen's head. Crackling static that made it hard to think. Ellen stood looking at the ominous missive for a full minute before she decided that it wouldn't go away. Resenting every effort and movement, she sat down and tore the envelope open.

The letter was typed, but she could see at a glance that the signature at the bottom was not printed.

> *Dear Ms. Homes,*
>
> *I am sorry to inform you that Melissa Homes has passed away. There is no obligation on your part to respond to this letter, but as a formality the next of kin are being notified and given the option to collect her remains. They will be kept at the county morgue until February 12th. If there is no reply to this letter, Ms. Homes will be interred in the county cemetery on February 13th.*
>
> *Melissa Homes died with no estate, and there is no legal obligation or inheritance. Again, this letter is a formal notification, no action is required on your part.*
>
> *If, however, you would like to contact my office for more information, such as place of internment, please feel free to call during regular office hours, 8 to 5, Monday thru Friday.*
>
> *Kindest regards,*
> *Frank Martinez*

Ellen stared at the strange, unwelcome words. What was the thought, if there was any, behind sending her this information? The words were clearly written, typed or printed, each word had its own, individual definition and the sentences were complete, and yet the resulting communication meant nothing, it made no sense to Ellen. Swirls of memories, all horrible, rushed at and around her, chasing the next worse one as they roiled past.

Ellen tested out a summary. Her mother. The woman who had tortured and then deserted her. Dead.

That was fine, what was weird was that her mother had been alive all this time and Ellen hadn't ever even considered that a possibility. She'd deliberately not given the woman, her actions, or her fate any consideration. Ellen had nothing but the vaguest image of this person who had abused her, burned her face into a grotesque mask, starved her, and then abandoned her to an uncertain, but almost certainly horrible, fate when she was five years old.

She did not want to know that the woman was dead. But even more, she did not want to remember that she had been alive.

Ellen thought, *My mother has been dead to me since I was five, and I didn't care then.*

She looked again at the piece of paper. Avoiding the bulk of the text, she scanned the other details in an attempt to distract herself, reading the heading, the date, the name and address of the sender and his office.

And the cc.

Someone had been copied on this letter. At first Ellen thought it must be some other government worker, a legality, a notification, and then she let the name register.

cc: Frank Homes

The name seemed to glow in a small pinpoint of light, and the white sheet around it went gray. At the same time, Ellen felt the blood drain out of her face and collect in the pit of her stomach, where it curdled and she found herself gagging back bile. She heaved, covering her mouth with both her hands as the room swirled, blending into the dark memories that churned the air around her with the fetid, half-remembered stench of that room where she had waited for three days with no food for a mother who did not return. The cold and the darkness descended, and Ellen, unable to process the pain, shut down.

11

"Ellen! Ellen!" Someone was rubbing her arm and calling to her. Ellen could feel the hard wood of the table on her right cheek, and slowly Temerity's face, anxious and frightened, wavered and then solidified in front of her.

"Hold on," a soft male voice said behind Temerity. A voice filled with concern. "Ellen, can you see me?"

Ellen shifted her focus from Temerity to just behind her. "Rupert?" Ellen asked.

"Yes!" exclaimed Temerity. "Oh my God, what happened?"

Ellen straightened up too quickly. Dizziness made her sway in the chair, and Rupert hurried behind her, placing his hands on her shoulders to steady her.

"I, uh, I guess I fell asleep," Ellen lied, wishing she could just go and curl up in her room with the curtains closed, dark and safe.

"You did not!" Temerity insisted, stamping one foot. "I was coming in from the hallway and I heard a loud thump. I called out to you, but you didn't answer and then Rupert was at the door so I let him in, and he told me you were unconscious. Oh, Ellen!" Temerity found the chair next to her and sat down heavily. "I was so afraid!"

Feeling horrible to have caused her friend so much anxiety, Ellen didn't see Rupert, on her left, reach down to pick something up from the floor. But as her brain cleared, she remembered the letter and turned to find and hide it.

Too late. It was in Rupert's hand and it was clear that he had seen at least a little of what it said. The first line was hard to miss. *Melissa Homes has passed away.* Rupert's eyes met hers with embarrassment. He hadn't *meant* to read it, it wasn't his fault. He was just picking it up for her.

Ellen wanted to be angry with him for this violation but she couldn't be. She dropped her eyes and held out her hand. Rupert handed over the letter, saying, "I'm so sorry."

Temerity's head shot around. "For what? What do you have?"

Ellen felt the unfairness of Temerity's blindness that excluded her from so many details obvious to others. She sighed and said, "It's a letter that came for me. The woman who . . . my mother, is dead. It's just a letter informing me, in case I wanted to know." To her surprise, she laughed, a flat, humorless sound. Ellen hated it.

"She was *alive*?" Temerity said.

Somehow, Ellen found the humor to say, "Right? That was my first thought, too."

Temerity's mouth was pursed into a tight knot. "Wait a minute. Was *that* what made you pass out?"

Ellen considered hiding the truth from her friend, but she knew that wouldn't do. "No, it was the fact that someone else got the same letter. Someone else was notified."

Temerity's face worked like a thick soup bubbling, and then, just as steam pops up through the surface, her mouth fell open. "Another relative? Who?"

Ellen couldn't speak, couldn't answer, the word had no resonance for her, no meaning. She had no relatives. She turned to Rupert, who looked down at the letter in Ellen's hands. He glanced nervously at her and she nodded. He read the name. "A Frank Homes," he said.

"Oh my God," Temerity repeated. "Do you think it's your father?"

Ellen reeled again, and she put her head down on her arms, trying to get control. The whirlpool was raging below her, and strong, watery feelers had snaked up in tendrils and were wrapping their cold fingers around her legs and stomach. She fought to stay calm, to keep above the turbulence. After a few attempts, she was able to draw in enough air to speak. "I don't think it could be. Wouldn't that mean he would have been involved, I mean somehow, in the legal paperwork that released me to the state? There was never any mention of a father, not in the paperwork they gave me when I turned eighteen anyway. This . . . woman never showed up in court to sign off on me, which I guess is why I got notified now."

Temerity stood up and moved, then stopped a few feet away and spun back. "*Her* father. It must be. Your mother's father." She said it again. "It must be, or, wait . . . maybe a brother. Frank Homes must be your mother's father or brother, and either way, he's alive." She came back and put a hand on Ellen's head, searching for her shoulder. When she found it, she gripped. "Ellen, you have a grandfather, or maybe an uncle."

Ellen raised her head, it was getting clearer now. "No," she said firmly, "I do not. I don't have any family."

"But . . . this is good news, right?" Temerity asked, sitting down next to Ellen, and that simple question confirmed to Ellen that Temerity equated family with good, and she was glad she hadn't told her friend about the boy in the basement.

Neither Ellen nor Rupert said anything. Even in her distress, Ellen could feel their discomfort like a responsibility. It wasn't their fault that her life had been so unhappy.

Ellen said, "Even if they are related to me, I don't know them or anything about them. They have no connection to me, and . . ." Something was bothering her, a sense of anger that pierced the un-summoned feelings of loneliness and memories of hardship. "And if they were there when . . . you know . . . then they must have made the decision to not have anything to do with me. So . . ." She almost choked. "It just doesn't matter. I can't . . . It doesn't matter."

Temerity leaned sideways and put an arm around Ellen's shoul-ders, squeezing with a firm, even pressure. "I'm so sorry," she said.

The spiraling, sucking force below Ellen was lessening as, with ex-hausting effort, she snapped the grasping tendrils. Deliberately anes-thetizing the pain by amputating the past. She asked, "It's not your fault. Why would you be sorry?" with genuine interest.

Temerity sighed. "Because it's got to be painful. Not the fact that that horrible woman is dead, but being reminded of it . . . all. I'm sorry that you have to deal with so much unhappiness."

Rupert had thoughtfully retreated and was standing in the kitch-en, pretending to be absorbed in the recipe book Ellen had left on the counter. He asked quietly, "Does anyone want some tea?"

Clenching her stomach and forcing her limbs to ignore the signals that told them to give up and just lie there, Ellen said, "No, I want to make cinnamon muffins."

She felt Temerity's hand move and land on the top of her head. "I think that's a much better idea!" she said. "Nobody can be unhappy while they are eating a warm cinnamon muffin. They're like weapons of mass happiness, little bombs of joy."

Except, a voice much like Ellen's own but more objective, said in her head, *it wasn't muffins—it was a bun.* The words cracked open time. Suddenly, without warning, Ellen was catapulted backward in time, to a day nineteen years before, when, starving and alone, the ache in her stomach had finally given a five-year-old Ellen no choice but to crack open the door and trust a stranger in a hostile place, not knowing if he would prey on her or save her.

She had worked hard to block that day out entirely, relegating any sensory or mental pictures to the muffled junkyard of her bad experiences, smothering them with tarps and locking the gates on an electrified chain-link fence topped with brutal barbed wire. Somewhere in her past, she had posted a sign on this barricade that said EXTREME DANGER. DO NOT ENTER, and, heeding her own advice, had forgotten it.

And there the memory stayed, trapped in her unconscious, but now, for a few crystal clear seconds, it came back with a gut punch. She remembered a man's face, bloated and smoke-stained, the image appearing in her mind as vibrantly as if it were on the big-screen TV. Ellen distinctly saw the repulsion of his expression as he registered her still-festering, wounded face. She heard the rustle of a plastic bag as he reached inside, and she saw the shiny, clean cellophane package, glinting in the dim stairwell as it arced toward her when he threw it.

A packaged cinnamon bun.

She put her head down on the table again and began to cry, though she did not understand why. Temerity just stroked her hair and told her it was a good thing, to let it out.

But Ellen could not permit this, and within a few minutes she had rethreaded the chain around the gates, fastened the heavy padlock, and turned her back on those rotting memories that meant only suffering.

She opened her eyes to see Rupert's hand extending a tissue to her. Without looking at him, she took it and wiped her face, blowing her nose as quietly as she could. She was mortified that he had been here to witness her breaking, and she stole a glance at him, expecting pity, or even disgust, but all she saw was Rupert. Standing by, in his clumsy, embarrassed, unobtrusive way, just being there. Solid, yet slightly, comfortingly squishy.

She felt a little lurch in her chest. Rupert understood. She patted Temerity's leg to let her know it was okay now and stood up. "So . . . let's make some muffins."

They went to work, Temerity producing bowls and mixers and measuring cups, Rupert supervising the blending of ingredients and the order in which they are added. Temerity explained the use of the oven, which did indeed speak, calling out the temperature and then signaling them with three sharp beeps when it was ready.

Ellen loved it all. She loved watching the dry flour and baking soda mix together with cream and melted butter into something smooth and thick and sweet. Loved watching the eggs add a golden hue to the concoction, loved the smell of the oven heating up. Following Rupert's surprisingly confident instructions, Ellen sprayed the muffin pans with cooking spray, ladled in the silky batter, and put the pans in the oven. She loved the way they looked in there, loved the delicious scent that began to waft around them.

But most of all, she loved the way that making this with her friends made her forget the letter. Not completely, of course, but enough. It flattened the erratic seismic scratchings of her emotional upheaval and lent her a sense of control. She could do nothing to change or erase her past. And now the containment of her pain had been breached, had proven to be beyond her control, but this activity she could master. She could take these ingredients—items that varied in texture, taste, color, and source—and put them together and make something entirely different. She could control this one small thing.

It felt good. And feeling good, Ellen was startled to realize, was exactly what she wanted, though she was still afraid to expect it.

When the little bell chimed, all three of them went to stand around the oven. Carefully opening the glass-fronted door, Ellen leaned back to avoid the blast of heat Rupert had cautioned her about, and then reached in and pulled out the pan of sweet-smelling, golden-brown domes.

Temerity was excited. "Coffee or milk?" she asked.

"Milk," both Rupert and Ellen answered in unison. Then they laughed. The hardest part was waiting a few minutes for the muffins to cool in the pan before carefully extracting them. Temerity produced china plates and linen napkins to mark this as a special occasion, and they all sat down together. They ate one, and then another, of the treats, and Ellen felt not only a contented sense of taste and of fullness, but of accomplishment.

She had made something, and it was yummy.

When they had put the plates in the dishwasher, Ellen took three of the muffins and wrapped them in a paper towel, then placed them in a brown paper bag. Finally, she put that inside a plastic grocery bag. Rupert was gathering his coat, and Ellen went to pull hers from the coat hooks as well.

"I'll walk down with you," she told him. "If that's okay." His face flushed to almost purple, all the self-assuredness of his baker's persona deserting him in an instant.

"Uh, okay," he said.

"I'm going out for a walk," Ellen called out to Temerity.

"Sure you are," Temerity said with a grin, sending Rupert's pigment into an onslaught of rosy hues ranging from pink to violet.

But as they stepped out the door, Ellen felt a light tug at her midsection and heard the sound of a clear, high-toned bell. She stopped in surprise. Temerity, who of course had heard the musical tone, came to the door. "What *is* that?" she asked. Rupert ducked under the string, which had been attached to the doorjamb on both sides with thumb tacks. It was tied off on the right, but on the other side, it dangled a single metal bell, which rang when the string was disturbed. Below the bell, tied with a ribbon, was a roll of white paper, neatly scrolled.

Rupert reached out and gently pulled the scroll free, studying it. "I think it's a special delivery for you, Tem," he said.

"Me?" Temerity said, surprised. "Why do you think that?"

Rupert unrolled the large sheets of what appeared to be blank paper. "Because of the bell, so you'd, um, see it, and because . . . it's in Braille," he said.

"Which we don't read," Ellen added.

Temerity took the sheets from him and ran her fingers over them. She smiled. "It's sheet music," she said.

Ellen couldn't help it. "I think we can assume the guy on two knows you're blind," she said. But Temerity didn't answer. She sat down and was smoothing the sheets gently across her knees.

Rupert unfastened the string, and carried the bell to Temerity. She rang the bell once more. It made a clear, calling sound. *Mellifluous,* Ellen thought. Then they closed the door and went down the stairs, leaving Temerity running her listening fingers over the music and humming the tune, a half smile of discovery on her face.

When they passed the second-floor doorway, Ellen could see that it was cracked open, but she said nothing to Rupert until they reached the street. There, they stood uncertainly at the door for a moment, both of them shuffling their feet. Ellen wanted to say thank you, to find the words to express to Rupert how much it meant to her that he had witnessed her outburst of embarrassing emotion with nothing but subtle acceptance, but she had no words, no practice at that, no skill in communicating anything as volatile as emotions.

So she said, "Come on, I want to show you something."

A fleeting, startled glance from Rupert sent a flush to both their faces. "Okay," he said, and turned quickly toward the street beyond the alley.

"No," Ellen said, "this way." Turning toward the dead end, she walked along the wall, staying close to it. When she came to the grating, she peeked carefully inside.

The child was there, hunched over his makeshift table with his back to them. She heard his cough, and so did Rupert, who drew back in alarm.

But Ellen shook her head and put a finger to her lips, gesturing that he should look. Rupert maneuvered his large body until he was up against the wall next to the grating and then leaned carefully down. He squinted as he looked into the dim space, and then, with a quick intake of breath, he straightened up and leaned against the bricks, his eyes wide open in surprise. He looked questioningly at Ellen.

Ellen put a finger to her lips again, then held up the plastic bag and took a step toward the dumpster. Rupert watched her, confused.

Shifting the plastic bag, Ellen reached out and grasped Rupert's hand in hers. Cello playing had made his fingers calloused and stronger than the rest of his body would suggest. She towed him along to the dumpster, where she let go, releasing them both from the unfamiliar intimacy. Lifting the heavy rubber lid, she gently set the fresh muffins on top of a stack of cardboard.

They started back up the alley, Ellen sinking her hands deep in her pockets to avoid the awkwardness of any further contact. Just before the grating, she stopped and said loudly, "Too bad we couldn't eat all those muffins, I hate throwing them away while they're still warm like that. Oh well. Thanks for helping me carry the trash down."

Rupert's mouth opened, then shut. Ellen gestured that he should speak. He blinked in panic, then a slow smile overran his usual startled expression. "Oh, yeah," he said with extra volume. "Too bad we're both on a diet, those muffins were really good." He winked and patted his large stomach. "Oh well, we have to get to work now. Can I walk you to the bus stop?"

"That would be great," Ellen projected. "We'd better hurry."

"Okay, let's go!" Rupert said, and they both made a show of stomping past the grating and on down the alley.

They rounded the corner and pulled up, waiting. After a moment, Ellen leaned around and looked back down the alley. As she had expected, the grating was angling out. She leaned back quickly and whispered, "Wait a second, and then look."

They changed places and Rupert did as he was told, working his back up against the brick at the very edge of the corner, and then easing just one eye around it. Ellen watched his face in profile as he observed the child. She could read it perfectly, so that she knew the moment the boy climbed out, she saw his pathos as he took in the boy's thinness and the hollow cheeks. She could tell the exact second when the child found the muffins from Rupert's triumphant smile.

After a full minute, Rupert leaned back against the wall and looked at Ellen. It was the first time, she realized, that they had looked at each other without their gazes flickering constantly away.

They didn't speak for a moment, and then Rupert pushed himself away from the brick and said, "Shouldn't we call someone?"

Ellen shook her head so hard it made it spin a little.

"No. He's probably run away from something worse than this. I don't know if you can understand that."

But Rupert was already nodding. "Okay, I get it. But he can't stay there forever."

"I know, I just need some time to figure things out. My guess is that if we call, say, the police, they'll send him back to wherever he was."

"But I mean," Rupert interjected, "if someone is mistreating him, he could call the police, or—"

He stopped speaking because Ellen was shaking her head. She said softly, "It doesn't always work that way. You can't always expect someone to listen."

"But what about social workers or . . . I don't know."

"Sometimes there isn't anyone. Sometimes . . . Usually, telling makes it worse. And he could be hiding from anything. Beatings, or even . . ." Ellen dropped her eyes, remembering some of the worst kinds of abuse she'd seen. Only her disfigurement had saved her from that particular horror, she was sure.

Thankfully Rupert seemed to understand without her having to put it into words. He puffed out his cheeks and blew the air out slowly.

"Well, we have to get that boy some medicine."

Ellen nodded. "I know," she said. "But he won't want to be found out, so . . . how?"

"What we need," Rupert said, rubbing a chubby finger along his jaw, "is someone with access to a prescription pad."

Ellen could only think of Amanda, and she was pretty sure Amanda would have to report the boy to the *authorities*.

And then she thought of someone else, someone in green surgical scrubs. Someone who didn't care what other people thought.

12

Two of the other cleaners, Kiki and Rosa, who were known to Ellen as the Crows, were in full caw when Ellen found herself working the aisle parallel to them later that night. Though she usually tried to avoid listening to their stream of gossip, she perked up when she heard the topic of their conversation.

"Did you see Thelma's girlfriend here last night?" Kiki was asking excitedly. "She was crying about something."

Through the deep shelves, over rows of plastic one-gallon relish containers and fifty-pound sacks of sugar, Ellen watched Rosa's face smile deviously.

So did Kiki. "What?" she demanded. "Trouble in gay heaven?"

Rosa planted her hands on her hips and frowned up at the much taller Kiki. It made her look even squatter than she was. "Now, be nice. I know it's not . . . normal, but I like Thelma, and she's always been nice to you, too."

Kiki had to concede that Thelma was a decent person, for a gay. "To each their own, I always say," Kiki added, a bit late. "But what's going on? Tell me."

"I happened to walk out to the parking lot with Thelma. You were already gone, remember?" Ellen grinned at that. She would have bet a month's paycheck that Rosa had planned, timed, and executed that exit perfectly to coincide with Thelma's. "Anyway," Rosa was saying, "I told her I'd seen her girlfriend and she looked unhappy. I asked if everything was okay."

"And she *told* you?" Kiki looked like she'd tried to swallow something that didn't quite go down.

"She most certainly did. I think she needed to talk to somebody. Anyway, it turns out that they can't have a baby."

"Well, of course not. That's just not possible," Kiki said with a snort.

Rosa slapped a hand against her thigh and insisted, "Of course it is. Lots of people have babies in lots of ways these days. Especially women. You can buy sperm, you know!"

Kiki looked affronted. She flicked a huge box of cornstarch with a rag. "Well, I know *that*. So what's the problem?"

Rosa, looking delightedly scandalized, glanced around and lowered her voice, but not enough that Ellen couldn't hear her. "Thelma has some kind of blood condition, Rc- or Rh-something, and now they found out that Beth, that's her friend's name, can't carry a baby either. And they're upset about it."

"No." Kiki clucked and shook her head. "Well, that's just a shame. Two mamas and no womb at the inn."

The two women snickered at the pun. Then looked over their shoulders to make sure that Thelma, or anyone else, hadn't heard the offensive slight.

The two women moved on down the aisle, dusting, wiping, and gossiping as they went.

Ellen found a container of relish leaking from a thin crack. She placed it carefully in the bin for damaged or tampered-with items, wiped up the sticky syrup that had oozed onto the shelf, and finished straightening out her section as she thought this through. So Beth *was* a doctor, maybe that could be useful, though Ellen didn't see how. The simple expedient of asking her for help did not even come to Ellen's mind. She had spent four years here out of sight and out of mind of her coworkers and she had no intention of drawing attention to herself.

Speaking of which: Ellen had been pleased to see that she had the dock restrooms on her work sheet for tonight. Normally, that would have been bad news, as the dockworkers were habitually disgusting in their bathroom habits, and of all the employees in the vast store, those callous-mouthed men were the most likely to make her work life unbearable if she drew attention. But tonight, it was *fortuitous*.

As she reached the end of the row of baking staples, with which Ellen felt a new affinity now that she had actually baked something, she swept a tiny dune of flour from one of the low shelves with a small whisk broom and deposited the white dust into her trash bag, then set out for the docks.

Careful to time it so that no one else was going in or out, she pushed the cart through the big loading doors that connected the docks to the store floor. Ellen headed to the restrooms on one side of the holding area. There were two—women's and men's—but the women's room was seldom used. Not that there weren't women who worked on the dock, there were, but not many, and most of them preferred to take the short walk to the ladies' locker room.

She started with the women's room, giving it a quick once-over. It was dusty, and the seldom-used toilets had rust stains that required some harsh-smelling product, which Ellen swirled with a rough brush and then left to soak. She wiped out the sinks and sprayed down all the handles, including the doorknob, with antibacterial cleanser to neutralize the legions of germs. As she was running her mop over the tile floor, she heard the distinct sound of a toilet flushing in the bathroom next door, and then the door opening and closing. She looked up. On what was the shared wall between the two, there was a metal vent, through which it was easy to hear what went on next door. Ellen shuddered. No wonder so few women used this restroom.

She packed up her cart, checked to make sure the area outside was clear, and scuttled back out onto the dock's holding area. She waited for a full five minutes for anyone to come out of the men's room, and when they didn't, she took her little sawhorse sign that read BATHROOM CLOSED, CLEANING IN PROGRESS, and set it in front of the door. She knocked, then backed rapidly away, ducking behind her cart.

No one called out or came out. Still, Ellen gave it another full minute. One of the drivers came to the door, saw the sign, and made a detour into the store.

Finally, Ellen went in, her reluctant movements the result of both her fear of surprising someone and the harsh stinging smell of urine that assaulted her nostrils as she proceeded in.

She regarded the small bathroom. There were two stalls, three urinals, and two sinks. All of them looked streaked with filth. Cautiously, Ellen took a short tour, checking the stalls and even the paper-towel holder, but she could not readily see anywhere a small cache of illegal contraband could be hidden. Cleaning this room took a good bit more commitment. Pulling the bottle of her most toxic green liquid from the cart, Ellen began by spraying a thick coating around the base of all the toilets and the urinals. Men, she thought, don't seem to have much aim. This wasn't something Ellen knew much about, or wanted to know any more about, but she had to wonder if it could really be *that* hard to hit the target. Next she went to work with the mop, giving the offensive areas a once-over from the handle's distance before donning her thickest rubber gloves and filling a bucket with steaming water from one of the sinks. Adding a generous dollop of pine-scented soap, she proceeded to scrub down the entire area with a huge sponge, changing the water several times. Then she mopped again, sprayed the mirrors and wiped them clean, letting her eyes glaze so as not to see the lewd comments scratched into them, and then stood back to check her work.

The room still had a very strong smell, but now it was mostly the harsh bite of bleach and pine, a definite improvement. As she surveyed it, she heard a sudden hiss up and to her left. Ellen dropped into a crouch and spun to look up. On the wall, near the corner, was an automatic scent dispenser. The artificial cherry scent didn't go far to cover the other odors, but it did its little bit.

Ellen watched it as she emptied the trash and replaced the plastic bag. In about a minute, a little red light blinked and another small spray released its odorous facade into the bathroom.

"Hmm," hummed Ellen. She took the bucket from her cart, turned it upside down, and stood on it. It was precarious, and she expected at any second for it to collapse like an accordion, but it held. Reaching up with a rubber-gloved hand, Ellen tested the cover. It was solid and did not come off easily, but when it did, she saw only a collapsing bag of red liquid inside. The plastic holder was small, about the size of two boxes of kitchen matches stacked together. Not big enough to hold anything but the deodorizer. Ellen was about to give up and climb down when she noticed that a ceiling tile above the sprayer was slightly askew.

It was out of her reach, so she stepped off the bucket with relief and a sigh of gratitude that it had let her live, and collected a broom. Using the handle, she pushed up on the tile. It moved, shifted, and Ellen could make out a large brown bundle resting just to one side.

I'll have to come back with a stepladder, she thought. Then wondered how, if she couldn't reach it, that Eric could. He was considerably taller than she was, but not tall enough to reach the ceiling. She looked around again, and then she spotted it.

The trash can was only about three feet high, but it was the steel bucket variety. It would easily hold the weight of a full-grown man, and, she hoped, hers. Ellen went to it and checked the rim. It was dented in several places, as though someone had turned it over and stood on it. She didn't relish the thought of balancing on that, but try as she might, she couldn't get the tile back in place using just the broom handle, so she dragged the trash can over, turned it upside down, and studied it.

It was twice as high as her squared plastic bucket and the base was narrower. Feeling like a performing poodle in a circus, Ellen put one foot on the top, which wasn't easy, because it was as high as her thigh and she had to maneuver her knee around her stomach. Then she put one hand against the wall and the other on the top of the trash can to counterbalance the weight on her foot and, with a heave, pulled herself up, wobbled dangerously, lurched, corrected, and steadied herself into a teetering but upright position. Leaning on the wall for precious balance, she reached one hand up and pulled out the parcel. It was a large manila envelope, and though she couldn't open it without risking cracking her skull, the contents certainly *felt* like the packages of drugs. She replaced the package and slid the tile back into its prefab framework.

Then she looked down.

Ellen did not like being up in the air. Ground was where she felt best, and this was definitely more like hovering. Ellen wasn't built for hovering, she was built for planting herself in one place and staying there, where gravity was her friend.

Through the vent came the sound of the sink running in the women's room. Someone was in there.

Help, Ellen thought. But of course she didn't say it, and didn't really mean it. Carefully, she shifted her weight to one foot in preparation for stepping down, but the trash can shifted and wobbled ominously. She reset the raised foot quickly, distributing her weight evenly again.

Great, I could be here all night. The floor seemed a long way down, but Ellen could see no option except to jump with both feet.

The very thought sent a presentiment of pain to Ellen's warning center. On a good day, her knees ached from carrying her extra poundage and the continuous bending her job required; she wasn't sure they could take the impact of a three-foot drop. *Probably,* she thought, *they'll explode.*

Or maybe, Ellen thought desperately, *I can lean against the wall and sort of . . . slide down.*

First she had to face the other way. She did this in half-inch increments, the metal trash can lurching slightly with each baby step, but eventually Ellen was able to rotate her back to the wall.

Thankfully, she made it all the way around without tragedy. Very carefully, she put both of her hands behind her and leaned her weight experimentally against them. So far so good.

She started to bend her knees, the plan being to get her weight against the wall, then slide down until she was in a sitting position. With some jockeying, she could get onto her butt and swing her legs onto the floor.

But . . . *The best-laid plans often go awry,* Ellen had heard Justice say, and though she hadn't known why, she found out now. She was starting the downward slide when the trash can lost its traction, slid across the still-wet floor, and Ellen's legs went with it, shooting straight out in front of her as gravity took hold.

The first thing that hit the linoleum was her bottom, it was well padded, and though it hurt, the friction against the wall had fortunately slowed her just enough to keep from doing any serious damage.

Unfortunately, the metal trash can went flying. It clanged across the floor, crashed noisily off the stall partition, which made its own distinct booming sound, and clattered back at her, every hit and smack reverberating like the steel drum it was, until it came to rest on her lap. Ellen's ears were ringing with the echoing din.

She sat for a few seconds, mortified at the commotion, and then tested her legs. They worked. She was moving the trash can off her lap when the bathroom door opened.

Horrified at the possibility of being confronted by one of the coarse dockworkers and being subjected to their cruel taunts, Ellen had to fight the impulse to pull the trash can over her head. Sheepishly, she looked up at the face in the doorway.

She was not looking at one of the callous men, but at Thelma, who was looking back at her with nothing but concern.

"Are you okay?" Thelma asked. "I was next door and I heard a crash."

"I'm fine," Ellen mumbled, rolling onto her knees and then struggling to stand. Thelma was next to her in a flash. With one hand under Ellen's arm, she helped her to her feet. Ellen stepped away the second she was upright. "Thanks," she stammered, staring at the floor. Pretending to wipe herself down, she swiped at the spot where she'd been touched, brushing away the contact.

"What happened?" Thelma asked as she picked up the trash can and turned it upright.

"I was changing the deodorizer," Ellen lied.

"Well, next time get a ladder. Safety first!" Thelma smiled at her recital of one of the many posters distributed around the employee-only areas of the store. "Are you sure you're okay? Maybe you should file an injury report—"

"Nothankyou," Ellen said in a one-word rush. "I'm fine."

Though she wasn't looking at Thelma, Ellen could tell that Thelma was watching her. "I know who you are," the produce manager said. "You're the one who . . . well, got shot last year. But I'm sorry, I forget your name."

As invisible as Ellen could be, getting shot was a surefire way to get yourself noticed, a pun that Justice had enjoyed. As friendly as Thelma was, Ellen was desperate to escape the tiny bathroom and the scrutiny, so she said, "Ellen."

Thelma nodded. "Right, of course, well, I'm Thelma, I'm the produce manager. I haven't seen you since that night, you just get back?"

She'd been back for more than five months, but because it was the path of least resistance, Ellen said, "Yes."

Thelma held out a hand. Trapped, Ellen extended her own to take it. The shake was firm, confident, and mercifully quick.

"Nice to meet you, Ellen," Thelma said. "Listen, if you want somebody to check you out, my girlfriend is a doctor, she has offices in the Venture Medical complex, and she takes our insurance. She's there every day but Thursday, that's the one day a week she works at the free clinic in midtown, at the Good Samaritan."

As trying as the encounter was for Ellen, some small part of her felt a thrill of recognition. "I know it. I live near there," Ellen found herself saying. She did know the clinic, it was only a few blocks away from the loft, toward the harder part of town.

Thelma wrinkled her nose. "I wouldn't recommend going *there*, but if you don't have a doctor, Beth's an awful good one. If you come by my office, I'll give you her card."

"Or maybe you could just leave it for me, like on the door or something, then I won't have to bother you." It was the best way to get the card and avoid further contact that Ellen could come up with at a second's notice.

Thelma nodded. "Sure." To Ellen's great surprise, Thelma's strong hand slapped against her back. "Okay, you, if you're sure you're okay, then we should both get back to work."

Without another word, Thelma turned and left the men's restroom, striding out as confidently as if she owned the place. Ellen was filled with admiration. If *she* had been seen coming out of a men's room, even with the excuse of cleaning it, she would have been mortified.

Of course, it wasn't much better getting caught crashing to the floor from an upturned metal trash can *in* a men's room, she thought as she gathered up her things onto her cart. *Well, at least I fell* after *I mopped. That's something.*

She checked carefully out the door, scanning the dock to make sure no one was lurking, before she scurried out, packed up her BATHROOM CLOSED sign, and hurried back to the store floor.

Though her next assignment was cleaning the glass of the huge sliding doors on the front of the store, Ellen went first to the outdoor section. Glancing up, she noted the location of the security camera for this aisle and was annoyed to see that it pointed directly at the area she needed to visit.

Oh well, she'd have to risk it. Pulling out her duster, Ellen began to run it across the displays of camping supplies and sporting goods. When she came to the item she was after, she took out her box cutter, turned her back to the camera, blocking her movements, and slit open the clear-plastic inventory control packaging. She removed the contents and shoved the plastic behind the other packages. Then she turned toward the camera, and feigned "finding" the trash, putting the mutilated packaging into the designated bin on her cart for damaged merchandise to be recorded by the night manager at the end of the shift.

She wasn't really worried. Ellen had watched the security guards in their little glass cube with the monitors. Mostly they dozed, and Ellen wasn't even sure that she would show up on a camera when she was invisible, she'd never tested it.

The contents of the package weren't cheap, it would take her more than two extra hours of work to "pay" for it. She patted the big pocket of her work smock. The bulge her prize made was small, about the size of two boxes of kitchen matches.

13

When Ellen got home early, Justice was having a breakfast of whole wheat pancakes and turkey bacon. Ellen eagerly agreed to a portion of her own. Though secretly she felt that turkey bacon was a poor substitute for the real thing, it was still . . . well, bacon.

As he reheated the pan, Justice asked, "So, how did the trip to the suburbs go?"

"Fine." Ellen wanted to say more. Justice was the easiest person to talk to whom she had ever met, and she liked listening to him, so she added, "There were lots of trees."

"Nice," Justice said. "Did Temerity tell you that Highland Park isn't far from where we grew up?"

Ellen sat up a bit at that. "Really?" she asked. "In that neighborhood?"

Justice laughed and tested the pan with a sprinkle of water from the sink; it sizzled. "No, about twenty minutes farther out, but that direction anyway. My parents still live there, in fact. It's a little bit more open where they live, not subdivisions, more land, and the houses are all different. Not like those housing developments with a choice of three floor plans."

Watching as the batter was poured into the skillet, Ellen thought about that. The idea of having even more land was daunting to her, but she liked the idea. "It's private, right?"

"Very." Justice nodded and lifted a corner of the pancake to test its doneness. Not ready. He let it fall. "The house is surrounded by woods, and they can't see another house from theirs. I mean, there are other homes nearby, you just can't see them."

She thought about being able to go outside without worrying that anyone else would be there to see her and with no threat of interaction. It sounded like bliss to her. "I think I'd like that," Ellen said.

"You *would* like it!" Justice told her, and then he put down his spatula and came to stand across from her. "And I'd like to take you." Ellen recoiled, leaning back and crossing her arms, but Justice went on. "They still haven't met Amanda. She's been so busy with her residency that I barely get to see her. It's no big deal, just dinner with the folks, it would only be them, and they'd really like to meet you."

"Why?" she asked. "Why would they want to meet me?" The idea of being anticipated was even more alarming than the prospect of meeting people.

Justice turned away to flip the pancakes. Over his shoulder he said, "Because they've heard such good things about you. And, complete disclosure, because they are both psychiatrists and they are fascinated by your story."

A story? Did she have a story? Ellen didn't really think so, but Justice thought about things differently, being an anthropologist. So she asked, "What story?"

With a sigh, Justice explained. "The way you were brought up, or rather, the lack of being brought up. The fact that you've been through so much, almost all of it on your own, and still become this rather remarkable person, is unusual. You must know that." Justice flipped the pancakes onto the plate next to three strips of bacon and carried it over to her.

Ellen could feel a frown on her face as she thought of the hundreds of other kids she'd crossed paths with, though she could recall only a handful of their names. She said, "Lots of people have grown up like me."

"True, though I doubt any of them can move through life invisibly, and I really doubt if any of them have thwarted a robbery-slash-murder attempt."

But Ellen didn't feel that those things were exceptional, just what she had done to survive, or because the moment had required it. "I'm boring, and you know it," she told him.

Mouse made a vocal appearance and would not be silenced without his share of bacon, though he sniffed at the turkey version suspiciously, as though he, too, detected an inferior substitute. Then he ate it.

"You think you're boring, huh?" Justice asked, propping his face on his hands across from her. "Let me ask you something. How's the kid from the bus—Lydia?"

"It looks like she really scored a nice family." Ellen poured syrup to cover her blush when she realized she'd just told him where she and Temerity had gone.

"Mm-hmm," Justice hummed. "And how many boring people have an undercover detective drop by to talk to them?"

Ellen's head snapped up. "What?"

"A Detective Barclay. He came by to thank you, he said. I told him you were at work. It seems like you both work nights."

That, at least, was a relief.

"You didn't tell me you helped him save the bus driver." Justice was beaming at her. "*And* you karate-kicked a three-hundred-pound, six-foot-four attacker who was high on meth cut with animal tranquilizer when he was about to go after the good detective, who was, apparently, trailing him because he's trying to find the source of the drugs." He shook his head and smiled. "I shouldn't tell you this, but they wanted to give you a citation. You know, get your picture taken for the paper and whatnot."

Ellen actually put her hands to her throat because she had stopped taking in air, but Justice hurried on. "It's okay, I told him you would much rather not. Actually, I said it was against your religion. Which is privacy."

Ellen sucked in a gasping breath and let her hands fall.

But Justice wasn't done. "And how boring is it that you're helping the kid who lives in the basement?"

"Wha . . . who?" Ellen feigned ignorance.

But Justice waved a finger at her. "You think I didn't know about that? I spotted him going through the grate when I got home from work about a week ago, but I didn't let on. I've been leaving him food and blankets. Of course, he doesn't know that either, I just left them in the dumpster, and made sure I forgot to lock it. I even talked to him, twice. His name is Seth."

Ellen's head felt as soaked with syrup as the pancakes on her plate. "And you didn't call the police, or, uh, anyone?"

Justice shook his head and looked concerned. "Before I met you, I would have, but now I decided to wait and see. No. I think where he came from is worse than where he is. I can't tell you why exactly, it has to do with some of the things he said about his uncle. But he's terrified to be sent back."

Her appetite left the room without excusing itself and Ellen pushed the plate away. "I thought it might be . . . I was sure it must . . . What should we do?"

Justice tilted his head sideways and regarded her. "I was kind of hoping you could tell me."

Stunned to find herself the resident expert on anything, Ellen tried to give it some thought. "Uhm, well, if he's fifteen, and he doesn't have a legal guardian, then he can choose—"

"He's twelve, and his uncle has custody. From what I can guess, the guy is a shyster, but capable of hoodwinking the forces-that-be when interviewed. And it sounds like he's the one who is . . . making money off Seth." Justice's face twisted. Ellen was afraid he might throw up or punch someone, or both.

"Is there anyone else?" Ellen asked, expecting a no.

"There's a mom, apparently, who 'signed off' on him, is the way he put it. And Mom's got a boyfriend that . . . I think that might be where the . . . trouble started."

Ellen nodded, her stomach twisting into a mass of knots. "So she relinquished custody and is out of the picture. Well, that means he has to wait at least three years, or find a way to get the uncle arrested *and* convicted." She felt hopeless. So many of the kids that had shared homes with her had been there for only a short time— the time their guardian had stood trial for abusing them. Only to be sent back when the overworked court system let the abusive parent walk. And if the child had said anything against them in the meantime . . . She couldn't bear to think about it.

"Arrested, huh?" Justice was thinking, tapping the fingers of one hand on the countertop. "I'm pretty sure Seth won't want to give us any information. Is there some kind of protective custody?" he asked hopefully.

Ellen stared past Justice. "There's supposed to be." The simple sentence was infused with sadness. Justice simply nodded his understanding.

Ellen elaborated. "To get away and stay away from the uncle, he'd probably have to testify against him, and that doesn't always work, especially if the uncle has a good lawyer. I've never seen it myself—I mean, I've never been to court—but I've heard about it . . . after. The kids tell their stories, you know, testify, and then the lawyers make them look like liars. Some of them do have juvenile records, so that's not too hard, but it doesn't mean what they said wasn't true." Ellen didn't add that one of the kids, whose story she'd overheard as he told it to another boy in the household, was the one who had taken his own life instead of returning to the abusive father.

"He's sick," Ellen said. "I think he needs medicine, and not the store-bought kind." She was hopeful. "Can Amanda get it for him?"

Justice shook his head. "I thought of that, of course, but here's the thing. Because he's a minor, the hospital would notify Seth's uncle. They'd have to." He sighed. "Plus, Amanda's legally required to report incidents of abuse, and I don't want to put her in the position of lying. She could lose everything she's worked for."

"I have another idea," Ellen said. As she shyly outlined it to Justice, her appetite returned and she pulled the plate back to her and took a forkful.

When she was done with the pancakes and the plan, Justice just stood smiling and nodding his head at her. "It could work," he said. Then he got her two more pieces of bacon from the pan and slid them on her plate. "And it is not boring."

Encouraged, Ellen ventured, "What do you know about illegal drugs?"

"You mean, like, meth, or heroin?" he asked. He blew out his cheeks and puffed. "Not much. I mean, I've never used anything harder than weed. Why?"

Ellen wasn't sure she wanted to tell him everything, not yet, he would worry too much. So she just said, "I think that this guy who works on the dock might be using the trucks to bring in . . . something . . . I don't know what it is. And I know he and some of the other guys are smoking . . . you know . . . weed when they are working."

Justice sighed. "Way too many people do. At least they're not driving."

"Yes, they are. I mean, forklifts and machinery and stuff."

"Ooh, not good. And you won't report this?"

Ellen just tilted her head and looked at him. They'd been through all this a year ago. The prospect of facing management, security guards, and then police and detectives was as repellent to Ellen as the idea of pole dancing naked.

"No, I know," he said. "Well, I suppose someone else needs to see it. You're still not connecting with anyone at work?" He asked this question as though it were completely normal, because for Ellen it was, which made it easy to answer.

Ellen opened her mouth to say no, and then she thought about Thelma introducing herself and shaking her hand. "Not really," she admitted, then amended her answer to "I mean, no." For all practical purposes—which is what this would be—"no" was accurate.

"Okay, so that limits our options," Justice said. "Are you sure this person is dealing drugs?"

Ellen thought about that. She'd seen Eric get high on the job, receive a shipment of what was pretty clearly some kind of illegal substance, bully Thelma, and lie to the general manager about the death of his own mother. "Pretty sure," she said.

"Then you need to probably stay out of it." Justice raised his eyes to the ceiling far above. "Like my telling you that is going to do *any* good. Does Temerity know about this?"

Ellen shook her head.

Justice said, "Well, then involvement isn't yet imminent. What about Seth?" Another shake. "Are you going to tell her?"

"I'm not going to lie to her."

The handsome man smiled at Ellen. "I don't think you should. In fact, I think she might be very useful for your particular plan. And you know how she loves to be useful! Ah! Here she comes now."

The hall door had just opened and Temerity came through it, making a beeline for the coffee. "I'm not here, I'm not up yet," she mumbled.

"Yes you are, I can see you," her brother teased. Ellen twisted around on her stool to look at her friend.

"Damn it. Sometimes I wish I were Ellen." Temerity grimaced with a crooked smile. "Hi, Ellen," she said as she came level.

"Hi," said Ellen, wondering how in the hell the blind girl knew she was sitting there silently, but when she shifted again, she noticed that the stool creaked slightly, and she knew.

While the water for her coffee was boiling, Temerity slid her hands across the counter until she found the plate of bacon. She sniffed it, then ate a piece.

"Did you tell Ellen that the detective came by?" Temerity asked, making it sound like that was nothing.

"Yep, she doesn't want a plaque." Justice picked up the breakfast plates and started to rinse them.

"What about the testifying part?"

Ellen had just been ready to slide off the stool, but suddenly her legs felt like yarn and she stayed put.

"Not yet," Justice said.

"No!" Ellen almost shouted. "I can't do that, you know I can't do that."

"Let's not worry about it for now, okay?" Justice soothed. "The absolute worst thing that would happen is that you could answer some questions on videotape, you wouldn't have to go to court."

But Ellen was shaking her head so hard it hurt. "No, no tape, no questions, no people I don't already know." She could feel the tears coming up. "It's been too much already, these last few months have been . . . I just . . . can't . . ."

"Then you don't have to." Justice was trying to calm her. "I don't think the detective would want to put you in a bad position."

As he was speaking, without saying a word, or seeming to respond to the volatile situation, Temerity set down the French press and walked around the counter. She sat down on the stool next to Ellen and leaned her elbows on the countertop. She didn't speak, she didn't touch. She just sat there.

It helped a lot.

14

To distract herself from the gaping black hole of possible police involvement, Ellen spent some time working out a plan for Seth with Justice and Temerity before she went up to bed. Because of Ellen's tenuous hold on her comfort zone, Temerity did not grouse about being left out of the developments so far, but Ellen could tell that her friend had felt excluded. By the time they had made the sign to post in the alley, Ellen had settled down and couldn't keep from yawning.

"Okay," Justice said, holding up their handiwork. "I'll post this, and Temerity, you man the phone."

Temerity's mouth twisted sarcastically. "Are you sure *manning* a phone isn't an obscene gesture?" she asked. Justice ignored her. "Well, I wouldn't know, would I?" she said. "You can't hear a gesture."

But Ellen thought if anyone could, it was Temerity.

Ellen looked at the small flyer. It read *Delivery person needed to run local errands. Please call* . . . then there was a phone number. It was to the point, and they had decided to place it near the edge of the main avenue, but on the alley side, so that Seth would be sure to see it, and hopefully not too many others.

Ellen was exhausted by now; it was almost nine a.m. She dragged herself up the narrow flight of stairs and stood for a moment, watching the apartment windows across the street. Her eyes swept the checkerboard of windows until she spotted the one directly across and below hers. At first glance, the window looked empty, and then Ellen saw that the woman's upper body was slumped along the sill. Her eyes were open and she was facing in Ellen's direction, but there was no acknowledgment. There never was.

Too tired to keep at it anymore, Ellen made a note of the scene in her notebook then climbed into bed.

When she woke up later, Ellen got dressed and went downstairs.

As she came into the main room, Temerity's phone rang and she pulled it from her pocket. "Yes?"

Though she couldn't hear the other side of the conversation, Ellen could tell immediately that it was about the sign they had put up that morning. Temerity said, "Yes, I am looking for help with deliveries. You said your name is Seth? When can you meet, tomorrow morning? Great, eight o'clock, then." Temerity gave the address and the loft number and hung up.

"Operation Antibiotic, stage one, complete," Temerity said with a content but sober grin. "That poor kid, I can hear how hard it is for him to breathe. Maybe I should have met him tonight?"

"No, it wouldn't do any good," Ellen said. "We have to wait for Thursday. In the meantime, you can get him to pick some stuff up for you."

"I'll send him to the drugstore," Temerity said, "and I'll have him pick up some cold medicine that I'll make him take. I'd have to be blind *and* deaf not to know he needs some mucus relief. It'll only help the symptoms but it'll be something." She seemed pleased with this idea. "Okay, get dressed, we're going back to see Maddy."

Ellen did not want to see the comatose woman again, but she knew that once Temerity had decided, they were going.

So within an hour, the pair was walking through the lobby of the hospital. Temerity stopped at security and said that she was visiting her friend, and they went right through. It was a short trek to the third floor, but then they had to stop and review.

"Now this part is up to you," Temerity told Ellen. "I think it would be best if we didn't run into that nurse again. She wasn't the friendliest."

"True," Ellen agreed, more with not wanting to meet the woman than with her general disposition. They crossed through the glass passageway without incident, and seated themselves in the waiting room across from the ward. Only when they were absolutely sure that it was empty except for the patients did they make their way cautiously to the bed where they had found Madeline Carson.

It was empty.

Ellen stood looking at the bed. The rumpled linens were still on it, as though the woman had been there recently. She noticed a corner of a sheet of paper that had fallen to the floor, halfway under the bed, and without even thinking, she stooped to pick it up. It was a copy of a transfer order, including the name and address of a state care facility.

Foiled and slightly shaken, the women retreated to the cafeteria, where they bought cups of hot tea.

Temerity broke the silence. "Do you think she's dead?" she asked.

Ellen said no, and told Temerity about the transfer order she had in her pocket. But she had another fear, one that had been growing since she had watched the happy Lydia surrounded by safety and warmth and good things.

She cleared her throat. "From that paper we found, she was probably moved into a state facility for the long term, so she was alive when she left, at least. But in a way, it might not be terrible if she did . . . Well, what I mean is, if her mom gets better, even partially better, then Lydia will go back."

Temerity's mouth made a little O and she said, "I hadn't thought of that. But I mean, it's her mom, and she'd want to, right?"

Ellen shrugged and said she didn't know that either. She'd only seen them together for a few minutes, and it had been impossible to judge. Lydia hadn't seemed frightened of her mother, and that was something. "I mean, I think that even if she does, if her mom is, you know, in a wheelchair or something, Lydia will be the one who has to take care of her."

"But she's only six!"

Ellen looked at Temerity and told herself that her friend just didn't know. "Who else is there?" Ellen took a sip of her cooling tea. "It happens a lot."

Temerity's eyes had filled. "How horrible," she said. "All of these things I never even thought of before I met you." She reached out and found Ellen's hand, which she patted and then drew back. "I just assumed that when a kid went into foster care, they found a new home and were taken care of. I mean, I know it can't be easy, but foster parents must *want* to care for these kids. Right?"

That, Ellen thought, was most definitely *not* always right. But she couldn't see what could be done about Lydia. She didn't want to hope that Maddy was dead or dying. On the other hand . . . if she stayed alive, Lydia would not become eligible for adoption. "Come on," she said. "There's not much use in staying here, let's go home." It was interesting to call it that, not that Ellen didn't think of the loft as home, but openly claiming it as their shared home felt new. Temerity didn't seem to notice.

They had arrived at their door when someone called out behind them. "Excuse me!"

Ellen shifted her weight into the deep recess of the doorway and looked cautiously back around it.

From the street, a man was rapidly walking toward them. He was dressed in jeans and a red leather jacket, his blond hair was slicked back around his ears, and the immediate overall impression Ellen got from him was *fraud*. She had known so many.

But Temerity couldn't see the smile that did not extend to his eyes, or the heavy gold chain around his neck, or the pointed cowboy boots with the silver tips. She turned and asked, "Can I help you?"

"I hope so." The man waved disarmingly and stopped a few yards away. "I'm looking for a boy, a blond boy, twelve, but small for his age. He was seen in this neighborhood."

Ellen held her breath and, leaning back hard against the cold metal door, she watched her friend's face.

It was twisted by a crooked smile. "Not by me," Temerity said. "I'm sorry." She switched her stick to the hand on his side.

"Oh, sorry," the man said, but Ellen could tell he didn't mean it. She peeked, just barely, around the lip of the bricks. The man was now coming closer, and his eyes were roaming freely over Temerity's body so leeringly that it might have existed for his personal pleasure. Ellen tensed.

"Do you live here?" the man asked, still watching Temerity. "Nice place."

"No, I'm visiting a friend," Temerity told him. "And I'm late. I'm sorry I can't help you."

"Well, could you maybe do me a favor?" the man said. "If your . . . friend has seen a kid, blond, small for his age, kinda thin, could you maybe let me know? He's my nephew and he's been missing for a few days. We had an argument, my fault, and he took off. I'm really worried about him."

In all her years of watching humanity, of observing behavior, good and bad, Ellen had never been more sure that a person was lying, and there was no way that Temerity could miss the false ring in every word. This was a man for whom the word *honesty* had no meaning.

"If they know anything, I'll have them call the police," Temerity said firmly. "You've notified the police, I assume?"

"Well, no, they aren't really very motivated by teenagers who haven't come home for a couple of nights." The man faked a sad laugh. "Can I give you my number?"

But Temerity took a step backward and said, "No, you can stay there. Don't take it personally, but I have to be a bit cautious around strangers, seeing how I don't know you and can't see you."

"No problem, no problem, I don't mean to scare you. Tell you what, I'll put some flyers in the mailboxes, so if anybody sees the boy, they can call me. Can you tell your friend?"

"Flyers. Sure." Temerity made a show of ringing the bell. Justice's voice came through the speaker box. "Hello?"

"Hi, Justice, it's your friend, Temerity. I'm here for the dinner you promised to cook me."

"What?"

"Are you going to buzz me in or not?" Temerity said pointedly.

There was one second of static, and then Justice said, "I'm coming down." The buzzer sounded.

When she heard the click behind her, Ellen leaned against the door and the two of them stumbled in. With a last, narrow-eyed stare, the man turned and moved away as the heavy metal door started to close. Above them, on the fourth-floor landing, they could hear the door to the loft open. Justice called out, "Tem? Are you okay? What's going on?"

Temerity locked the door behind them and exhaled hard. "We're okay!" she called upward.

Justice came all the way down, and Ellen told him about the man.

"It's the uncle, gotta be," Justice muttered. He told them to go up while he checked the alley and the grating to the basement. Both were deserted, he reported, when he came back up.

"Should we warn Seth?" Temerity asked.

"I'm not sure how, without telling him we're watching him," Justice said. "The kid's pretty savvy, maybe he already knows."

"You think it's true someone told him Seth was in this neighborhood?" Temerity asked.

Ellen frowned down at the floor. "It's possible. You'd be surprised how much some of the homeless people know about what goes on." She fidgeted a bit. "I know most people think all of them are crazy, but they aren't. Could have been one of them."

"True." Justice sighed. "For someone whose home is the street, a new youngster in the neighborhood would be as obvious as someone sitting in our living room would be to us."

"What can we do?" Temerity asked.

Justice paced a bit. Then he said, "Nothing for tonight. He's coming over tomorrow, right?"

"Eight o'clock," Temerity confirmed.

"Well, we might just mention that someone was asking about a kid his age, you know, give him a heads up, but not let on that we know it's him."

Ellen thought that was probably smart, there didn't seem to be much else they could do. "I've got to go to work pretty soon," she said.

"And I'd better start dinner," Temerity said, moving toward the kitchen. "You want me to make you a sandwich to take?"

"Yeah, thanks," Ellen said, thinking that she would leave it for Seth, if she could. She went upstairs, showered, dried her hair, dressed, and collected her things. When she went back down it was dark outside the big windows. She entered the open area and came to a stop.

Justice must have retreated to his room to work, because Temerity was alone in the room, in the middle of the large open space. Ellen canted her head, and in a moment the sound of music found her lesser ears. Searching for the source, she saw Temerity's small tape recorder on the coffee table, playing back an unfamiliar piece of violin music that Ellen guessed she'd recorded earlier. Her face was rapt, her eyes were half closed, and she was dancing where she stood, her arms raised, like they were resting on a partner's shoulders, and her body turned in a graceful circle. Ellen slunk through the room and left as quietly as possible, leaving her friend to dance alone to music only she could read.

15

On the way to work, Ellen leaned her head against the window of the bus and thought about Lydia. She remembered the way it had felt to have Lydia in her lap, trusting her. She imagined the slight weight on her chest and experienced it as a spreading warmth.

Ellen got off the bus and walked across the huge parking lot, then around the giant block of a building, and took her usual route through the docks toward the locker room. Hearing voices inside, Ellen stopped just outside the break room. She leaned an ear against the door and made out a constant flow of words in a man's voice, not one she immediately recognized. She drew herself inward, took a quiet breath, and opened the door soundlessly.

At one of the tables across the room, two men were sitting. The talker, who Ellen now recognized as Daniel, the dockworker who had shared Eric's mean-spirited opinion of Thelma, was leaning forward across the tabletop at a forty-five-degree angle, while the guy across from him leaned away from it proportionately, his chair tilted back, seemingly determined to keep an even distance between them.

Ellen couldn't blame him, the flow of babble from Daniel was incessant and not particularly coherent. Neither of the men noticed Ellen, or even glanced at the door, as she slipped through the room.

She disappeared into the ladies' locker room, put her bag in her locker, took out the small package she had borrowed the night before and placed it in the pocket of her smock. When she was ready, she went back to the exit. She listened but heard nothing. Wary, she pushed the door open a crack and looked out.

The second man had fled, but Daniel was still there, muttering in a constant stream, though now under his breath. As Ellen watched, he took a small baggie from his pocket and a popsicle stick, which he used to scoop out some of the powder. Then he sniffed it up his nose. He made a harsh sound and shook his head, as though it burned, and returned the baggie to his pocket with a glance at the entrance. His movements were both furtive and nervously manic.

Ellen let the door to the locker room slip back two inches, concealing the crack and her presence, and waited until she heard Daniel leave. With a sigh of relief that she hadn't walked in on him—*Always have a plan*—she went to collect her supply cart and check the work assignments. She had the produce section tonight, but she let her eyes wander on down the list until she found *dock restrooms*. They had been assigned to Irena, a Russian immigrant for whom Ellen had done a small favor nine months ago. She was one of the only people in this work environment to whom Ellen had ever willfully spoken.

Knowing that Irena, like herself, felt like an outsider and preferred to arrive early and not deal with too many other people, Ellen waited for her in the supply room. As she waited, her eyes roved around the stacked shelving and she spotted a folded stepladder slotted into a narrow space between the shelves and the wall, like a slice of bread in a toaster. Ellen would have liked some toast with butter and a thick smearing of strawberry jelly. When the door opened a few minutes later, Ellen saw the tall, thin Irena come in, and for the tenth time, she thought how much difference a few months and the demise of an abusive husband could make.

Irena had filled out and the dark circles under her eyes had faded, but the changes weren't just physical. She no longer stooped and scurried, mouselike, in terror from place to place. Ellen remembered coming in on Irena and their then boss in this very room almost a year ago, when the boss had been attempting to molest the terrified woman. Ellen had enjoyed anonymously putting a stop to that. She had been happier still when Irena's murderous husband had gotten what was coming to him.

Ellen braced herself and said softly, "Irena?"

Irena jumped and turned toward the corner where Ellen was standing behind her cart. "Oh, Ellen, you startle me." The woman's use of English was growing more solid, but the finer points were still slippery.

"Sorry, uh, I have a favor to ask you."

Irena smiled at her. "Your face, it is good, almost healed completely. Only, a bit red, but good."

"Uh, thanks." Ellen had no idea how to react to a positive remark about her physical appearance, as up until now they had been uniformly hurtful. "Listen, would it be all right with you if I took the dock restrooms tonight? You can spend an hour in produce instead."

The eyebrows above the high cheekbones went up. "You . . . *want* to clean there?" Irena's nose wrinkled. "Okay by me."

"Thanks." Ellen started to push her cart away and then felt that she should make some sort of reference to their frightening, shared experience months before. "Uh, how's, uh, the baby? Do you ever see him?"

Irena shook her head but smiled broadly. "No, but Susan, she send me pictures sometimes. Ivan is big and has six teeth now! A very healthy boy."

Ellen thought about the sickly child that had been dumped on Irena, while his cruel father ran off with another woman. It was good to hear that the child was healthy now and safe with his adoptive mother. "Oh, that's . . . uh, good."

"And your friends, they are well?" Irena asked.

"Very well, thank you. I'll tell them you asked."

"Yes please, thank you." Irena's Russian accent still rumbled her consonants heavily in the back of her throat.

"Well . . . bye." Ellen scooted out as quickly as she could, searching her pockets for a stashed chocolate Power bar, which she ate to restock the nervous calories it had cost her to interact. The carbs took effect almost immediately, settling her quivering anxiety and smoothing her jitters with their fluffy-stuffing comfort.

She made her way to the docks and found a safe, dark corner to wait in until the shift changed and she could get to work. At 10:02, she'd been watching the restroom doors for so long that she knew it was safe to go in the men's room, which she chose first.

She put out her BATHROOM CLOSED sign and went in. Normally, she propped her cart in the doorway of the restrooms to discourage any attempted entry, but tonight she took it all the way in and shut the door behind her, then pushed the cart up against it. She pulled the stepladder off the top, where she had precariously balanced it, and set it up below the automatic scent dispenser. In a few minutes, she had replaced the contents and snapped the cover back on. Then she climbed back down to the reassuringly flat floor and went on to clean the rest of the room.

It was amazing how disgusting thirty or so workers could make a bathroom in a day or two, but Ellen worked diligently and soon the smell of pine cleanser was sharper in her nostrils than urine. She mopped her way out after checking that the space outside was clear, did a quick cleanup in the women's room, and was pouring the mop water down the sink when she heard the scream.

It was followed by shouting. Ellen left the bucket on the floor and went to look out the door. At first she couldn't see anything but crates, but she moved cautiously forward until she had a view of the commotion.

It was bad. One of the dockworkers, who had been wearing a headset, she noticed, had been hit by a forklift. The lower part of his leg jutted at a strange angle from below the knee, and he was grimacing in pain and clutching at his thigh. "Don't touch my leg!" he screamed as Thelma dropped to her knees next to him.

"I won't, don't worry, Bruno," she told him, putting a hand on his shoulder instead. "Somebody call 911," she called out. All around them, people were either moving eagerly forward to see the drama or standing stupidly and doing nothing. Picking a face out of the crowd, Thelma barked sharply, "Eduardo, 911, do it now!" Eduardo peeled away and ran for the office.

Eric was there, too. He leaned down over the injured man and said, "Okay, buddy, just lie still. You'll be okay."

"'Okay'?" Bruno opened his mouth in a silent scream that muted him temporarily. When he could breathe again he said, "I am *not* okay. Christ." He grimaced again and whimpered, dropping his head forward and baring his teeth against the pain. "What the . . . ?! That hopped-up idiot ran right into me!" The man gasped between clenched teeth. "How could he not see me? Ahhhh!" He let his head fall back.

Ellen looked at the forklift. No one was in the driver's seat, but standing next to it, twitching, was Daniel. As she watched, Ellen noticed Eric checking to make sure no one was watching him, then he jerked a thumb toward the open edge of the dock. Daniel nodded fearfully, slipped backward, step by step, and then bolted down the stairs and into the darkness.

The Crows arrived, elbowing their way to the front of the crowd. Rosa and Kiki looked thrilled as they took in the carnage, memorizing details for future use. Ellen knew that a few minutes of listening to them throughout the night would keep her up-to-date on any of the ensuing details.

While everyone was distracted, Ellen retrieved her cart and escaped to the main floor. She went to the produce section and began to clean out the emptied bins with a ferocious energy. Something was driving her to stay busy, to scrub and focus here, only here. Her busyness was fueled by the need to avoid a prickling, stinging feeling. She did not hear the ambulance arrive, or see the injured man taken away. She did not know who was questioned or blamed, she did not listen to the other workers whispering or exclaiming openly about the "accident." She didn't want to, not yet.

She felt that she'd been stung by a wasp on the inside and the insect was still buzzing furiously in her chest, searching for more tender tissue to assault. Only if she kept busy could Ellen avoid the inevitability of it landing and piercing her again and again with its stinger. But she couldn't. All her well-trained practice in not feeling, in pushing aside the nagging awfulness, was not working. This was something different than the hurt that had happened *to* her in the past.

The Crows came back and headed into the wine section, their heads close together, talking fast. Ellen followed them down the parallel aisle to listen.

"Snapped the leg, twisted it almost all the way around," Rosa was saying. "Bruno was lucky he wasn't crushed."

"And Daniel just ran off, and you know why!" Kiki was almost ecstatic with the adrenaline rush of insider information. Ellen watched them through the cases of wine.

Rosa gasped and put a hand to her chest. "You mean he did it on purpose?"

Kiki shook her head, pursing her mouth into a prissy little pout. "No, but he's always *on* something. Can't you tell? If you listen to him talk for two minutes, you will. Why he hasn't been fired, I don't know."

"I do!" Rosa's brown eyes were huge and sparking as if static electricity was being repeatedly discharged. "I told you that I caught Eric giving Daniel a package and taking money from him one day! When Eric saw me watching, he said Daniel was returning money he'd lent him and told me to mind my own business. Then he made a point of mentioning that my nephew's son, Jimmy, works for him. Like a threat!"

Kiki nodded. "Maybe you should tell Billy. I heard him talking to the police. They said that Daniel will be in trouble for fleeing from the scene of an accident." The tall, sharp-faced woman seemed pleased with her assessment.

"Hit-and-run," Rosa agreed. "And with a forklift! Those things scare me. They weigh tons! I don't even like to go out on the dock, and when they come in *here*, I stand clear."

"Well, you've got some sense. Those guys out there are always trying to prove how macho they are." Kiki huffed.

Rosa and Kiki looked at each other knowingly, then at the same time they both said, "Men!"

The two women cackled, and then went back to whispering, but Ellen could hear no more as they moved to the far side of the aisle.

It was a full hour later, as Ellen paused to wipe the sweat from her brow and straighten her aching back, when she finally recognized the sensation she had been feeling. With a searing hot slap of shame, she called it by name. *Guilt.* She could have prevented the pain that man Bruno was feeling. The pain he would most likely suffer for the rest of his life had been caused by someone whom Ellen had known was incapable of being safe. More, she knew why he'd been in that state and who was responsible. If Ellen was someone different, if she was a person with the ability and the courage to speak up, the accident would not have happened.

For the first time that she knew of, Ellen understood what it was like to feel guilty for *not* doing something.

But what else *could* she do? It just wasn't possible for her to be other than she was. She thought about this long and hard as she threw herself back into her work. If Eric was selling drugs to the other workers and encouraging them to use them, something like this, or worse, was certain to happen again. The thought made her feel frayed all the way down her spine. She did not have the courage it took to speak up, and she knew it. But, she reminded herself, she had other . . . *talents*, as Justice put it, and in that moment of recognition, she decided that she would make up for her failings. Ellen was an observer. She would catch Eric at his own game, and, like Temerity had said, he would never see her coming.

That she could do as well as anyone else.

16

Though Ellen was exhausted when she arrived home at seven a.m., she knew that Seth was supposed to come over at eight, and the appearance of the uncle had increased her interest and concern. So she had a cup of Justice's thick coffee, with a healthy dollop of heavy cream and two teaspoons of sugar to mute the taste. Considering the nervy tension from the night, she added a spray of whipped cream on top. Just watching the dense white foam as it whooshed out of the can calmed her.

She made herself breakfast, peanut butter toast with bacon, and watched Temerity fuss about. Justice came out, dressed, but his hair still wet from the shower, and asked, "Is he here?"

"Do you see him?" Temerity asked.

"No. Do *you*?" he responded testily.

"Maybe that's because he's not here yet. Obviously," she shot back.

Ellen realized they were both feeling nervous and she intervened. "It's not eight yet." It didn't work.

Justice said to his sister, "Oh, and you are Queen of the Obvious."

"Better than being King of the *Oblivious*," she retorted.

Ellen moved to the big windows and looked down at the street, letting the nervous tension blend away behind her. She didn't really expect to see Seth, but it always calmed her to watch from above.

"Someone got hurt at work last night," Ellen interjected into the stream of quarreling.

That stopped them. "Who?"

"A guy on the docks, he was hit by a forklift and it broke his leg. Badly."

"Ouch!" Justice exclaimed. "Is he okay?"

But at that moment, the buzzer sounded. Temerity jumped and then crossed the floor to the phone. "Yes? Oh, good morning. Come on up to the fourth floor, it's the only door. I'll open it now." She hung up. "It's him," she said, sounding excited and nervous.

"Okay," Justice told her. "Just play it cool, like we practiced."

Ellen was already at the hallway door and didn't hear the reply. She hurried up the narrow stairs and reached for her notebook, and then thought she'd better wait or she'd miss the meeting downstairs.

Turning around, she crept back down and positioned herself just at the end of the hallway inside the door, opening it a crack so that she could see and hear what was going on in the big open space beyond.

"Hi, come on in! My name is Temerity, and this is my brother, Justice."

"Actually, we've met," Justice said, affecting surprise. "Hi. Seth, right?"

Ellen couldn't hear the mumbled reply, which was lost under a rolling cough. Switching off the hall light, she opened the door a few inches more and sat down on the floor. From this angle she could see straight to the table area, where Temerity had put out juice, milk, cereal, and some pastries.

"Are you hungry? Help yourself. Would you like some hot chocolate or tea?" Temerity moved into the kitchen area. Seth's eyes tracked her like she was a windup toy and he was figuring out how she worked.

"Do you have coffee?" asked Seth, moving toward the table but keeping his distance from both of them. Ellen was reminded of a stray cat, curious and wanting, but too wary to approach. "Black," he added, still studying Temerity with fascination.

"Yeah, I don't know if you want to do that. My brother's coffee is pretty much a punch in the gut. How about if I mix in some hot chocolate? I love a mocha, don't you?"

Ellen saw the boy's face relax slightly. "Sure," he said. His eyes continually flicked to the goodies on the table. Justice was standing a few feet behind Seth and he stepped up next to him to take a bear claw. The boy feinted and slid away, around the other side of the table. *He's as fast as an alley cat,* Ellen thought. Justice pretended not to notice the reaction, just took a bite of the pastry and sat down, gesturing for Seth to join him. The boy reached for a donut, took a huge bite, and chewed with purpose.

"Sit down," Temerity said. "Let's discuss terms. You available to run some errands today?"

"Sure," Seth said, sitting, but leaving an empty chair between himself and Justice.

"Good. I was thinking maybe ten dollars an hour? Would that be all right?"

"Eleven would be better," Seth said, almost automatically, and Ellen recognized the bargaining skill of someone who lived dollar to dollar. The boy began to cough again and Justice handed him a paper napkin. Seth blew his nose, a fruitful sound. His nostrils and upper lip were red and raw. Justice leaned behind him to a shelf under the bar and grabbed a box of tissues.

"Here, put a bunch of these in your pocket, they're the lotion kind. Easier on the nose. So, Seth, you live around here, I assume, because I've seen you in the neighborhood."

"Are you in school?" Temerity asked.

Seth squirmed in his seat a bit, he was almost painfully thin, and though he hadn't taken off his jacket, he shivered slightly. "I'm on break right now."

"In winter?" Temerity asked.

"Yeah. Split schedule. I go in summer."

"That's right, public school is year-round now," Justice commented. His voice had a slight warning tone directed at Temerity. She must have picked up on it, because she didn't ask any more questions about school.

"This won't be an everyday thing, probably about three times a week for . . . say, three or four hours. Can you do that?" she asked him instead, opening a cabinet. She found a round box and let her fingers run down the tape to identify it, though Ellen could read the powdered hot chocolate brand name from where she sat.

"Yeah, okay." Seth was still considering Temerity with his runny but sharp eyes. "You're blind, right?" he asked bluntly and without embarrassment. "Is that why you need somebody to get your stuff?"

Temerity paused, and Ellen knew that her friend was fighting the impulse to declare her independence, but practicality won over and she said, "Only my eyes. But you're right, sometimes it's easier, especially when I'm busy."

Now Seth's eyes played around the huge apartment. It was far less cluttered than most homes. Part of this was because of the size and open floor plan, but in fact, the lack of decorative furniture or knick-knacks made it much easier for Temerity to negotiate, and were without value to her anyway. Justice seemed to like the sparse, open atmosphere, and Ellen, never a hoarder of *things*, preferred it as well. But Seth took in the comfortable sofa and chairs, the big-screen TV, the view through the huge windows, and a sort of hungry deficit showed in his expression.

"Nice place," he said. "Must cost a lot."

"Well, it's not free, but we actually own it," Temerity told him. "We had grandparents who ran their own grocery store, then sold out to a big chain. So when they passed away, Justice and I inherited some money. Not a fortune, but enough to buy this place and fix it up. It used to be a garment factory. It was a real mess at first. You like it?"

"Sure. Except most people have, you know, stuff on the walls."

"Most people have vision," Temerity said lightly. "But maybe we should. If only for the sake of my more discerning guests, like yourself. Now, some sculpture, *that* I could appreciate. Do you like art, Seth?"

The boy shrugged and then realized that was inadequate. He said, "Don't know anything about it. I like the big pictures in the library on Grant, the ones of the ships."

"Oh, those are great," Justice said. "Tall ships."

"I don't know how tall they are, but I like the sails," Seth admitted.

"They are called 'tall ships,'" Justice explained. "Have you ever seen one? I mean, in real life?"

Another shrug. "Never been to the ocean."

"Well, then it's something to look forward to," Justice said. "Cereal?" he asked, casually pouring Lucky Charms into a bowl. Ellen felt a smile cuddle up into her cheeks. Justice had bought the cereal for Seth. She'd never seen Justice eat sugary breakfast cereal in all the months she'd lived there. He added milk and set the bowl in front of the boy without waiting for an answer. Then he served up a small portion for himself and took a tentative bite.

Seth was shoveling the name-brand treat into his mouth, pausing only to gulp down some orange juice. When he'd gone through half the bowl, his hunger seemed abated enough for him to take another look around. He did so and then asked, "So, what do you do?"

"Me?" Temerity asked. She finished making the mocha and brought it over. She felt for the chair backs, and held out the mug in Seth's direction. "Here," she said. He reached out and took it, placing the hot drink carefully on the table, and then letting his fingers slide around the warm ceramic, relishing the heat as a treasure he could feel through the pads of his fingertips and palms. Temerity pulled out a chair and sat down across from Seth and Justice with her back to Ellen, but not blocking her view of either of them.

"Both you," Seth said through another full mouth of frosted-oat cereal and marshmallows.

"Well, I am a musician, I play for the city symphony orchestra, and Justice is an anthropologist."

"A wha . . . ?" Seth's eyes had gone round.

Justice said, "An anthropologist is someone who studies humans, basically. Their behavior, like in society and stuff like that."

"Is there money in it?"

Justice laughed. "Actually, yes, depending. Oh, by the way . . ." Justice leaned back in his chair and wiped his mouth with his napkin. "Some guy was asking about a runaway boy yesterday, blond, about your age, I thought the kid might be a friend of yours."

Seth had tensed, but Justice was so casual, not even looking at Seth while he took an exaggerated sip of his coffee. Seth said, "No idea."

"Didn't seem like the guy was too concerned anyway. He hadn't even told the police or anything," Justice said, giving a dismissive shrug of his own.

Ellen saw Seth relax at that. "So, what do you want me to do?"

Temerity said, "First things first. You have a bad cold."

A new coughing fit sent his face into the tissue again. "It's no big deal," Seth said thickly, and blew his nose again. Justice pushed the tissue box closer and Seth took a few more.

"Maybe," Temerity said. "I need you to go to the drugstore any-way, so you can pick up some cough syrup. I don't want you to be out sick on your first day!"

The boy dropped his eyes and stared at his dirty fingers. "I don't have money for that, not right now," he said.

"Oh, that's okay," Justice told him. "We'll buy it for you. You know, a job with benefits." He smiled and winked at the waif.

Seth had started on the mocha. After a cautious sip, his eyes closed in delight, savoring the sweet, bracing heat, and he gulped at it eagerly. He held the mug's warmth to his chest, just under his chin so that the scent would rise. Ellen liked that, though she doubted he could smell or even taste very much with all that congestion.

Seth, now full of the hefty carbs that meant being sated for a few hours, looked around him more leisurely. "Who cleans this place up? It's big, you got somebody to do that?"

"Not really," Temerity said. "We have a service that comes in once a month, but mostly we do it."

"You need somebody," the boy stated this as a well-known fact. "I could do it."

"You clean?" Justice asked.

"Sure," the boy said with forced ease. "I had to clean my last place, it wasn't this big, but I could do it." His eyes roamed the big open room again. "Easy," he added, and buried his face in his mug.

Justice was watching Seth thoughtfully. "It's certainly a possibility. We have a roommate who is a professional, maybe she could give you some pointers. Why don't we start with the errands and go from there." In the dark, Ellen smiled again. She was a *professional*, it sounded good.

Seth immediately set down the mug and stood up. "I'm ready. I can go now."

Temerity laughed. "No rush. I still need to make a list. Tell you what, you need to use the restroom or anything?"

"I could?" Seth asked, and for the first time, Ellen heard the defenselessness in his voice. She could guess how he was treated, sneaking into restaurants to use the facilities and being hustled out, refused admittance to anything but the most unmonitored of public restrooms. She wondered how long it had been since he'd had a hot shower or clean clothes.

Justice stood up. "Right this way. I'll show you. And there's some towels and soap in there. I notice your hands look a little dirty, you can wash up if you want." He moved nearer to Seth, intending to show him the way.

"That's okay," Seth said quickly, backing a nervous step away from Justice. Ellen cringed for him. To have been abused . . . in that way . . . made it hard for Seth to even stand near a grown man he didn't trust. And, she guessed, he trusted none.

Identifying the fear, Justice reversed his motion, sat back down, and pointed toward Ellen and the door. "I'm sure you can find it yourself, just go through there and it's the first door on the right. I have to go to work, so I'll see you later. Nice to meet you, Seth." Justice extended a hand.

Seth stood a few feet away, looking at the outstretched arm. Then, biting his lip and watching Justice suspiciously for any sudden moves, he sidled forward, just close enough to touch the hand, shook quickly, and bolted for the far door.

Ellen barely had time to get behind the door before it opened and Seth came through. She watched him from the shadows as he looked nervously around before creeping down the hallway, his head rotating from side to side, scanning for danger. Finding none, he opened the door to the bathroom, switched on the light, and scoped it out. Ellen watched his eyes spot the huge tub. His mouth dropped open, and then he emitted a long, low whistle. His face hopeful, but cautious, as if even this treat of a clean bathroom could not be trusted and might be snatched away, he went in. Ellen heard the door close and lock behind him.

She went out.

Justice was handing Temerity some cash. "Here, this is enough for the store, and forty bucks for Seth. Make sure he gets a receipt and tell him I'll count the change. If we're too trusting, he won't trust us back. Hi, Ellen, did you hear?"

She nodded. "I think you're right," she said quietly.

Justice looked up at her, uncertain what aspect of his being right she might be referring to, but understanding came to him almost before his eyes settled on her.

"I do, too," he said sadly. "Which is why I'm vacating. See you guys later." He started for the door.

"Justice?" Temerity called.

"Yeah?"

"Thanks. I guess you're an okay brother." She smiled slyly. "But I still hate your coffee."

Justice pulled on a stocking cap to cover his damp hair and winked at Ellen. "That's why I make it that way. Love you." He went out.

Ellen thought, *Sibling relationships are complicated.*

"You want me to write the list?" Ellen asked Temerity as Justice went out.

"I already did it," Temerity said, pulling out a folded, printed sheet of paper. She was twitchy, turning to listen for Seth's return. "Why can't we just move him in with us?" she asked suddenly.

"Because he won't trust you, like Justice said, and he needs to be independent, I guess. And there's, you know, laws and stuff."

Temerity did know. She nodded. "Okay, but I . . . it's so awful for him."

Ellen smiled and actually reached out to pat Temerity's shoulder to reassure her, not even realizing that it was the first time she had done so. "It will be better now. He'll have food and some money. After tomorrow, he'll hopefully have the medicine he needs, too."

"He sounds bad, doesn't he?" Temerity asked. "How does he look?"

"Gooey," Ellen confirmed. "But the medicine today will help some. Let's hope. Make sure you tell him that you need him tomorrow. I'll try to find out what time tonight." Ellen was watching the door nervously now. It wouldn't do to have Seth come back in while she was *there.* "I'm going to sleep now."

"Okay," said Temerity. "I'm not."

Ellen smiled at that as she hurried back upstairs.

When she awoke, Ellen dressed quickly and went downstairs, where Temerity was waiting for her.

"How did it go?" Ellen asked.

Temerity sighed and said, "Good. I guess. I mean, I got a dose of medicine in him, and sent the rest with him. By the time he left, he wasn't coughing so much."

There was a large saucepan steaming on the stovetop and Ellen enjoyed the savory scent of beef stew. She went over and looked in it.

"Help yourself," Temerity said, tracking Ellen's movements with the direction of her head. "I tried to get Seth to eat some, but he couldn't get out of here fast enough once he had that forty bucks in his hand."

Ellen got down a bowl and used the ladle propped on the spoon rest to fill it. "He wants to buy something specific," she said, remembering the same situation in her own life. After years of having literally no personal possessions and no food options other than the bland dishes that were served at the group foster home, when she'd received her first paycheck she had headed straight to a grocery store to buy herself a treat she'd always wanted. Braving even the trauma of being seen by the pretty, young checker when she turned to give Ellen the perfunctory customer greeting. A greeting that had died in an openmouthed gawk of horror that changed into nervous glances at the bag boy as she tried to avoid looking at Ellen's face, disfigured and drawn down on one side by the burn. The bag boy, apparently experiencing no such discomfort, had stared without embarrassment, as though he'd bought a ticket to a freak show and wanted his money's worth. Ellen remembered that, and she remembered what it was she had wanted so badly. Fancy crackers and two kinds of cheese, just like she'd seen one of the group home supervisors have with wine every evening but never share. Ellen dismissed both memories and then she added to Temerity, "I mean, probably."

"Okay, so what about tomorrow?" Temerity asked. "By the way, there's some good bread in the bin."

Ellen opened the wooden bread box and pulled out a heavy loaf of something brown with multicolored seeds. Nine months ago this would have frightened her, but she'd come to prefer the grainy bread over the white Wonder Bread that was all she'd ever been given. Though she missed the friendly, polka-dotted packaging, the healthier bread was more satisfying, once you learned to like it, and she had. Ellen cut herself a thick slice and dipped it in the rich beef broth. Then she carried the bowl to the table and sat down across from Temerity.

"I'll give you the address. What we have to do is send him with a note, and tell him to wait for a reply." Ellen remembered this particular scenario in a paperback she'd read, and it seemed to suit the current situation.

"What if he doesn't want to stay?" Temerity asked.

Ellen paused with the spoon in midair. "Then we'll think of something else."

"All right, spill about the work drama."

Ellen took another big bite before she answered. "Well, the guy on the forklift was . . . uh, high." The expression sounded alien to Ellen, who seldom used slang. "And I think that the dock manager sold him the drugs."

"Really? How do you know that?" Temerity asked.

"I don't *know*. But I think so, because I saw him get them from someone and I know where he's hiding them."

"Where?" Temerity was almost breathless.

"In a ceiling tile in the men's bathroom."

Temerity sighed. "And how, may I ask, do you know that?"

"I clean the men's room," Ellen said, chagrined. As an afterthought, she added, "It's always pretty disgusting."

A spurting laugh erupted from Temerity. "I bet it is!" she said with a snicker. "And before you ask how I know that, let me just say that not being able to read the signs on restroom doors makes for some amusing moments." She laughed again. "At least no one can accuse me of peeking! But what I meant was, what's up with the smell in those men's rooms?"

Ellen grimaced but decided to go for it. "Not the toilet seat, that's for sure," she said, and her friend laughed harder.

Then Temerity said, "So, this guy is selling drugs at work, we think, and someone got hurt because of it, possibly. Is there any other reasonable scenario or explanation?"

Ellen thought about it. There was always another possibility, but in Eric's case only one word came to mind.

Guilty.

17

Temerity had a performance that night, and three more through the weekend, so she changed and went out the door with her violin. Since it was barely six o'clock, it was too early for Ellen to leave for work, but she had something else in mind.

She dressed with slightly more care than usual, and went downstairs. She found a city map in a drawer in the kitchen, where she'd seen it months ago. She found the address she was looking for, made a note of the bus route, and put on her heavy coat. The temperature had been dropping all day, and as she stepped into the street, she thought, *It smells like snow.* Where she ever got the idea that you could smell snow, she didn't know, but she liked it.

The trip turned out to be easier than she had thought it would be. The long-term facility was in a rougher part of the city, not far from where Ellen used to live. The bus actually went past her old apartment building, and Ellen twisted in her seat, straining to look at it as she went past, but she could see nothing in the window of her old place except a dark blue curtain. Strange as it was to know that someone else was now living in that small one-room apartment, she was not displeased to see that they had hung curtains. It gave her a tremor of almost jealous pleasure to know that someone was caring for the little space. Her little hideaway before meeting Temerity and Justice.

Five blocks on, she changed buses, and a short trip dropped her near the state facility. Ellen stood looking in. There was a security door on the building, but no guard or receptionist that Ellen could make out. Her guess was that not many visitors came here, and if they did, they would know whatever routine was required.

But how would she get in? Giving this some thought, she circled the building. As she arrived back at the front, a van pulled up, on the side it said UNION LINEN. The driver got out and opened the back. Carrying a large canvas sack filled, no doubt, with his product, he pressed a button next to the door. A loud buzzer sounded almost immediately and the man opened the door, blocked it with the bag, and returned to the truck to get more.

Ellen looked down at herself. She was dressed for work, and it happened that she had brought her work smock home to be washed. She quickly took it out, removed her jacket, and pulled it on. Then she slipped through the open door while the driver was in the back of the van. With any luck, if she was spotted, she'd be mistaken for a cleaner. Which, after all, she was.

Inside, there was a hallway that branched off in three directions. Ellen veered quickly left, into the most neglected-looking of the three and found a storeroom marked JANITOR. It was unlocked, and she gathered a bucket and filled it with a few cleansers and rags. Over her shoulder, she saw the linen man go out carrying what she assumed were dirty linens, and then she heard the security door close with a clang.

Ellen began to explore. She saw no security cameras. Near the front was a door marked OFFICE, the hours clearly stating nine to five, and it was after six, so it was closed and locked. Next to the door, hanging on a hook, was a clipboard, across the top of which was taped a printed notice that read PATIENT LIST.

She was amazed that it was right out in the open until she realized that, unlike a normal hospital, a person would need an appointment to get in, except of course her. Ellen quickly ran a finger down the list until she found Madeline Carson's name, and next to it, the number 231.

Ellen backtracked to a stairwell door near the janitor's closet. She went up one flight and carefully pulled the door open.

It wasn't like a hospital. The rooms were smaller and there was no large nurses' station, only another small room, marked STAFF, with, Ellen could see when she peeked inside, file cabinets and a desk. The hallway was cluttered with shelves of medical supplies, haphazardly stacked, which made it easy for Ellen to move along without having to be exposed for more than a few yards at a time. When two people dressed in scrubs passed her, Ellen turned her back and used a rag to wipe down one of the shelves. They didn't even glance in her direction.

It took her only a few minutes to find room 231, but what she had not expected was to find it filled with people. Ellen stepped back hastily to a cubby between stacked linens on the shelving and waited. The door was cracked open, and Ellen could hear voices from inside. Straining, she could make out the controlled calmness of Serena Hoffman, though the conversation itself was no more than a muted murmur.

In a few moments, four people exited the room. Lydia was there, in the arms of the older man Ellen had seen at the dinner table with her, her tear-streaked face buried in his shoulder. The plump, gray-haired woman was there as well, and she kept one hand on Lydia's back, massaging gently, her eyes red-rimmed, revealing that she, too, had been crying. At the end of the pack was Serena Hoffman.

The social worker was speaking. "Lydia, sweetie, I need to talk to Mr. and Mrs. Rush. Let's go back to the little waiting room and you can look at a book, okay?"

The child's face was the definition of dumbstruck; that she couldn't understand what was happening was so clear to Ellen. They started down the hall and Ellen leaned against the wall, peering at the party through a small space between the linens and the next shelf. As the grim procession passed, everyone kept their eyes either on the floor or straight-ahead.

Except for Lydia. Her face against the man's chest was turned in Ellen's direction and in the two seconds that Ellen was in her eye line, she saw the girl spot her, and recognition and hope lit up the child's face. She sat up a bit, but Ellen put one finger to her lips. Lydia's eyes darted around at the other adults, but she nodded, and then they were gone down the hallway.

When they turned the corner, Ellen followed after them, passing the doorway to the small waiting room, as the older woman was explaining to Lydia that they would be right back. Ellen stopped just behind a deserted monitor that blocked most of her. She spotted a trash can and opened the lid, pulling out the bag, as though changing it, as the three grown-ups exited and walked a few feet in the opposite direction, where they began to speak in hushed voices.

"So, it's unlikely that she'll regain consciousness if she doesn't within the next week," Serena was saying.

Mr. Rush responded. "And how will that affect us trying to adopt Lydia? I mean, it doesn't seem like she has anyone else."

Serena sighed, and Mrs. Rush leaned into her husband for support. He put an arm over her shoulder. "We have to wait to be certain that no one does show up. The state is required to perform due diligence looking for relatives, but right now there are no leads, which is good . . . and bad."

"Why?" Mrs. Rush asked steadily, but in such a gentle voice that Ellen wished she would say more.

"Because unless Madeline Carson either signs off on her daughter or, well, dies, Lydia won't be eligible for adoption."

"Where does that leave Lydia?" Mrs. Rush asked.

"Well, she can stay with you for up to two years, and then we would need to place her in a different home."

"And how, in God's name, is that supposed to benefit the child?" Mr. Rush asked.

"The idea is for the child to not become overly attached to any family so that when it is time to go back, it won't be too much of a jolt."

There was a long sigh from Mr. Rush, and he muttered, "Insanity. How can Lydia 'go back' to her mother? She's in a vegetative state! Poor woman." He sounded so genuinely sorry for Maddy that Ellen instantly liked him.

"The system isn't perfect, I know," Serena said quickly. "But I'm sure you can understand, if it was your child and you were ill, you wouldn't want someone else to be able to take them from you while you were unable to act. That's the reason for the law." She dropped her head and studied her ever-present clipboard. Very quietly, she said, "I'm sorry. In view of what the doctor just told us, I'd like you to fill out some further paperwork. You are willing to commit to long-term with Lydia, for now?"

"Of course," said Mrs. Rush emphatically. "For as long as she needs us."

"Good. Um, I saw an office with a desk back here, let's go in and get this done, it will only take a few minutes."

Mr. Rush let go of his wife and walked back to the waiting-room door. "Lydia, sweetie? We just have to sign some papers, we'll be right back. You okay?"

Ellen couldn't see Lydia, but she guessed that the girl had responded, because Mr. Rush smiled, said, "Good girl," and turned back to the two women. He extended an arm. "Ladies." They preceded him down the hall and the three of them disappeared.

With an eagerness that amounted to yearning, Ellen slipped into the tiny waiting room. Lydia was sitting in a full-size chair, her feet dangling well above the stained carpet. Her face, turned to the wall, was blank of everything except confusion.

"Hi," said Ellen.

Lydia turned toward her and her expression transformed. She leapt from the chair and rushed the few feet to Ellen, wrapping her small arms around Ellen's thick thighs. Ellen responded, reaching down and patting Lydia on the back. Then, on impulse, she lifted the child and sat down in one of the chairs with her in her lap.

"I'm so glad you're here," Lydia whispered. "Do you think my mom is going to wake up?"

Ellen shrugged, feeling the child's weight shift against her breasts with the movement. "I don't know," she said honestly. "I haven't had a mom since I was five."

"Did your mom go to sleep, too?" Lydia asked, pulling back enough to look Ellen in the face.

"No," Ellen told her. "My mom left, when I was smaller than you, and I went to live with some other people, too."

"Were they nice?"

Ellen's throat squeezed so tightly that she almost choked, and the scars on her upper arm ached. "Not like your people. The Rushes are special, I think. Do you like them?"

Lydia nodded, a little uncertain. "They have a really big house, it's scary."

Ellen chuckled a bit at that. She could just imagine that Lydia had probably shared a small apartment or room and even a bed with her mom. The Rushes' home would seem vast.

"Do you have your own room?" she asked Lydia.

The girl nodded. "It's really far to the bathroom, and scary at night."

"I'll just bet," Ellen said. "But I know that you are a very brave girl. Remember, I saw you being brave, so I know. I think you'll be safe there. It just takes a little while to get used to it. Do you understand that?"

Lydia was watching her with her round brown eyes so open that Ellen felt like she could have just walked right in through the irises. The girl nodded slowly. "It's nice to play outside. And there's always food there!" Her voice rose slightly with this wonderful proclamation. "I miss Mama, though." The last was spoken so quietly that Ellen felt the words more than heard them. She had no response.

"I'll tell you what," Ellen said, worried that the grown-ups would return and she would be caught trespassing, or stalking, or whatever it was she was doing. "I'll come and see you there, okay? But don't tell the nice people I was here today. I just wanted to make sure you're okay."

Lydia's smile showed that she was glad to share a secret. She put one finger to her lips, the way Ellen had done, and said, "Shhh." Her eyes sparkled.

"Good girl. I have to go now. But I'll come check on you, okay?"

Lydia looked into her eyes and laid one hand on Ellen's cheek. Ellen winced before she remembered that the horrible scar was mostly gone. "Do you promise?" Lydia whispered.

"I promise," Ellen said. She stood up again, hugged the fragile Lydia to her, and then put her down on the chair. "I'll see you soon, Lydia Carson." And she slipped back out into the hallway, where she found a spot to wait until the adults came and took the little girl away. Her last glimpse of the child was a tiny wave over Mr. Rush's shoulder.

When they were gone, Ellen found Maddy's room again and went inside. It was small, with two beds. The second was not occupied. The room was cluttered with equipment, which left Ellen feeling bulbous and invasive. Maddy lay completely lifeless. Ellen stood for a few minutes, and then she leaned forward, the way she'd seen Temerity do, and whispered, "You don't need to stay if it's too hard. She's going to be okay."

Then she turned and left that sad place.

18

Ellen was cleaning the office supplies section that night. She didn't care much for this area because the entire row was stacked, three huge shelf levels high, with imposing boxes. Though the regular cleaners were only responsible for the lowest level, the only one they could reach, there was something about all that unfathomable technology occupying the air above her that made Ellen feel both apprehensive and ignorant.

The other thing she didn't like was that the Crows had been assigned to the produce section just at the end of her row, a bit too close for Ellen's comfort. Though Ellen was entirely ignored by Kiki and Rosa, who, as usual, were so preoccupied with their gossip that they noticed nothing that wasn't repeat-worthy. Beyond them, Ellen could see Thelma constructing an elaborate, prefab cardboard display for gourmet dried fruit, something Ellen didn't care for—unless it was covered in chocolate.

Even from a dozen yards away, it didn't take long for Ellen to learn from the Crows' carrying banter that Bruno had been taken to the hospital, where X-rays had shown his lower leg was broken in two places and the ligaments around the knee had been torn when the leg had been twisted. The very thought of it made Ellen grimace and reach down to rub her own knee, sore from kneeling while she worked. She also found out that the worker who had hit him, Daniel, had not been found, but the police had discovered drugs in his apartment. Something called methamphetamine.

So, the drugs in the dock men's bathroom ceiling were methamphetamine. Ellen knew next to nothing about it, except for what she'd heard on the radio news, and that wasn't much. She wondered again what she could do, short of telling someone and announcing herself as a witness. The thought of facing "authority" triggered her stomach fluids into a bubbling, acerbic water ballet. Then she thought of Detective Barclay and how brave he had been, taking on a violent aggressor and putting himself in danger to stay and help the injured bus driver. The memory made her grateful that people like him were out there in the world. Somehow it counteracted the faceless entity that was the government—not enough to balance the scales, but it gentled the world somewhat.

She had only been working a half hour when she heard the sound of a heavy machine and turned, expecting to see Johnson and the floor polisher, but it was Eric who was himself driving the forklift tonight. Ellen watched him and the movement of the lift from the corner of her eye, recalling the smell of marijuana smoke as she had passed through the dock on her way in earlier, but Eric seemed to be expert at maneuvering the machine, even fully loaded with double-stacked boxes of printers, secured by strapping. He stopped in the first part of the aisle, just past where Rosa and Kiki were working.

Glancing up, Ellen saw that there was a relatively open space on the very top level of shelving, maybe twenty-five feet up, under the roof supports. Eric set down his load on the floor of the aisle in a clear position, then, with the mandatory *beep beep* sounding, he backed up, jockeying into position to bring down the almost empty pallets on the top shelf.

Both Rosa and Kiki were wiping down shelves at the end of the row of shelving where it opened onto the grocery section. Ellen could only see them through a small space above the stacked reams of paper below the spot where Eric was working. With the teeth of the lift raised to their highest level, he was trying to insert them into the base of the pallet. Judging from the angle of his seat so far below, Ellen could tell that it was probably not an easy thing to do.

She returned to her work, and for a few minutes she heard nothing but the constant maneuvering of the forklift and its beeps. And then, over the din, she heard a shout. Turning to look past the forklift into the produce area beyond, Ellen saw that Thelma was running forward, waving her arms and shouting, though Ellen couldn't make out what she was saying.

Then she looked up.

Jockeying the pallets far above him, Eric was sliding the heavy pallet with the printers into position without realizing that it was pushing against another one behind it, stacked high with large boxes marked PAPER, 5 REAM BOXES, toward the end of the aisle, and it was almost halfway off the end of the shelf, hovering directly over Kiki and Rosa, who were whispering together, completely unaware of the danger in the air above them.

As Thelma ran forward, Eric looked up at her, and Kiki and Rosa both turned to look at the shouting woman. Just before the pallet toppled, Eric, who could not see what was happening on the diagonal, raised one hand and gave Thelma the finger. Thelma wasn't looking at him though, she had her eyes fixed on the threat above. Almost in slow motion, Ellen watched as the crate began to tip. Kiki looked up, screamed, and immediately scrambled to one side, but Rosa was still staring at Thelma in confusion. The pallet and its heavy load began its downward descent. Thelma, in a full-out run, threw herself into the air and tackled the shocked cleaner, carrying both of them clear a split second before the boxes crashed to the floor, exploding in a ticker-tape parade of single sheets of white paper.

Eric shut down the forklift and ran around to the aisle's end to survey the damage. Rosa was lying on her side, moaning and gasping, her hands clutching her chest where she had taken Thelma's shoulder, which had knocked the wind out of her. Ellen slipped quietly up just behind the forklift, where she could see through the shelves.

Kiki was standing over her friend, exclaiming loudly, "Oh my God! Oh my God! We could have been killed. Oh, Rosa, thank God you're all right." Rosa, still gasping, looked up at the tall, thin woman, and though she had no breath to speak, Ellen was just betting that what she would have liked to say was "No thanks to you!"

"Son of a bi—" Thelma was exclaiming when Eric interrupted her.

"What the hell do you think you're doing?" he demanded of Thelma. "Why didn't you tell them to stand clear?"

Thelma rose to her feet and stood panting and shaking. "Me?" was all she could manage. "Are you actually trying to blame *me*?"

"Well, I couldn't see them from around the corner, could I?"

"You . . . Then why did you . . . *What*?" Words seemed to fail the produce manager.

But she didn't need any. Kiki was in the tall man's face before he could even formulate a reply.

"How dare you!" she was shrieking. "You almost killed us both, and Thelma saved my friend's life. You say one more word and I will slap that smug righteousness right off your face!" The rant continued

178

but Ellen didn't hear any more of it. Knowing that anyone who witnessed the accident would have to give a report, she had turned and was making her way back to the locker room.

But she was thinking, *Perfect.*

It was only a short time later when Rosa limped into the locker room. She was supported by Kiki, who was still ranting in a constant stream. "The nerve of him! I've never lodged a complaint against that man and his behavior before because Jimmy works for him. I know he's your nephew's son, and I was worried Eric would fire Jimmy if we ever said anything against him. Ooh, I'm so mad I could spit!"

Rosa sank onto the bench that surrounded the central lockers in a large U shape and leaned against the wall. "Ouch," she said, rubbing her chest. "Same here, but I'm going to report him this time! I know I smelled marijuana on him! You think I don't know that smell? My daughter has fifteen-year-old twins!"

Kiki shook herself and made fists out of her calloused, long-fingered hands. "But what if Jimmy loses his job? He's got a baby on the way. Uh!" she groaned. "I suppose you're right, I can't imagine Eric will stay after that, anyway. Did you see Billy's face? He was furious, and six people saw what happened!"

"If he *doesn't* get fired, and messes with me or Jimmy, I'll . . . I'll . . ." Rosa trailed off.

"I know," Kiki said soberly. "Eric is the kind of guy who might do something crazy, you be careful. But I'll tell you this—I will *never* say another word against Thelma. That woman is a hero! And if I hear anyone else bad-mouth her again, they are going to answer to me!"

After the barrage leveled at Eric that Ellen had just witnessed, she didn't doubt it.

"You just sit tight," Kiki told her friend. "I'm going to get you a bag of ice." She hurried off to the break room. Rosa groaned a little and leaned her head back, closing her eyes.

Summoning solidity, Ellen said softly, "He's selling drugs."

Rosa's eyes flew open and she turned toward the darkest corner, where Ellen was sitting, partially blocked by the lockers. "What?" she said.

"Eric. He's selling drugs to the other workers. Maybe if you told him you knew that, he wouldn't fire Jimmy, or make more trouble for you."

Rosa was peering at Ellen with a shocked curiosity. "How do you know?" she asked.

"I saw him, and I saw the drugs when they came in."

"Why didn't you tell someone?" Rosa asked breathlessly.

"I . . ." Ellen faltered, almost at the end of her brief episode of bravery. "Because I would have to prove it and . . . because I don't do that. I mean, speak up. I can't."

Rosa sat absolutely still and unblinking for a moment, and then she nodded. "You're the one who was shot last year. It was you and your friends who helped Irena." Ellen didn't respond. Rosa seemed to sense her discomfort and dropped her eyes. "I understand," she said. She leaned forward to smooth her smock and pull her skirt down over her knees.

When she looked back up, Ellen was gone.

Ellen did not return to the scene of the accident. Instead, she moved on to her next assignment and spent a pleasant few hours dusting the books and music section. It amused her to see the titles of the books that were "best sellers." Occasionally, she would select one and flip it over to read the description on the back. Very few of them interested her. Though she liked the heft and weight of the hardcovers, she'd spent so long reading paperbacks that these seemed unruly. Then she came to a picture book. It had beautiful black-and-white images of old-time movie scenes. She thought of Rupert telling her about the dim and quiet movie house and imagined seeing those images bigger than life and moving, telling the whole story. She flipped the pages, intrigued and curious. The silver photos were so expressive and filled with character. She checked the price. It was on clearance for only $4.99. Ellen slipped a copy underneath the stack of trash bags on her cart and continued working. She saw no more of Rosa or Kiki that night, but would have bet a month's paycheck that Eric, and most likely she herself, were the subject of much discussion.

When the shift ended, Ellen slipped the book into her bag and decided to work off the book next week. This Thursday morning she had something else she needed to do.

19

Ellen got home and dropped her bag and the mail shortly after seven. Just before eight, she slipped out again and went to wait, hidden in the busy commuter foot traffic of the sidewalk, just at the edge of the alley.

At about eight fifteen, Seth came down the alley, his hands stuffed into the pocket of his too-small coat, and his head bowed against the cold wind. There was a light dusting of snow on the sidewalks, too powdery to stick, that blew into tiny ridges and swirled in the doorways. Seth's nose and cheeks were flushed and red and his breathing was labored. He had the look of someone who was so cold they would never get warm again.

Moving stiffly, he turned left onto the avenue, and then left again at the next corner. Ellen fell into step behind him, letting him keep a long lead because she knew where he was going. Eight chilly blocks later, he stopped in front of a dingy storefront, whose windows had been painted white, and checked an address on an envelope he was holding. Then he went in.

Ellen went slowly to the door and stood waiting until a big man, shabbily dressed with lesions on his face and leaning heavily on a cane, came along and opened it. Past him, Ellen saw a small but busy waiting room. She followed in the large man's wake and slipped into a chair squeezed in a corner to watch. Picking up a magazine, she opened it in front of her. It was dirty and old, some of the pages were torn, and it was in Spanish, but she wasn't going to read it anyway.

Seth was standing at a reception desk that resembled one found in a high-security bank more than in a medical clinic. The harassed woman behind the thick glass was entering information in a computer while Seth shifted his weight from foot to foot and occasionally coughed into his hands.

The woman seemed to be annoyed by this. She leaned forward and said through the low opening, just large enough to pass paperwork through, "Just write your name and take a seat. You need to put this on." She slipped a cotton mask through the opening and Seth picked it up, looking at the folded white rectangle with elastic straps hanging from both sides without comprehension.

"I just have a message for someone," he said, passing an envelope through the space. "I'm supposed to wait for a reply," he told the woman, and then the effort of speaking had him doubled over with coughing. When he finally straightened up again, he was flushed and swaying from lack of oxygen.

The woman behind the desk was watching him with a combination of disgust and concern. "Young man," she said, "have you seen anyone about that cough?"

Seth shook his head and wiped his mouth with the back of his sleeve. He swayed again, leaned against the counter, and then just melted, his weight slipping like limp goo before he flopped onto the floor in a heap. Ellen stood up, but the receptionist had already rounded the desk and opened the security door. She was kneeling next to Seth on the floor in seconds. Leaning over him, she put one hand to his forehead. Seth's eyes fluttered open and he moaned, then tried to sit up, floundering wildly with his arms as though fending off an imagined attack.

"It's okay. Just lay back," the woman said. "Beth!" she called out through the door, and two more people appeared. One was a sturdy man Ellen guessed was a nurse, and the other, Ellen was relieved to see, was Beth in a white doctor's coat over green scrubs.

Beth went straight to Seth and began speaking calmly. "Okay there, buddy, let's get you into an examining room and take a look at you." Seth tried to object, but allowed Beth and the man to help him up. As they started through the door, Beth was already asking questions. "How long have you had this cough? Have you been to a doctor? Do you have someone we can contact to let them know you're here?" Seth was answering as best he could, but at the last question, he shook his head furiously and tried to pull away. Beth just held on tighter. "It's okay, don't worry, we don't have to call any-one if you're afraid, let's just take a look at you." She and the man led him down a short hallway with a door off each side, and the recep-tionist closed the security door behind them.

Ellen was amazed at the astuteness with which Beth had rec-ognized and dismissed Seth's fear, but now that she had time, she looked around her. There were no less than three teenage girls there alone and looking terrified, a dowdy woman with a black eye hold-ing an ice pack to a split lip, a young man who pulled a bloodstained bandage from his upper arm to check under it. The round hole on the fleshy outside of his arm looked suspiciously like a bullet wound. It took Ellen five seconds to realize that the majority of work that was done here was done anonymously, or at least unreported to "family" and/or authority, otherwise, these people would not have come.

Ellen expelled a quiet sigh of relief, and when the street door opened to admit a harassed, exhausted woman with two small children and a screaming baby, Ellen slipped out around them.

She made her way to the side of the building, looking for a place to wait until Seth came out. Along the wall of peeling stucco, there were two small, heavily barred windows. They were both hung with dingy vertical blinds, but a few of the slats were damaged or askew, so by standing on an abandoned orange crate, Ellen could see inside through a small space. The first window revealed nothing more than a cluttered office, but the second looked into one of the examining rooms. The window was cracked and a shard was missing from the lower left of the windowpane. Someone had stuffed a wad of fabric in the four-inch space to staunch the flow of cold air from going in. Ellen doubted it worked very well, as it did little to stop the sound from coming out.

Closing one eye and clinging to the cold bars, Ellen positioned herself so that she could see through the narrow slit left exposed by a broken blind to across the room, where Seth was sitting on a rickety examining table. He had his shirt off and his legs were dangling as Beth listened to his chest with a stethoscope. His rib cage and arms were painfully thin, but he had the scrawny, wiry look of a tough little survivor.

Beth listened to his back as well, waiting between coughs, her face tight with concentration. She had given him a white towel and instructed him to hold it over his mouth when he coughed. He seemed to keep forgetting, or maybe the coughing was coming so rapidly that he just didn't have time.

Finally, Beth sat down on a chair across from him and wrote on a pad. "You have bronchitis, young man," she told him. "You're a step away from pneumonia. You shouldn't be out in this weather, or doing anything but resting. I would put you in the hospital but—" Seth began objecting immediately, so Beth held up a hand. "Let me finish," she told him. "I'm going to give you a round of antibiotics instead."

"I don't have money," Seth wheezed.

"It's free," Beth told him. She went to a cabinet, and removing a ring of keys from her pocket, she unlocked the formidable-looking latch and pulled down two yellow boxes. "Each of these is a week's dose. You need to take two of these pills a day, one in the morning and one at night, for fourteen days, and then I want to see you again. If the infection has cleared up, good. If not, we'll go from there. Also, if your fever rises over a hundred and three, you need to get yourself to the hospital. Do you have a thermometer?"

Seth shook his head, looking abashed.

"Here." Beth got up and rooted through a cabinet until she came up with what looked like a pack of disposable thermometers. She handed them to Seth. "Just hold this under your tongue for thirty seconds and then look at these dots. The one that's blue will tell you that your temperature is the corresponding number. Right now you're at a hundred and one. You need to get home and to bed."

"Okay," Seth said. "I just have to wait for your answer."

"My what?" Beth asked.

"It's my job. I do deliveries for a blind lady, and she sent me with a letter for you. I'm supposed to wait for your answer. The lady in the front took it."

Looking very curious, Beth stood and went out. Seth lay down sideways on the table, curling his knees up to his chest. Ellen could have sworn he was relishing the relative safety and warmth of the clinic, though he must have known it couldn't last. In a minute Beth returned with the folded letter in her hand. She sat back down in the chair and pretended not to notice Seth leaping up and pretending he hadn't moved since she'd left.

"Did you know what was in this?" she asked him.

Seth shook his head.

"It's a request for me to see you and an address where to send a bill if there is one. This is your employer?"

Seth nodded again, more hesitantly this time.

Beth sighed. "Well, she's looking out for you, and a good thing, too. A cough like that can get very nasty if you don't take care of it. Now, I want you to go home and get some soup in you." Beth was watching Seth. His eyes were now roaming the room.

"You do have a home?" Beth asked.

"Oh, sure," Seth lied, and Ellen was certain that Beth knew that. She saw the doctor hesitate, considering whether to challenge him or not. Then she stood up. "Well. I tell you what." She scribbled on a pad and tore off a sheet. "You take this note back to Ms. Bauer, and tell her to get you these things. I'll let you go now if you promise me you will do two things."

Seth looked back at her expectantly.

"You will come back if this gets worse, or if your fever spikes. And . . . you will come back when you finish the pills so that I can have a listen and make sure that nasty congestion is cleared up. Do we have a deal?"

The boy nodded eagerly, relieved to be allowed to go. But Beth wasn't quite finished. "While I have you here, is there anything else you'd like to talk about? Anything you want to ask me?" The questions were spoken factually, casually even.

"How did you get to be a doctor?" Seth asked.

Beth smiled. "That's not what I meant, but I went to school, and studied really hard."

"Did you always want to do this?"

The doctor nodded. "Yes. I always wanted to help people. Since I was little, I used to set up a clinic with my dolls. Quite a few of them have stitches now where I did a little surgery." She laughed a bit at the thought.

"I'd like to go to college," Seth said. "If I was smart, I would."

Beth regarded him, then she said, "You seem pretty smart to me."

He shrugged. "I don't do so great in school. Sometimes I have too many other things to do, so I can't go."

"What other things?" Beth asked.

Head down, Seth shrugged again. "You know, things for . . . work."

"School is really important," Beth said, and Ellen had to lean in to hear her.

"So is food," Seth said, and smiled disarmingly.

Ellen could tell that it was difficult for Beth to keep her expression calm, her mouth twitched a little, but she said, "True enough. Is there anything else wrong you'd like to tell me? Any injuries or concerns?"

"No, just the cough," Seth said, illustrating this with a long rasping session.

"Is there any possibility you might have a sexually transmitted illness?" Beth asked when he had settled again.

The boy's ears went scarlet but he did not speak. Just twisted the white towel in his thin fingers.

Beth stood up and came around the side of the table so that she was facing Ellen, who stooped lower. Beth put two fingers on Seth's ribs and pressed lightly. "What about these bruises? How did you get these?"

"Oh, uh, I fell down. You know, in the park."

"It looks like you fell on someone's fist." Beth lifted one of his arms and began checking over the rest of him, including parting his hair and examining his scalp. "What are these marks on your head?"

"Nothing," Seth said. "I hit my head in a doorway."

Beth's eyebrows went up. "Low doorway."

"Yeah, it's . . . uh, my garage. The door was down halfway. I'm pretty clumsy."

The doctor finished looking him over and said, "Put your shirt back on." As Seth slid to the floor and reached for his shirt, Ellen saw his back for the first time. The left side was marked with purple and red bruises, almost like splattered paint, but more mottled. She drew in a breath and felt her nostrils flare.

Beth faced the wall while Seth dressed, and was making notes. She stopped and turned back to him, holding the clipboard against her chest.

"Are you sure there isn't something else you want to tell me?"

"No," Seth said, staring at the floor.

Beth said nothing, just stood looking down at the top of his head. Then she reached out and put one hand on his shoulder. "Listen . . . Seth, is it?" She glanced at the pad. "I want you to know that you can come back here whenever you need to. We're really busy, as you can see, but if I'm here, and I always am on Thursdays, I'll find time to talk to you. Okay?"

"I'd like to work here," Seth told her.

Beth seemed taken aback, but pleasantly. "Well, we'll have to see about that. You're a little young yet. But in the meantime, you can come in if you need medical attention or . . . *help*." Beth stressed the last word quite differently than the others, and Seth's eyes darted up to her face, the hollowness in his eyes revealing, if only for a fraction of a second, that it was desperate to be filled. Then he shrugged off the hopeful weakness and resumed his facade of self-reliance. Beth's face tightened, but Ellen knew she'd seen it before, and understood. "If I'm not here, I want you to take this." She pulled a card from her clip and handed it to him. "That has my cell number on the back. If you need advice, or just need to talk, you can call me."

"Thanks," Seth muttered, and slipped the card, very carefully, Ellen noted, in the back pocket of his loose pants, which were being held up by a short length of rope.

Then he made his way to the door. Beth pretended to be writing again, but Ellen could see that she was watching the boy walk away, her eyes filled with concern. When he'd gone, she set down her work and put her face in her hands. Then, with a little shake and a forcefully exhaled breath, she picked up the clipboard and went to the door, making room for the man in scrubs. He came in and began to wipe down the table, pulling out a fresh sheet of white paper to erase and cover the place where Seth and his infection had been.

Ellen waited a minute to give Seth a lead, and then she headed for home, her head heavy with thought, and the craving for sleep.

20

B ut sleep, Ellen could see when she arrived in the alley, was
going to have to wait a while.

Taking her usual precaution, Ellen paused before she
turned the corner, to scan the alley. The first thing she saw was Seth,
he was looking all around, checking to see that he was unobserved
before he went into his hidden den.

The second thing Ellen saw was the man. The wind was biting,
and the man had taken shelter beside the dumpster, out of Seth's
view, but he was clearly interested in the boy. When Seth started for
the grating, Ellen looked around desperately for some way to distract or warn him, but there was nothing nearby but the empty street.
The man was tall and slim, his skin was dark, and even though his
collar was pulled up over his chin and his hat was pulled down to
his eyebrows, something about him struck Ellen as familiar. With a
last glance behind him, Seth moved toward the grate. At that moment
the man emerged from the shadows and started toward the boy.

And Ellen recognized him. "Detective Barclay!" she called out in
a croak. The detective, distracted by hearing his name, especially as,

from the clothes he was wearing, he was obviously still undercover, stopped and looked up the alley in surprise.

Fighting her flee impulse, and feeling as though the wind had bit through her unprotected self, Ellen waved one hand to keep his attention while Seth disappeared through the grate, pulling it closed behind him. When the detective looked back, his eyes rested on the grate for a second before he started toward Ellen. "Ms. Homes, I'm glad to catch you."

Unable to run away, she forced herself to walk toward him. "Why?" she asked, terrified that he would say she needed to come with him, to speak up, to face others.

But he said, "I really wanted to thank you personally. It turns out that we won't need you to testify. The prosecutor has such a strong case, and the perpetrator was dealing the drugs he was using, so he's plea-bargaining. The case won't even go to court, so . . ." He hesitated, searching for a polite way to say the next bit, Ellen assumed. "After talking to your friend, Justice, who told me you'd prefer to stay out of it, I wanted to stop by and let you know you're off the hook." He smiled apologetically.

"Oh, okay, thanks." Ellen would have felt relieved if she hadn't been in a state of panic.

"I also thought you'd like to know that the bus driver is fine. Back to work, in fact. And the little girl you were so kind to, Lydia? Has been placed in a great home."

Ellen knew she should have feigned surprise. But once again she was reduced to single syllables. "Oh. Well. Good."

They had reached each other now, and were standing almost directly in front of the loft door. The detective looked at it pointedly. "Are you just coming home?" he asked. "I understand you work nights." He nodded ruefully. "Me too."

Wondering if the detective could see her face flushing and realize that all she wanted to do was evaporate, Ellen said, "Yes."

A brief pause and then, "Would it be all right if I came up for a minute?"

"Why?" Ellen asked, drawing back without being able to stop herself.

"Because I have something to give you," he said. "They wanted to have a ceremony, but your friend convinced me that that would be unwelcome, so I asked if I could just drop it off."

"Uh, I guess," Ellen said. She unlocked the door and went up the stairs, hyperconscious of the detective's footfalls behind her. The echoes grew more exaggerated with each flight, multiplying in her alarm until Ellen felt she was being followed not by a single person, but by an army of pursuers. When she reached the fourth-floor landing and heard voices on the other side of the door over Runt's frantic scratching and barking, Ellen was flooded with relief. With any luck, Barclay would be distracted by Temerity or Justice and she could fade away.

When she opened the door, Runt jumped up, celebrating her return with his usual abandon, then stopped, sniffed the air fearfully, and began to bark a steady rush at the detective, repeatedly looking back at his people to make sure they were paying attention.

Justice called out, "Hey, Ellen! You're late. Did you stop for some—" His words cut off as the detective stepped in behind her and in a friendly, confident voice ordered Runt to sit. Runt sat. Justice switched gears. "Well, Detective! Good morning."

Temerity, who was sitting at the table with a cup of coffee and toast, snapped her head up and around. "*Who* is it?" she asked.

"Temerity, this is Detective Barclay. He's the gentleman who helped Ellen on the bus."

"Actually," said Barclay, his white teeth gleaming, "it was the other way around. That's why I'm here." Ellen crossed quickly to put the kitchen counter between her and the unfamiliar presence.

"And you *saw* Ellen downstairs?" Temerity asked incredulously.

"No. She saw me." Barclay's face sobered. "Speaking of. Have any of you noticed a young man who might be homeless outside your building?"

Ellen looked at her friends. Both of them were pictures of innocence. "Well, there are certainly homeless people around," Justice said, not committing.

"I miss a lot of details," Temerity said evasively, but honestly.

"This is a boy, eleven maybe twelve, I think he might be living somewhere in your alleyway. I've seen him twice now. If he's a runaway, he needs to get back home."

Temerity rose. "You never know these days," she said. "Depends what he ran away from. Can I get you some coffee, Detective?"

"Oh, no thanks. I'm headed home to sleep after this. So, without further ado." Reaching into his black leather jacket, Detective Barclay produced a large envelope. "I hope I didn't crush it," he muttered, and pulled from it an official-looking document, thick parchment with colorful designs. With a grin, he held it out to Ellen. "I'd read it, but since it's just us, I'll let you."

Ellen took it between two fingers, almost afraid it would be hot to the touch. She was still distrustful that it was a summons of some kind, and she stared at the fancy wording. Justice came to stand at her shoulder.

"What does it say?" Temerity asked impatiently.

"It's an accommodation from the city, thanking Ellen for exemplary bravery and assistance to law enforcement in a time of need," he told his sister. "Well, isn't that something."

Ellen thought it was something, too, but she wished it would go away. This was why she didn't get involved. She only wanted the detective to go away. It wasn't that she didn't like him, or thought that he meant her any harm. It was only that she didn't want anyone to look at her. She had talked to three people in the last couple of days. That was more than in the last six months combined, and she felt besieged.

"Well, that's great!" Temerity said. "Congratulations, Ellen. See? I told you that you were brave. Now you have it in writing, so that proves it!"

Barclay cleared his throat and looked slightly abashed. "On a personal note, I'd like to add that I owe you. If you ever need a favor, please ask."

Justice was watching Ellen, she could feel his eyes on her from the side, and though she had learned not to mind Justice's regard, it was one more set of eyes now than she could bear. She shuddered involuntarily, and Justice, turning briskly to the detective, stepped sideways to shield Ellen from his view. "So, how about some toast, or juice? Sit down, sit down. What can you tell us about the rest of the people on the bus? What about the woman who was injured?"

Barclay went to the table and took a seat. Ellen gratefully shifted over to the seating area and sank into the winged armchair, out of view. She pulled Mouse onto her lap and curled over him, making herself as small as possible.

"I was just telling Ms. Homes. The driver is back at work and the little girl has been placed in an excellent foster home."

"So that means that her mother . . . ?" Justice asked.

"Is not doing well. I can't say much, except that she's in a coma, and it's not looking like she'll come out of it." He sighed. "So unfair."

"What will happen to the guy on the bus? Will he get off by plea-bargaining?" Temerity asked, incredulous.

"Oh, no. Too many previous arrests and, of course, he's responsible for the bus crash. His sentence will be shortened a bit because he was on a certain kind of methamphetamine we've been trying to track down and he offered to turn in his source."

"So much for honor among thieves," Justice said.

The detective smiled grimly. "Or drug addicts. We keep getting close to the ring producing this stuff, but it's been tricky. The street meth they're producing is particularly toxic, we've had nine related deaths so far. Evil stuff. Usually meth is produced in small batches and it's hard to track, but this stuff has been cut with animal tranquilizer. It makes people jump-off-buildings crazy." He shook his head. "And it's being mass-produced." He leaned back. "Get this: our friend from the bus told us that it was delivered packaged as 'gourmet food.'"

Ellen's head jerked up. *Gourmet food?* But before she could muster a voice, Temerity was back on track, allowing Ellen to dismiss the coincidence.

"So . . ." Ellen could hear the purpose in Temerity's voice, but she doubted that anyone else would. "What does the fact that her mom is in a coma mean for Lydia?"

"The little girl?" The detective grimaced and thanked Justice for the glass of juice he handed him. "It depends. The way the law works, she will stay in foster care until her mother, or some other relative, can care for her again."

"And what if they can't?" Temerity asked pointedly.

"Then, hopefully, she will be adopted."

Ellen couldn't help it, in spite of the burning in her cheeks heating to the point of spontaneous combustion, she said, "That didn't work for *me*. They never found my mother, or anyone else to sign off on custody, so I *couldn't* be adopted." She didn't mention that no one had wanted to adopt her—that wasn't the point. Lydia was the point. Just putting herself out there enough to make the comment leeched energy from Ellen, and despite the tension in every muscle, she felt the exhaustion of her stressful interactions over the last few days weaken her bones.

"Yes, that can happen," the detective said.

"But what if Lydia's mom dies?" Temerity plowed on.

Justice exclaimed, "Tem, please, how awful!"

"Well," Temerity said, crossing her arms. "What if?"

"Then she would be an orphan," Detective Barclay said. "And that's a very different circumstance."

Temerity drummed her fingers against her upper arm. "Is there any other way? I mean, let's say that Lydia's mom, or anyone in that condition, doesn't wake up, but doesn't die, is there some other way? I mean, it doesn't sound like it's fair to the kid in that situation."

The detective took a long sip of juice as he studied Temerity over the top of the glass, taking her in. "Well," he said, "a judge can have the mother declared physically incompetent, but it has to be extreme. It can't just be that she's, say, in a wheelchair. I'm talking legally brain-dead."

"And who would be in charge of that?" Temerity asked.

The detective pursed his mouth and thought. "Well, her doctors, of course, but someone would have to instigate the investigation, then there would be a hearing for competency . . . but that would be at least a year off," the detective said firmly. "That's the minimum time to wait and see if family steps forward. Or if we can flush them out, more likely," he ended grimly.

Ellen thought about the letter she'd received, with its mysterious copy to Frank Homes, and hoped Temerity wasn't having the same thought. Wasted wishing of course, because, much to Ellen's distress, her friend asked, "And what if a relative did show up? I mean, months, or even years later?"

The detective set down his glass and addressed Temerity a bit more severely. "You have quite a few questions. Are you interested in this topic for some specific reason?"

Please don't say it, Ellen was thinking desperately.

"Well," Temerity said, and Ellen's fingers on Mouse's head jerked. He twisted and bit her lightly. "I didn't know anything about the foster care system—I expect most people don't—until I met Ellen. She was raised in foster care and it wasn't exactly a warm and fuzzy experience for her." Temerity gestured in Ellen's general direction. "But let's just say, for the sake of argument, purely hypothetically, that Ellen found out she had a relative she never knew about." Ellen's heart stopped as though it had been flash frozen and broken into little, icy marbles, like a plastic bag of peas in a freezer. Temerity went on. "How could she find them?"

"I'm going to bed," Ellen half shouted at the same time, unable to take even one more reference to herself or one more second of the pressure of notice without ending up compressed into a small, petrified lump of organic matter. "Really tired. Night." She loped for the door to the hallway. Once it was safely closed behind her, she stopped and pressed her ear against it, but all she could hear were the low murmurs of polite conversation.

Ellen hurried up the stairs and into her room, and sat on the edge of her bed, trying to catch her breath and calm herself. It was too much, she couldn't do it. She counted four new people, *four*, whom she had willfully interacted with in the last two days. The scrutiny and the involvement were like subjecting herself to lethal, airborne chemicals or mercury contamination or . . . something, she didn't know, but it was poisoning her.

Sliding off the bed, she went into the bathroom, locked the door, drew a warm bath, turned off the light, and felt her way into the water. The waves of displacement rocked her quietly as she let herself float. She stayed there, in the warm, gently swaying blackness, feeling as little as possible, and listened to the thrum of the hot-water heater on the other side of the wall. It was a constant but fluctuating sound, not unlike a heartbeat heard from deep inside the womb.

21

It was much later that Ellen made her way out of the bathroom and into her bed. A solid eight hours of sleep ended and she opened her eyes to a darkened window. Night had fallen and she had slept straight through. Slightly panicked, she checked the clock radio. It was only seven thirty, plenty of time to get to work.

Ellen got up, dressed, and went downstairs. Temerity was playing the violin under the big windows, and the sound plucked at Ellen's heart. Though it was beautiful, it sounded to her like loneliness calling her name. On the floor at Temerity's feet were the plain white sheets of the perforated music score that had been delivered. Temerity stopped when Ellen crossed the floor.

"Sleep well?" she asked.

"I thought you had a concert tonight."

"Nope, this afternoon. Special show for schoolkids. I'm already back," Temerity said.

"Have you heard from Seth?" Ellen asked as she made herself some coffee.

Temerity's brow furrowed. "No, not since this morning, but I didn't really expect to. Did you?"

Ellen sat down on one of the stools and told Temerity about her visit to the state facility, her exchange with Lydia, what the grown-ups had discussed, and finally, about Seth's exam at the clinic that morning.

Temerity listened eagerly. When Ellen had finished, she said, "He shouldn't be in that freezing basement, he won't be able to get better. What time do you need to get on the bus?"

"Nine is good."

"Terrific, then there's time." Temerity actually rubbed her hands together so briskly that Ellen half expected sparks.

"For what?" Ellen asked.

Temerity faced her almost directly and smiled radiantly. "You never know what the day will bring."

"Or the night, as the case may be," Ellen said, turning to look at the bleak, freezing evening outside.

"Oh, is it dark? I hadn't noticed," Temerity said drolly, and then she laughed. A laugh that was round and unapologetically fat, but filled with life and fearless delight—Temerity's laugh. "Makes no difference to me."

Ellen wished she could say the same, but she couldn't.

She preferred the dark, where it was easier to hide and there were far fewer eyes to see, except, possibly, Temerity's.

What the night would bring, Ellen discovered, was a party at a gallery. Temerity had been invited and she wanted Ellen to go with her.

"You want me to go to a *party*?" Ellen choked, the calm from her extended bath and sleep evaporating instantly.

"You don't have to wear sequins and toot a horn," Temerity told her. "You don't even have to go in. I just need you to check it out for me. You know, give me the layout. Usually, I wouldn't go to an art show, what's the point?" she said with a cackle. "But the artist is the sister of someone in the orchestra, so I said I'd make an appearance." Temerity laughed again.

Ellen didn't like the look of the gallery at all. It was brightly lit, with huge sidewalk-to-ceiling windows through which she could see an open space with nowhere to hide. Huge, colorful canvases were dramatically lit on the brick walls, and in the center of the room sat a grand piano, the player with his back to them.

"Okay, this is as far as I go," Ellen told Temerity. "The door is about ten steps ahead on your right."

"Can you see in?" Temerity asked, unfolding her stick as she let go of Ellen's shoulder.

"Perfectly. It's like a big fish tank."

"Adult swim. Not your favorite thing, the adult swim," Temerity said grimly. "Okay, thanks for helping me out. Wish me luck."

"'Luck," said Ellen, though she didn't for a second think that her fearless friend would need it. Ellen watched Temerity go in and then she shifted herself to stand just off the curb between two parked SUVs. One of the bumpers was the right height to perch herself on, so she did, bracing one foot against the bumper in front of her. It must have been overly warm in the gallery, because the door was propped open, and Ellen could hear the murmur of conversation. The evening was frigid, and Ellen's breath hung in the air in front of her. She blew into her hands in their loosely knit mittens, purchased at the thrift shop, and hoped that Seth was keeping warm.

Watching Temerity enter a new space was always a worthy exercise, not because of Temerity, who did almost everything with complete confidence, but because of the other people watching her. Tonight the "other people" were stylishly dressed, painstakingly groomed beautifuls. "Beautifuls" were what Ellen called the type of people who would watch themselves go by in a window reflection, completely oblivious to the fact that a murder was being committed just inside. Ellen saw them on the street often enough, constantly checking to make sure they were being noticed while pretending complete disdain for the presence of the unattractive others. Ellen's keen observing had long ago taught her that these people thrived on the attention of those others, without whom they were nothing. And now these people, their self-worth so obviously reliant on their physical appearance, so certain that they were more valuable than their less-attractive fellow beings, were faced by a person for whom physical appearance had no meaning, and they had no idea how to respond to that. Temerity and her blindness rendered them worthless.

It was fun to watch.

Temerity stopped a few feet inside the gallery and turned slowly, unaware, except perhaps for the change in the conversational murmur, that everyone there had turned to watch her warily.

Ellen watched the beautifuls shift uncomfortably. Suddenly, with a little cry of delight, a tall, effeminate man called out, "Temerity Bauer, sexy, darling, *gorgeous* girl!" and rushed toward her. Temerity smiled and turned toward him as he descended on her, wrapping an arm around her waist and leading her toward a group of people who were obviously her musician friends. He snatched a glass of champagne from a tray and pushed it into her hand that wasn't holding the stick. Temerity laughed and Ellen relaxed.

She settled in to wait. Temerity hadn't said she should, but she had some time before she needed to reboard the bus, and watching this spectacle through the picture glass was enjoyable, like a parade from the safety of a balcony.

The cold air could not stop the warm sensation of pride that Ellen felt as she watched her friend mingle and amuse. She was obviously popular. No surprise there, Ellen thought. She had never known anyone so kind or so brave, and Ellen treasured even the twinge of jealousy that Temerity's admiration inspired.

A tall, swarthy man positioned himself near her friend. He leaned down and spoke in Temerity's ear, and Ellen could tell from the way Temerity shifted away and crinkled her nose, her smile stiffening, that she did not care for him. The man's shirt was unbuttoned too far down, revealing a furry chest. Ellen smiled. Between Temerity's reaction to the man's scent and the hair, she knew this must be the infamous bassoonist.

Ellen wished she could go in and rescue her friend, but it was unthinkable, and it wasn't like Temerity was in danger. Ellen mused on what it would be like to meet someone and not be able to see what they looked like. She realized that she based the majority of her assessments on the physical. Not if someone was pretty, or skinny, or old, but the way they dressed, they treated others, their mannerisms all told her so much. Without that . . . Well, for Temerity it was different, she knew.

And then she saw exactly how different. Temerity was listening to the lascivious bassoonist with her head tilted slightly away from him, looking rather bored. But in an instant her face changed and she turned away, straightening up. Then, after a word to her suitor, who looked affronted, she began to drift toward the piano.

Through the open door, Ellen could hear the punctuated murmurs of conversation, laughter, and piano music filtering out onto the sidewalk. Listening hard, Ellen thought she recognized the music the pianist was playing, and she felt excited. *I know that music,* she thought proudly, though she didn't remember from where.

But the connection was made as she watched Temerity stop a few steps away from the piano and stand with a look of fascinated concentration on her face. Ellen couldn't see the man at the piano, because his back was to her, but she could see him watching Temerity. When the piece ended, Temerity raised her hands and clapped with delight, but was immediately intercepted by a group of women, who began an animated conversation with her.

The piano player stood and crossed to where they were standing. Ellen caught her breath as she recognized him, though he looked considerably different from when she'd seen him in his pajama pants on the landing. He stopped behind Temerity, very close, but not touching. He pretended to study one of the large pictures, but Ellen could see that he was taking in Temerity. She watched as her friend seemed to sense his presence, and she knew Temerity had "recognized" him, too, though in her own way—from his music or his scent, instead of his face. She half turned, and one hand went to her throat, but then one of the women took her arm and led her away, laughing, to another group of people.

The cold seeped more deeply into Ellen. She knew, of course, that Temerity had other friends, but this was the first time she'd seen her in a social group like this, and old feelings of isolation loomed up. She felt boneless, frightened that she might lose what she had such a tenuous hold on. Temerity was part of something bigger, but the idea of joining in was as foreign and as frightening to Ellen as leaping from a plane. The thought of going back to a life without Temerity and Justice felt like a screaming wind rushing past her as she fell, out of control.

Ellen turned and made her way back to the bus stop, where she stood in the cold, wondering if she would ever be brave enough to do more than stand on the side and watch.

And then she remembered something that Temerity had said about the piano player. "Why disappoint us both?"

And she knew that her courageous friend, too, had chinks in her armor. Vulnerabilities and uncertainties about her own worth in a world that valued what she couldn't even appreciate.

Stupid world.

22

A half hour later, Ellen was rounding the side of the building, making her way to the loading dock entrance, when a side door, an emergency exit that Ellen had only ever seen closed, suddenly opened. She stopped and slid between two dumpsters, up against the cement-block wall, a few feet away from the six or so stairs that led to this door.

Eric was standing in the doorway, and he wasn't alone. "I'm sorry about this, I really am," Billy, the general manager was saying, "but this was one too many incidents, and I have to fire you."

"This blows!" Eric shouted, clearly in a rage. As he stepped onto the small landing and spun to face Billy, Ellen could see that two security guards were behind the general manager. "This is Thelma's fault and you know it. I'll sue for wrongful termination."

Billy was tense, but he kept his voice low. "That's not the story everyone else told, including the security cameras. I don't know if you've been drinking, or doing drugs—"

"How dare you accuse me!" Eric raged.

"You've been seen," Billy interrupted him. "According to a few other employees, they've observed you using drugs, and I just can't take that responsibility when people's safety is at stake. Be grateful I didn't have you tested last night. I would have, if someone had gotten hurt."

"What *other* employees?" Eric demanded. "Who? I want names. I'll bet it was that little gnome Rosa, and her stick-figure friend."

Billy shook his head, the yellow light over the door rimming his balding head with a strange halo. "That's enough, Eric. The fact that you took a swing at Thelma *tonight* means you have to go—no matter what. You're lucky *she* isn't pressing charges. You've cleaned out your locker and you'll receive two weeks' severance, but I do not want to see you back here."

"Oh, you won't see me again," Eric said meanly. "But I'll be around. You'd better watch your step."

Billy leaned forward. "Are you threatening me?"

Eric, who had now descended the steps and was looking up, shrugged and said, "Take it any way you want to."

The GM sighed and shook his head. "Just go. Do yourself a favor and don't come back." He went inside, past the guards, who waited, arms crossed, until Eric had performed another rude gesture and strode away into the parking lot.

Ellen waited until the door closed, then she hurried on through the building and into the locker room. She changed, took her notebook and pen, and went to the broom closet. Sitting on the folding chair, she wrote down in her book what she'd heard, adding the comment *If the drugs are still there, he'll have to come back.*

When she was relatively sure the halls would be sparsely peopled, Ellen checked the chart and got to work. She had the bakery section of fresh foods, and though she usually didn't care much for the open area, tonight she was glad, as it gave her a chance to watch Thelma, who, to Ellen's relief, seemed uninjured.

Just before the meal break, Rosa approached Thelma, who was stacking netted bags of onions into a pyramid on a raised countertop. The squat cleaner was holding a brown paper bag. She cleared her throat. "Thelma?" she said.

Thelma turned and looked at her. "Oh, hi, Rosa. I'm glad I didn't hurt you too badly last night."

"I'm so happy that Eric finally got fired!" Rosa told her. "He almost killed me, and if it wasn't for you, I . . . might not be here tonight." She shook her head and pressed her lips together in anger. "I cannot believe he tried to hit you. I'm so sorry."

Thelma stopped what she was doing and put her hands on her hips. "*I'm* not, if it means he's gone. I only wish I could have kicked him back!" She laughed.

Rosa giggled. "I'm glad it was me who saw him do it! That'll teach him to mess with us tough ladies."

"I hope so! Thank you for speaking up, by the way. I know that isn't easy. Eric is just one of those people who absolutely cannot admit to making any kind of mistake. They have to blame it on everyone else." Thelma paused and looked at the bag, neatly folded at the top, that Rosa was holding.

"What's that?" Thelma asked.

"Tamales. I made them for you. I hope you and your . . . girlfriend, like them."

"Oh my gosh," Thelma exclaimed, a big smile splitting her face. "We *love* tamales. That is so nice of you Rosa, thank you. You really didn't have to, but . . . I'm glad you did!" She took the bag as Rosa thrust it at her. "Beth will be so excited."

Rosa blushed. "Chicken and pork. It's no big deal. I just wanted to give you that. So, I'll see you later."

Thelma offered her hand to Rosa, who looked taken aback at the—in her world—male gesture, but she shook it shyly and then hustled away. Opening the bag, Thelma put her face in it and took a long sniff, then came up eyes gleaming. "Yum," she murmured. She put the bag carefully on the pushcart holding the sacks of onions and went back to work.

It was close to quitting time when Ellen made her way to the dock. The restrooms looked deserted. Ellen went to the men's room, knocked, and shimmied behind some boxes. When no one came out, she gathered the stepladder and a broom, went in, and climbed up to check the loose ceiling tile.

The package was still there.

So Eric hadn't had time to remove it before he was escorted out by security, as she'd expected.

When the shift finished, Ellen did her usual slink out the dock. She was snaking her way through the employee parking lot toward the street when she saw a suspicious shape moving furtively among the parked cars. Stooping down, she watched the man, dressed entirely in black, through the windows of a sedan.

As he turned toward her, Ellen got a quick glimpse of Eric before he lowered a black ski mask over his face. Then he slipped behind a minivan and did not emerge from the other side.

Ellen glanced back at the building, but the dock looked deserted at the moment. Then she heard voices coming from the direction of the employee entrance, and twisted to see Rosa and Kiki walking toward the van with Johnson and a younger man she didn't know. When they were twenty feet from it, Johnson split off. "Good night, ladies.

'Night, Jimmy! Drive careful!" He went to an ancient Toyota, pulled out his keys, got in, and sped away as though escaping a war zone.

The other three proceeded to the minivan. Kiki went to the driver's door, and Rosa and Jimmy went to the passenger side, waiting for Kiki to unlock the doors. Ellen's palms were sweaty on the sedan. She saw a small shape break the outline of the back of the van as Eric leaned out around it. Ellen felt a scream rising in her throat, but it was choked off by fear. She *couldn't* make herself known, and what could she do against a full-grown man bent on hurting someone thirty feet away? Then there would be police to talk to, too many questions. The very thought of it made her feel that her chest had been opened by a zipper that was rusty, broken, and would never close again.

Ellen searched around, desperate for some way of alerting the three people to the danger without revealing herself. A brick to throw, anything. Then, in the car she was crouching next to, she saw a small blinking light on the dashboard.

At the van, Ellen saw the dark shape of Eric emerge from the back and advance toward Jimmy and Rosa, who had their backs to him. Eric's hand, holding something, rose into the air, and Ellen lifted up, turned around, and sat down as hard as she could on the bumper.

The car rocked and the alarm blared, magnified by the pavement, to assault the quiet of the predawn. Ellen bounced, ungracefully, down onto the asphalt, but as she did, she caught a glimpse of Eric's form running away. Kiki was staring toward the blaring sedan, but Rosa was stooped over Jimmy, who was sprawled on the asphalt. Ellen could just see his head and shoulders next to the wheel of the van.

"Jimmy!" Rosa was screaming. "Help! Jimmy's been hurt! Somebody, help!"

On her hands and knees in front of the sedan's bumper, Ellen scrambled, still on all fours, along the row of cars until she came to the last one, then she stood up and ran for the shadows without looking back.

Because she needed a long sit in the park to calm down, Ellen didn't get home until after nine. When she did, she was surprised to find Rupert standing in the kitchen, a large apron tied around his larger midsection.

"Hi, Ellen!" Temerity called out. "Rupert is making a cake for my parents' anniversary. It's their thirtieth, and we're all going for a lunch today. We can't do dinner because of my concert tonight."

Ellen waved shyly at Rupert but couldn't make any eye contact. This wasn't a big problem because Rupert seldom could either. She put her stuff down and came over, drawn by the magic. "What flavor?" she asked.

"Red velvet," Rupert said. Ellen was intrigued.

"Is that, like, strawberry?" she asked with interest.

"No, it's more of a fake chocolate, but it doesn't taste like chocolate," Temerity said. "You'll have to wait and taste it later."

"But you're taking it to your parents'," Ellen reminded her.

Temerity hummed and swayed happily. "I'm taking you, too."

Ellen jerked in surprise, then she remembered Justice asking her to visit them. "I can't do that."

Temerity performed an exaggerated sigh. "Okay, listen. You don't have to participate, at all. You can sit in a corner, or go outside and walk around in the trees all by yourself. Both my parents are psychiatrists, like I said, so they won't have any judgment if you prefer to keep to yourself. I want them to meet you, though, and I thought you'd be more comfortable doing it there. Also, Justice doesn't know this yet, but we're going to stop by and check on Lydia on the way."

That changed things a bit. Ellen *had* promised. Though her scalp was prickling with the trepidation she always felt when there was a possibility of being observed, Ellen had to concede that the parents of Temerity and Justice were most likely discreet people.

"When you say 'check on' . . ." Ellen began.

"I mean that, while we're on our outing, we're going to drive past, see if anyone is home, and if they are, sneak into the trees and check up on her."

Well, that sounded okay, but the door buzzer sounded before Ellen could finish formulating a decision about the "outing," a word that worked on two levels for her.

"It's Seth," Temerity said as she hung up the phone. "He's on his way up. I'm going to have him go to the post office and the grocery store. You know, get him a couple of hours' work."

Ellen nodded, wanting to hide, but she had a question first.

"Did you talk to him?" she asked.

"Who?" Temerity said.

"The, you know, the piano guy, from downstairs. He was at the party last night."

Temerity colored slightly and started toward the door. "No, I didn't see him." The joke was familiar, but for the first time it lacked buoyancy.

"He saw *you*," Ellen said. "And he looked really pleased about it."

"He was just happy that at least one person wasn't shouting over his playing."

Not wanting to push her, Ellen went to the hallway door. Leaving it partway open, she waited just inside the hall until Seth arrived at the landing. It seemed to take an inordinate amount of time. When the knock came, Temerity opened the door. Runt was barking and making his usual ruckus, then he went out onto the landing and began to whimper. Ellen heard Temerity call out, "Come on in."

But no one did. From across the large room, Ellen couldn't see out the front door, but she could see Rupert standing in the kitchen, focused on whatever was through the doorway with his brow furrowed. Suddenly he moved. Dropping the measuring cup in his hand back into the bowl, he hustled across the room with his hitching, rolling gait and gently but firmly moved Temerity aside. As he did, he called out, "Ellen! Justice!"

Without even thinking, Ellen threw the door open and rushed to the doorway. Seth was lying on his back on the landing, his eyes rolling upward as he gasped for breath and tried to orient himself. Ellen spun and ran back to the hallway. She knew, of course, which door led to Justice's bedroom, but she had never even knocked on it. She did so now without a second's hesitation.

Justice opened the door immediately, having apparently heard Rupert's plea. He was wearing pajama pants, and at the large bed behind him, Dr. Amanda was stooping for a robe. Ellen averted her gaze. "It's Seth," she panted.

She felt the wind as Justice bolted past her. In a few seconds he had lifted the semiconscious boy and carried him to the sofa, with Rupert helping the best he could. Temerity trailed behind, finding the throw blanket and tucking it around the shivering child.

Amanda appeared in a dressing gown and knelt beside the boy. "What do we have here?" she asked steadily, and Ellen knew that her projected calm was good medicine.

"He has bronchitis, and he's on antibiotics, but listen, he cannot go to the hospital, unless it's absolutely necessary," Justice told her quickly. "Not yet," he added.

"We do have another option if we need it," Temerity told her.

"Justice, get my bag," Amanda instructed. "I need the stethoscope and the blood pressure cuff. What's his name?"

"Seth," three people said at once.

At the sound of his name, the coughing boy's eyes fluttered open in alarm and he gazed around in a fevered panic.

"Okay, Seth," Amanda said soothingly. "You're going to be fine. We just have to clear your lungs a bit. I'm going to need you to sit up." She rocked him forward, resting his chest along her left forearm to support his weight, and began to strike his back with the open palm of her right hand, not too hard, but you could hear the liquid thump. Seth coughed again, this time fruitfully, and Rupert pulled a dish towel from where he'd tucked it in the tie of his apron and held it for Seth to spit the mucus out. In a few minutes, the congestion had lessened and Seth was able to sit, propped up by pillows, while Amanda examined him.

Ellen put the water on for tea and then stood, feeling helpless, a few feet back from everyone else.

Seth lay there, panting and exhausted, pale, sweaty, and shivering, until Amanda had finished. Then she smiled at him and told him to try to relax. "Can I see your medicine?" she asked him. Seth waved a weak hand at his bag, which was lying by Runt's paws. Amanda handed the bag to Seth and he looked through it until he came up with the packs of antibiotic Ellen had seen Beth give him.

Amanda read the labels. "These are good, but they take a couple of weeks to work, and you should be resting while they do. Why are you out in this weather?"

Temerity chimed in, "We all gotta work to eat," as though it were the most natural thing in the world that this twelve-year-old was killing himself to run errands. "Amanda, can we talk to you?"

Everyone stood silently, looking at each other for an uncomfortable moment, unwilling to leave Seth, and unsure if they should. The whistle of his restricted breathing punctuated the tenseness. Then, quite unexpectedly, Rupert took charge. Perching his bottom on the edge of the easy chair next to the sofa and placing a hand on the armrest nearest to Seth, as though claiming the area and the boy, he said to them, "I'll sit with him. You guys go on." He jerked his head, looked shyly at the boy, and turned bright red. His unease was so obvious that Seth seemed to sense there was nothing to fear. He laid his head back against the pillows and closed his eyes.

The other four went to the hallway, where Justice pushed the door shut behind them.

"What's going on?" Amanda demanded.

"He's living in the basement," Justice began.

"In this weather?" Amanda looked horrified.

Temerity explained. "He ran away from an uncle who is abusing him, and, we think . . . selling him. If we tell anyone he's here, he'll have to go back because the uncle is his legal guardian."

"If he's being abused, then they'll take him away . . ." Amanda began.

It was Ellen's turn. "Not necessarily," she said. Not sure how to sum up all her life experiences in a few sentences, and not wanting to, she settled for adding, "It could go really badly for him if there's no proof."

"Listen, honey," Justice said, putting a hand on Amanda's shoulder. "There are two reasons I didn't ask you for your help right off. The first is that this kid trusts nobody, with good reason, so if he thinks we'll turn him in, he'll disappear. The second is because this is a legal mess. We want to help this kid, but our interfering without having some way to protect him first could backfire—big time."

Amanda looked indignant. "I would have helped you!"

"We didn't want to put you in the position of not reporting the abuse," Temerity told her.

"And how abusive is it for this kid to die of exposure?" Amanda countered. "He cannot go back out there!"

"Does he need a hospital?" Justice asked, setting them back on track.

Amanda sighed. "He could use some fluids, and probably some intravenous antibiotics at this point, not to mention blood work so I can even be sure. That infection needs to be aggressively attacked, but without admitting him to the hospital, there's no way I can get my hands on those kinds of supplies and lab work without violating about sixteen laws, including theft and illegal distribution of prescription drugs."

Justice said softly, "That's why we didn't ask you."

Amanda grimaced, but nodded, resigned to the truth of what he was saying. "You said you had another option?"

Justice and Temerity both turned toward Ellen. Even without the benefit of sight, Temerity's face was set with so much determination that she reminded Ellen of a small bulldozer. But they were leaving it up to Ellen.

She took a deep breath, thought of Seth's white face gasping for air, and said, "Call her."

Temerity put a hand on Ellen's back and murmured, "Good girl." Ellen was reminded of Mr. Rush saying exactly that to Lydia. She felt like she was six, too.

They returned to the living room and Ellen hovered in the background while Temerity knelt next to Seth. "Seth?" she asked gently, finding his forehead with her palm and pushing his sweaty hair off his skin. "Remember that nice lady who helped you at the clinic?"

Seth rolled his head to look at her, and nodded. For once, it was not a wasted movement, as Temerity's hand moved with him.

She smiled. "Good. And you know she won't say anything to anyone, right?" Another nod. "Good, we need to call her. Do you have her phone number?"

Seth pointed to his bag again. Justice asked permission to look in it, and found the card. He dialed the handwritten number on the back and then nudged his sister with the phone. She took it.

"Hello? Is this Dr. Howell?" No one else in the room spoke. "My name is Temerity Bauer. You were kind enough to help a friend of mine yesterday, a young man named Seth." There was a pause. "Actually, not well. He collapsed on my doorstep and we've had a doctor friend look at him, but we can't send him to the hospital because . . . I'm glad you understand. Is there any way we could bring him to the clinic, or you could come here?"

Ellen's fingers hurt, and looking down, she saw that she'd crossed them, on both hands, and curled them tightly in. She shook them out.

"Oh, thank you! Yes, she is. Hold on." Temerity took the phone from her ear and called out, "Amanda, she wants to talk to you."

"I'm right here," Amanda said from behind her. They passed off the phone, and Amanda walked a few feet away as introductions were exchanged, and then came a stream of medical terms that Ellen didn't understand.

"All right," said Amanda, returning to the group. "She's waiting for her wife to get home so they can go by the clinic to pick up what she needs and then drive over. In the meantime, let's see if we can get some tea or broth in you, young man. And maybe we should give him a little space." She swung her head to point out the fact that five large adults and a huge shaggy dog were clustered around one small boy.

"I think," Temerity said, picking up the suggestion first, in spite of having missed the pointed look, "that we should finish making that cake. Rupert?"

Rupert rose and Amanda took his place. Justice said he would take Runt for his morning walk, though the dog seemed reluctant to leave the boy, and Ellen went upstairs. She was uncertain whether to show herself to Thelma again or not. Her trained instinct was to *not*. Yet it was odd. Somehow, Ellen felt that she knew both Thelma and Beth because of watching them in an unguarded moment, and the fact that Seth was their focus, and not her, lessened the sensation of being trapped in searchlights.

Maybe, Ellen thought, *when people behave well when they don't know anyone is watching, you can trust that's who they really are.*

23

After forty-five minutes of doing battle with the voices telling her to be afraid, the desire to find out what would happen to Seth won out. Her ingrained reticence was unconquered, however, so she didn't just march back downstairs. Instead, she waited until she heard the door buzzer, then took up her position just inside the half-open hallway door.

"Hello, thank you for coming," Temerity said when she opened the door to Beth and Thelma. Ellen observed both women try for eye contact, take in Temerity's blindness, gauge the situation, and then adjust and proceed as needed. She had expected no less. Easy.

Justice and Amanda were both sitting near the sofa. They'd turned the TV on to some cartoons for Seth, but the sound was almost off. They both rose to shake hands with the newcomers and discuss the situation. It was strange to see Thelma in the loft. Two familiar things to Ellen that she had never expected to see united, it made them both feel unfamiliar. Then the two doctors had a hushed discussion near the door while the other three stood talking politely a few feet away. Finally, Temerity pointedly invited "everyone who is not Beth" to gather in the kitchen for coffee and snacks.

Ellen could see Beth perfectly through the crack in the door, but she couldn't see Seth for the back of the sofa. The doctor had brought a large bag, and she handed it off to Thelma, who smiled at her warmly and went to join the others.

Beth leaned over the sofa and spoke softly. "Seth? Are you awake?" Ellen saw the top of Seth's towhead pop up above the sofa back as he jerked upright. The sound of coughing was all Ellen could make out for a few moments. Beth helped him take a few sips of tea, which seemed to help calm the spasms.

"So, Seth. Looks like you're in luck. These nice people want you to stay here until you get better. How do you feel about that?"

"Why?" Ellen heard Seth rasp.

"Because they don't want anything bad to happen to you," Beth tried to explain. Ellen felt her hands form into tight fists again. It wasn't Beth's fault, but there was nothing for Seth to grab on to there. This was a kid who lived a life in which nothing came for free. Adults were not to be trusted.

"Why?" Seth croaked again.

Beth exhaled. "I know that it's hard for you to understand that some people just want, or actually *need*, to be helpful. And I don't blame you." She sat down on the coffee table and rested her chin on her fist. "Take me, for example. I don't *have* to work at the clinic, I have a good private practice, but I like to help people. There's no reason for you to trust us yet, but let me put it this way. If you want to get better, you have two choices. You can go to a hospital. And I think I understand why you don't want to do that," she added quickly as he recoiled against the cushions. "Or you can stay here so that I can give you the medicine you need through an IV. You have to stay in one place for several days, no moving around, no going outside, and no working."

"I'll be okay," Seth said, trying to stand up.

Beth put a hand on his shoulder and shook her head. "Seth, if you walk out that door, you'll be in a hospital by tomorrow, or worse."

"But I don't know them," Seth whispered, glancing fearfully at the group of adults conversing across the room.

Beth was nodding. "I know, me neither, actually," she whispered back, as though they were conspirators. "But I do know that they sent you to me because they knew I could help you without having to turn you in. They know you've been living in the basement, Seth."

"What do they want?" Seth asked. "Why would they want to help me? I can take care of myself." He was panicked and confused, this was out of his realm, and Ellen realized that the only person there who truly understood was her.

She stood up, tested her voice a bit with a small hum, and went out. She walked straight to the back of the sofa, and then around it. She could see Justice watching her curiously, but he did or said nothing to draw attention to her. Temerity, too, knew she was there. Ellen could tell, because her friend turned her head in her direction and tilted it slightly, listening.

The smell of the cake baking filled the air with a delicious scent and Ellen with courage. When she had come around almost next to Beth, Ellen spoke. "They want to help you because that's what they do," she said to Seth. "They've done it before. That's why I'm here." Both Beth and Seth looked up at her in absolute surprise, as did the five people in the kitchen. "Hi, Thelma," Ellen waved, wanting to shrink small enough to crawl under the couch.

"Ellen! Oh, so *that's* how this happened," Thelma said with a huge grin. "I thought I recognized these two." She pointed a thumb at Justice and Temerity. "You're the ones who saved Irena's butt last year. Wow, nice to meet you, I mean, officially." She was beaming at them. Seth was staring from one person to another.

Ellen was concentrating on Seth, though. "I'm like you," she said. "I didn't have anyone or any family. I grew up in foster care. I'm not saying you should trust us, I know you can't and shouldn't yet. But I'm telling you for sure that this is for real."

Seth was squinting up at her. "What happened to your face?" he asked.

Ellen's hand flew up to pull down her hair, to conceal the large angular patch of redness and the remaining white crisscross of scarring. But she forced herself to stop and lower her hand, leaving the surgical scars and still-healing skin exposed. Truth, she knew, was absolutely crucial if this boy was to ever trust them. Ellen tested her courage, steadied its wobbly legs, and took a step. "My mom burned me, on purpose, when I was young. I didn't have a very happy childhood." Ellen turned to point at Amanda. "That woman there? She helped me get some surgery to fix it. I know it's still not pretty. I won't ever be that, and that's okay, but it's much better than it was. Before, I would never let anyone see me." Ellen dropped her eyes to the carpet. Not since being taunted or mocked at school had she had this many people focused on her, and she had to fight to remind herself that this was not the same situation. "I still don't like it," she added quietly, shrugging.

Seth stared at her for a moment longer, then his eyes trailed around the room. "It's nice here," he said. "It's warm."

Ellen grinned. "And the bathtubs are huge!"

Beth was looking across at Thelma. Ellen didn't know what passed between them, but she saw Beth acknowledge something and nod.

Then she said, "Seth, I want you to meet my friend Thelma. She works with Ellen, and she told me all about her. Thelma is my favorite person, and I'll bet you'll like her, too." With a small movement of her head, she gestured for Thelma to come over.

Thelma picked up the medical bag and joined them. "Waz up, Seth?" she asked and extended a fist to be bumped. Seth did it, one corner of his mouth curling upward slightly at the familiar gesture.

"Not me," Seth said.

Thelma threw her head back and laughed. "True that," she said. "Listen, obviously you're a person who can take of yourself. Me too. Very independent." She thumped her chest and pretended to flex her muscles somewhat comically. "But you know, that doesn't mean that we always *should*. Beth here, she taught me that sometimes I'm stronger when I lean on something. Kind of like a swing set. You know, if it didn't have those angled pieces, it would fall over." Thelma had formed a triangle with her hands. "Sure," she shrugged, "you can do everything you need for yourself, but I know from experience that that can get awful lonely. For a while there it was just me and my parrot." Thelma rolled her eyes up, as though admitting a shameful secret. "What can I say? I've got a thing for pirates."

The boy was clearly amused. He smiled up at her.

"So, can we get a commitment that you'll stay here, at least for a few days?" Thelma asked, but casually, as though it didn't really matter to her one way or the other.

Seth's untrusting eyes flickered back and forth between Beth and Thelma, and then settled on Ellen, who nodded, almost imperceptibly.

"Okay, for a few days," Seth agreed, and fell back in exhaustion.

"Good man," Beth said. "Thelma, get out the IV kit and the saline drip. We'll start with that and then add in the antibiotic."

While Beth explained carefully and thoroughly to Seth what she was going to do, Thelma asked Ellen if there was anything they could use to hang the IV bags. "Ceiling's a little high in this place," Thelma said loud enough to be sure that Seth could hear her, looking up, way up, at the ceiling twenty feet above them. "It's as high as the top of a ship's mast. Usually we'd just fasten a hook somewhere, but to get up there we'd need some major rigging, not to mention a nimble cabin boy or a spider monkey. And they both bite." Seth snickered.

"I've got a hat rack in my room," Justice offered.

"Perfect!" Thelma told him. "Bring it on out!"

Grateful to be forgotten in the general activity, Ellen made her way back upstairs and burrowed into the heavy covers of her bed, exhausted. Ellen would normally have been drained by the exchange with other people, and she was, but for some reason she also felt fuller. Maybe it was the fact that the others were helping Seth, and maybe it was something else. Ellen fell asleep wondering what the something else might be, but as hard as she tried to catch it, it evaded her.

She slept for only four hours, but awoke knowing she wouldn't go back to sleep. She dressed hurriedly and went downstairs.

The living room was quiet. From what Ellen could tell, Thelma and Beth had gone, and so had Rupert. She didn't know where the twins or Amanda were. The hat stand next to the sofa trailed its tubes down until they disappeared behind its back, so Ellen knew that Seth was there.

She started into the room cautiously and then stopped when she heard a laugh from the floor next to the sofa. Circling it in a wide berth, Ellen was surprised to see Thelma sitting on the floor next to Seth. A small table with a game board was between them. Runt was sitting against the sofa with his head resting on the cushion under Seth's arm, who scratched his ears. As Ellen watched, Thelma said, "And that's a six. I'll take two hundred dollars for passing Go, thank you very much!"

Seth, using one hand, carefully counted out the bills and passed them over. Thelma gave him the dice.

"Where is everybody?" Ellen asked.

"Oh, hi there. Well, let's see. Your amazing baker friend finished that masterpiece and left." She pointed to the counter where a confection of creamy white swirls and red flowers sat on top of a cake stand. "I told him it was cruel to make that in front of us and not give us any, so he made a small one, too!" Ellen saw two plates on the coffee table, one scraped clean and the other holding a slice of cake that had only been nibbled on. "Everybody else went to get ready for an anniversary lunch, I think they said? And I'm hanging out with Seth until you guys get back."

Seth smiled weakly at Ellen. "She's beating me," he said.

"No mercy!" Thelma exclaimed, and then laughed. "Actually, he already owns all of the valuable properties. It's only a matter of time before I'm bankrupt."

Ellen had no idea what they were talking about. Board games didn't come for one, so she'd never had much interest.

Remembering that Thelma, too, had worked all night and not yet slept, she observed, "You must be tired."

This reminder produced a yawn, but Thelma waved it off. "I'm fine. I'm off tonight, and I prefer to stay up and sleep later. It's the only way Beth and I get a day together."

With a shiver, Ellen realized that since no one else was around, that made her the hostess. "Do you guys, uh, want, um, soup, or something?"

Thelma scrunched up her face at Seth. "Soup?" she asked. He shook his head, clearly too tired to eat, to judge from the piece of untouched cake on his plate.

"Nope," Thelma said. "Not much appetite just yet. It'll come. We're good, thanks. Roll away, buddy!"

Temerity came out, wearing jeans and a bright orange sweater. "Ellen? Is that you?" she called out. When Ellen answered, she said, "Are you ready? We have to leave in about ten minutes."

"Yeah, I don't think I'm going to go," Ellen said as Temerity joined her.

"You know"—Temerity crossed her arms and assumed a familiar tone—"sometimes, even though we know we can do everything by ourselves, that doesn't mean we should."

"All right! I get it," Ellen said, and stomped back upstairs. It was so like Temerity to use an argument back on her that Ellen had endorsed. It was cheating, of course, but what could she do?

They waved good-bye to Thelma, who put a finger to her lips, and pulled the wad of fake money from Seth's limp hand as he slept against the pillows.

"Thank you so much," Justice whispered, shushing his sister, who was filling her lungs to call out a good-bye. "We'll be back before six. This one has to go to work and support us." He pointed at Temerity.

"Oh yeah, right," Temerity said under her breath. "The arts are so lucrative, I'm just raking it in."

"Classical musicians are such mercenaries. It's all about the cash," Justice agreed, earning himself a thump in the ribs from his sister. *"Oof."*

Amanda laughed and said in a low voice to Thelma, "Are you sure you don't want me to stay? I could."

But Justice took her arm. "No, you are going to meet my parents.

It's been nine months, and they understand residents' long hours, but they're beginning to think I've made you up."

"Oh . . . okay," Amanda said, sounding very nervous.

This floored Ellen. Amanda, nervous to meet her boyfriend's parents? Who would *not* like the brilliant, beautiful, funny doctor as a girlfriend for their son? Amanda was like the bonus jackpot. It stunned Ellen to realize that even someone seemingly perfect could be afraid of an introduction.

Amanda said, "Well, if you're *sure*. Call my cell if you need anything, Thelma."

Thelma dismissed them with a casual wave. "Go!" she said. "Beth's already on call and I'm really glad to do this. Beth is always the one who gets to be all useful, it's nice to have a turn." She smiled at them, and then turned a concerned face back to Seth.

Ellen trailed down the stairs behind the other three, thinking about that word. *Useful.*

It was, she knew, important.

24

We need to make a quick stop," Temerity said brightly once they had exited the garage.

"Did you forget something?" Justice asked.

"Not at all. We just need to cruise by and see Lydia. If they're not home, we won't stay."

The car braked slightly and Justice turned to look at his sister with a creased brow. Amanda, who was sitting in the backseat with Ellen, asked, "And this would be the same Lydia who . . . ?"

"Oh," Temerity said. "She's the little girl that was in the bus accident with Ellen. We found out where she's staying and stopped by one other time. It's a nice place, and everything seemed good, but then Ellen saw her again, at the facility where her mom is, and promised to check on her."

The frown deepened as Justice said, "And do these people who are taking care of her *know* you are coming?"

"Well, we haven't officially met them, seeing how we had to Sherlock Holmes the address. But they didn't know the last time we went by either, and that worked out fine."

Justice rolled his eyes. "Stalkers!" he enunciated very clearly. "You guys cannot do this. Detective Barclay told you she'd been placed in a really good home, can't you be happy with that?"

"I could," said Temerity, screwing her mouth sideways like she was thinking really hard, "*if* that were the end of it. But see, we told her mom that we'd check up on her and let her know how she's doing."

There was a quick swerve that pressed Ellen against the leather interior of the car as Justice pulled over and put the car in park. He spun in his seat and looked at Ellen. "Explain, please."

Knowing there was nothing else for it, Ellen began. "We found her mom, Maddy. She's in a state facility, in a coma." Ellen left out the fact that they had used Amanda's computer to find her originally. "I went to check on her, see how she's doing, and I saw Lydia. I promised her I'd visit her."

Justice twisted so that he could look directly at her. "And did you speak to anyone else while you were there? Say, anyone with any *authority*?"

Even the word made her uneasy. *Authority*. Ellen looked down and shook her head.

"Great." Justice addressed his sister. "That's why you were asking the detective so many questions, isn't it? You guys are getting involved again."

"Well!" Temerity exclaimed, throwing her hands in the air. "I mean, how could we not? You understand that if Maddy lingers in that state, without someone to help her, Lydia will just be shuffled through the foster system. She won't be allowed to stay with one family, no matter how good it is for her."

Amanda was looking from one of them to the other. "I don't understand," she said. "You want to go and *spy* on this little girl?"

"Your girlfriend is exceptionally bright!" Temerity said to her brother. "Too bad about you."

Justice growled, but Ellen could tell that he was considering it. "What is it you think you can do for her?"

"Don't know yet," Temerity sang. "We're winging it."

A groan came from the long-suffering Justice. "Oh my God, you two will be the death of me, or at least the reason for my incarceration. I know you were able to help find a new home for the baby that your coworker Irena was saddled with by that criminal who tried to rob Costco. But Ellen, Irena was a work associate, and be honest, it was dumb luck that you knew someone who was looking to adopt and could put them together. It doesn't mean you should open an agency!" He sighed, but Ellen knew that that success, dumb or not, was influencing him. "All right, but just a drive-by! Okay?"

Temerity gave him the address, and Ellen was amazed that the trip that had taken over an hour on the bus was reduced to twenty minutes in the sleek BMW. They drove slowly around the cul-de-sac where the Rushes' house sat, but could see nothing from the street.

"Can you let me off, up here, just for a minute?" Ellen asked.

With a grunt of resigned frustration, Justice pulled over just past the driveway, where the house was blocked from the road by the trees. Ellen climbed out and made her way into the pines, heading for the vantage point where she could see into the windows and the backyard. She stopped suddenly when she heard a woman's voice: "Lydia!"

Ellen dropped into a crouch behind a bush.

Through the backyard fence, Ellen could see Lydia on the swing set. She was swinging for all her tiny frame was worth. At the top of the arc, the girl looked over at the porch, at the back door of which stood Mrs. Rush, who called out, "Lunch in five minutes, okay? Don't forget to wash your hands."

"I'm coming," Lydia answered, but she only increased the angle of her body as she rose high in the air, pumping with all her might, watching the sky rush down at her with every upswing. The door to the porch closed.

Reaching into her pocket and pulling out the paper she'd prepared, Ellen crept forward, across the thin strip of open lawn, until she was up against the fence.

"Lydia," she whispered. "Lydia, it's me, Ellen."

There was a muted scraping sound as Lydia put her feet down and dragged herself to a stop. She got off the swing and started toward the fence.

"Don't come over," Ellen said quietly. "I'm going to leave you a note. You can get it later, okay? It's got my phone number on it, so if you need to call me, you can." Ellen didn't have her own phone, so she gave the number at the loft. "Everything okay?"

Lydia, eyes sparkling from the mystery, came a little closer and whispered, this time loudly, "Everything okay." Then she glanced up to the house and pretended to be interested in something in the grass. Stooping down, she said, "Mommy woke up. We're going to see her on Monday. Are you coming back?"

"Yes, but I don't know when. I'm not supposed to know you're here."

Lydia looked a little disappointed, but she nodded and then scrunched up one side of her face, forcing one eye closed, in what Ellen assumed was her attempt at a wink.

"Gotta go. See you later," Ellen said, and she bolted back for the trees.

When she got into the car, Temerity asked, "All good?"

"Yes," Ellen told her. "She seems really happy there." They drove on, Ellen staring out the window at the fancy houses and the open spaces. After Justice's reservations, she would tell Temerity in private about Maddy waking up so that they could decide what to do, and then tell him. It would be different to grow up here, away from the grays and browns of the inner city. *So much green,* Ellen thought as the trees slid by.

After another fifteen minutes, the BMW turned onto a long driveway that curved between trees until it ended gracefully in front of the most beautiful house Ellen had ever seen in magazines or on TV. This one was mostly wood with tall, narrow windows of smoky glass that reflected the dense trees around it. It looked like it had grown there instead of being built. They came to a stop, and Justice turned off the car.

Ellen didn't want to get out. Then she felt someone take her hand and squeeze. Startled, she looked over.

It was Amanda. She was grasping Ellen's hand and looking at her with a kind of desperation. "Come with me," she whispered as the twins climbed out.

Amanda had done so much for her that Ellen didn't see how she could refuse. In a kind of stupor, she climbed out of the car and reluctantly trailed the others toward the house. Then the front door opened, and Ellen came to an abrupt stop.

Standing in the doorway were two people. The woman was an older, very beautiful version of Temerity, and the man had no face.

That he had been badly burned, Ellen knew at a glance. His skin was rough, tight and pulled; his nose was little more than two slits; there were next to no lips, only a crooked suggestion; but the most shocking thing was the huge, unguarded, toothy smile.

"Welcome!" the man said. "Come on in. Your mom's been cooking all morning." He reached out a hand—also scarred and missing two fingers, Ellen could see—to Amanda, who took it and smiled back at him, as he said, "I'm Andy, and you must be Amanda. It is so great to finally meet you."

Amanda, who must have been prepared, didn't register any surprise at the ruined face. She said smoothly, "I'm so sorry, I've been so busy. Final year of residency, you know the drill! Thank you for inviting me."

"Of course, of course," chimed in the woman. "I'm Dory. Glad to finally meet you!"

Hugs were exchanged between the family, with one for Amanda, too, and then a pause while everyone turned to Ellen, still several feet back.

No one said anything, and then Andy spoke. "Well, we should all go in. If you'd like to join us, Ellen, we'll be in the den. It's straight through. If not, feel free to make yourself comfortable on the porch, or take a walk, whatever you like." The big smile came again, and then Andy stepped aside to allow everyone else to go in. "So, Amanda, are you planning on specializing?"

Ellen didn't hear the answer because her head was ringing inside. Distantly, she recalled something that Temerity had said to her not long after they met, when Ellen confessed that she was sorry that Justice had had to see her face. Temerity had said, "Justice wouldn't care."

It wasn't the burn damage that had startled Ellen. It wasn't the shock of the grotesque that had frozen her, she'd looked at her own for too long. It was the fact that Andy's affliction, as extreme as it was, *didn't define him.*

The porch was a big one, screened in, and there was a porch

swing, laden with pillows. Ellen stumbled to it and rocked herself calm. Swinging not for the joy of it like Lydia, but for the soothing motion. After ten minutes or so, she felt strong enough to get up again, and drawn to go farther.

Tentatively, Ellen pushed open the door and went in. She went through a large, beautifully decorated, but cozy living room, and stared in wonder as she passed into the kitchen/den.

The entire back of the house was glass. Outside, there was a small lake surrounded by trees, dense and lush, as far as she could see. It was as if the kitchen were part of the forest. The peace of the view landed on Ellen's heart like a sparrow to its nest, and for the first time in her life, Ellen allowed herself to wish for something she knew she'd never have.

Justice was sitting next to Amanda, who looked radiant, already at ease. Ellen side-slipped to an armchair next to where Temerity was sitting and curled back into it.

"You want anything to drink?" Temerity asked her from the side of her mouth.

"No, thanks," Ellen said.

Dory gave Ellen a simple smile but didn't stop telling the story she had begun. "So, this lady sniffs, she actually *sniffs*, and says to me, 'I was looking at that jacket yesterday.' Like I had stolen it off her back. I told her, 'And now I'm *buying* it.' I mean, really! Did she think they should keep it there in case she happened to change her mind? If someone else hadn't wanted it, she wouldn't have, either. Classic coveting behavior."

"You should have given her a card," Andy joked. "Sounds like she could use a good therapist."

Dory leaned into her husband's shoulder and nestled her head against his cheek. "No way. That jacket was a gift for our anniversary and I didn't want her to know where to come looking for it!" She turned her head and kissed him, smiling into his eyes.

The conversation continued around the table, with plenty of laughter. Ellen found herself included in the smiles and occasional eye contact but was never called on to participate. They were good to their word. When Justice did an imitation of a priggish work associate discovering a caterpillar in his salad by leaping up and emitting a high-pitched squeal, she actually laughed out loud.

They had lunch at a table in front of those huge windows. It was when Ellen's plate was loaded up with roast beef, mashed potatoes, green beans, and homemade bread with honeyed butter, and Temerity was explaining about Seth that Ellen surprised herself by speaking. She didn't mean to, it just happened. She found herself drawn out by the insights of Dory and Andy about the effects of what Seth had most likely been through.

"But," Ellen asked, after Andy advanced a theory that abused children sometimes become violent parents themselves, "it makes a difference how they deal with it at the time, right? I mean, Seth ran away from it."

"True," Andy agreed. "But people will still be controlled by the fear and anger that builds up in them if they don't understand it. Most abused kids go on to abuse their own children. It's a cycle."

Ellen asked, "What if you, say, had a bad childhood, but you just decide not to think about it anymore, because . . . uh, it's too hard?"

Dory responded to this. "Well, too often the bad feelings fester, they don't just magically go away. All of us are products of our emotional and environmental past, and when something triggers those emotions, they flare up."

"Don't we have a choice?" Ellen asked, surprising herself again.

"Well, that depends," Dory responded, pursing her mouth, "on whether or not we choose *consciously*."

Ellen didn't want to hear that. She said, "Let's say a kid is bullied, and all they want is to be left alone. Why can't they just go be alone?"

"The problem with bullying," Dory said, "is that most often it leaves a person feeling powerless. And being alone won't alleviate that."

Ellen felt a surge of energy, as though she needed to make them understand this. "That would be because, most often," she said, more forcibly than she intended, "they *are* powerless."

Andy wiped his gash of a mouth with a napkin and said, "To answer your question about choosing how to react, there *is* a way to take control, but it takes work. It involves reaching back and examining those unconscious emotional minefields so that we know the effect they have on us. Eventually, we can lessen the effect, until, even when those bombs are triggered, we understand the onslaught of panic, or sadness, or whatever feelings come up, for what they are—*shadows*. The more we understand they aren't real now, the less we are controlled. *That's* how we can choose."

Ellen stared at her plate, her need to stay unknown wrestling with her need to understand. Then very quietly, she said, "Once, when I was moved to a new school, two older girls held me down while another one wrote on my face with a marker." No one responded, there was no outcry or expression of pity, just polite attention. "They wrote 'freak,' and they drew arrows pointing to my scars. That wasn't a shadow, it was a Sharpie. It took a week to wear off. Every day I would leave for school, go into the gym, and spend the day in the basement. That was the only way I could 'control' it. I made that choice."

Andy nodded. He seemed interested, but not to the point of being intrusive. "When you think of that incident now, how does it make you feel?" he asked.

Ellen shrugged. "I don't think of it."

"But you just remembered it now, so how do you feel?"

Ellen gave the question some consideration. Underneath the embarrassment of speaking up in a group of people, she did feel something else, but she couldn't identify it. A sharp spike of annoyance at these confident, happy people surged through her, threatening to make her lash out. But even as the anger pierced her, Ellen's gaze landed on Temerity's father, watching her with his kind, respectful eyes from his ravaged face, and she knew that he was not responsible for the way she felt, for her . . . "Anger," she said. "If I let myself—and I don't—I guess I would feel angry."

Andy and Dory both nodded. "I'll bet you would," Dory said. "And with good reason." She stabbed a piece of roast beef with her fork. "I hope they got theirs. Little bitches."

There was a second of shocked silence at this condemnation from such a gentle, self-possessed woman, and then the table erupted in a chorus of laughter. And Ellen found that one of the voices was hers.

"Can you pass me that gravy?" Andy asked Ellen. "Go ahead and help yourself first. More potatoes?"

And so the unpleasant memory returned to its confinement deep in Ellen's past, but strangely, it seemed to have lightened by a fraction. A tiny piece of the anger had been worn away by contact with the outside.

After all, Ellen knew from long experience that very little in life is easy. Maybe it isn't supposed to be. Maybe what is important is that, whether it's easy or hard, we accept it, and do the best we can.

On the drive back into the city, Ellen stared out the window at the thickening of buildings and human occupation. More buildings, with less space per person, were multiplying as they sped by. She thought about how Andy Bauer seemed to get on with his life without letting his disfigurement stop him. He had made his life *useful*. It made her think. *Am I doing my best?* It was a question she'd never even considered before, and the sudden tightness in her chest made her want to stop thinking about it now.

25

They steadily climbed the stairs to the fourth floor, but halfway up the last flight, Temerity paused and sniffed the air.

"What?" Ellen asked.

"It's . . . like a summer garden, but where's it coming from?" Temerity answered, and they continued up. Ellen put a hand on Amanda's arm to silence her reaction, as the two of them, along with Justice, saw what was causing the now strong floral smell. Temerity set one foot on the landing then drew it back. "What the . . . ?"

Ellen said, "Go ahead, walk." And shared a smile with Amanda and Justice, who were looking at the scene before them, eyebrows raised.

Between the top step and the door was spread a path of flower petals. Temerity had stopped in response to the soft, yielding feeling beneath her feet. With each step, the crushed flowers released a new wave of scented delight. "What is this?" Temerity asked.

"I think piano guy wanted to send you flowers," Ellen suggested.

"So he threw them on the floor?" Temerity asked.

Ellen nodded, realized that was insufficient, and added, "I think he wanted you to enjoy them, you know, the best way *you* could."

A soft breath caught in Temerity's throat, and her eyes, dark and thoughtful, shone. But she said nothing, only walked to the door and back, and then to the door again, breathing deeply, her nostrils slightly flared with a smile that crinkled the corners of her eyes. "Okay," she said. "Pretty cool move." But that was all.

They went into the loft quietly, in case Seth was sleeping. What they found was not just Seth, but Thelma and Runt asleep as well. Thelma was stretched out on the floor next to the sofa, her head on a throw pillow and her jacket tossed over her. Runt was curled up at her feet. Justice shook Thelma gently to awaken her. She sat up and rubbed her eyes, then immediately checked on Seth, then her watch.

"It's time for another dose of antibiotics," she told Justice.

"I'll do it," whispered Amanda. She leaned over the coffee table, where they'd laid out the supplies, and selected the bag. "Then I have to get back to the hospital. Twenty-four-hour emergency room shift."

Temerity was standing near her brother's shoulder. She said, "We need to move Seth into a bedroom. He can have mine."

"No, when he wakes up, I'll move him into mine. That way he can have the TV in there," Justice insisted.

Temerity grinned. "And will you go stay at Amanda's? She's met the parents. Next step, arguing over wallpaper. Pointless, as far as I'm concerned, unless it's a choice between velvet or faux fur."

Next to the hat stand, Amanda blushed and shot a look at Justice, who was frowning at his sister. "Okay, first of all," he said, "Amanda and I will decide when it's time to make the next step and what that will be. Second, I'd like to be around to help out right now. And thirdly, fur wallpaper is a really good idea."

Temerity shrugged, but Ellen could see from her impish expression that she'd accomplished what she'd wanted. "Okay, fair enough. But women like Amanda don't grow on trees you know."

"Yes, I know. Thank you," Justice enunciated pointedly.

Thelma seemed amused at the exchange. "Well, I've got to go pick up Beth for date night."

"I've got to get ready for work," Ellen said, eager to vacate. She started toward the hallway.

"Me too!" Temerity said. "Justice can you drive me? You'll be back before Ellen leaves, right Ellen?"

"You want me to stay with Seth?" Ellen turned back, alarmed. "Alone?"

"He'll be fine," Amanda said. "Most likely, he'll sleep most of the time for the next few days. He should, anyway."

Everyone split up. Ellen got dressed in her work clothes and then came back downstairs, where she sat awkwardly on one of the stools with her notebook, writing down what had happened at the Bauers'.

A voice spoke behind her. "I have to get up."

Ellen turned. Seth was sitting up, his blond hair sticking out at the back. He was holding up his left arm, which trailed the IV. Ellen didn't know what to do.

"Uh, well. Can you wait a little bit? Justice will be back soon."

Seth looked at the floor. "I have to go to the bathroom," he said, his face reddening.

"Oh. Okay." Ellen got up and went to look at the contraption. She could make no sense of it, and she was afraid if she unplugged it, the way she'd seen Amanda do, that all the expensive medicine might leak out. She wanted to go back upstairs and leave this for someone else. The idea of going with a boy, or anyone, to the bathroom had her shoulders twitching involuntarily. She had no idea how to help him and that panicked her. Then she thought, *Be useful, do your best!*

The IV line was about six feet long. Okay, she could do this. She walked around the sofa until she was standing beside the hat stand.

"Can you stand up and walk?" she asked Seth as she tested the balance of the hat rack by picking it up.

"Of course," Seth said grandly, but when he tried, he swayed a little and sat back down.

Ellen shifted so that she could hold the stem of the rack with her right hand and get her left under Seth's arm. Slowly, they shuffled their way to the hallway and the bathroom, no easy job without tangling the tubes, especially with Runt glued to Seth's legs. Ellen set the rack down in the bathroom, made sure that Seth was steady on his feet while Runt panted happily up at him, and then she went out, closing the door behind her. "Just yell when you want to go back," she called from outside the door. She retreated down the hall as far as she could go without being worried she wouldn't hear him, and waited, trying to ignore the sensation that a swarm of bees had settled and were crawling frantically over her face and arms.

"You were right about the bathtub. The first time I came in here, I thought it was a pool," Seth called from behind the closed door. Ellen couldn't help smiling. She took two steps closer and called back, "I told you!"

"It's gigantic! Why does it have feet?"

The bees stopped swarming and stood still, but Ellen could still feel the hum of them waiting. She moved forward another two steps so she didn't have to shout. "I don't know. It's called a claw-foot tub. I guess it's kind of old-fashioned."

"Man, old people must have really liked taking a bath."

"They didn't have showers," Ellen told him. It was all she knew to contribute. She leaned against the wall outside the door. The bees lifted off her, flying as a unit, and Ellen rubbed her face and arms to dismiss the crawling sensation they had left. She heard a flushing sound, and then the water in the sink running.

"Okay, I'm done," Seth said.

Ellen opened the door and they repeated their tramp back to the sofa, this time with an iota more grace. Seth sank down gratefully, as though the short trip had exhausted him, and Runt took up his position with his head on Seth's chest. The boy lifted his arm and examined the insertion point of the drip. It had been taped over with clear tape. "This is so cool," he said.

Ellen looked, felt a wave of dizziness, and averted her gaze. She remembered Seth telling Beth that he would like to be a doctor, though of course Seth didn't know she'd heard that. "What's cool is that Beth knows how to do that. *I* never could," Ellen said. She sat down in one of the armchairs. "I pass out when I see blood. Mostly my own."

Seth looked like he might laugh. "No way!" he exclaimed. "How do you know?"

Ellen started to shake her head and opened her mouth to say, "Just do," when she caught sight of his eager face, waiting and listening. "'Cause I got shot once," she said.

The reaction was very satisfying. Ellen couldn't ever remember telling anything about herself that had been so well received. Seth's eyes opened wide and his mouth dropped open. "You *did*? When? How? What happened?"

Shyly, weighed down with natural reticence that lifted away as she went on, Ellen began to tell the story of Irena and her abusive husband, his attempt to rob Costco, Justice's daring intercession, and how the bad guys had been foiled. For all her love of gathering stories, it was the first time Ellen had ever told an adventure of her own.

It went over big. She finished by explaining how they had used her own skin to repair her face.

"Can I see?" Seth asked. "I mean up close?"

The bees came back. Ellen could hear the alarming hum of the swarm in the air around her. *Do your best, she thought. It isn't easy, but it won't ever get easier if you don't try.* So she braved her vibrating nerves and went to kneel next to the sofa, holding her hair back on the left side. Seth leaned in, inches from her face, and examined the area with intense interest. Finally he relaxed back.

"That's so cool!" he said. "I bet I could learn to do that. It's like sewing. Sometimes I have to sew things, you know, things that need to be fixed."

"Me too," Ellen said. "But I couldn't do it to skin." The very idea made her shudder. She heard footsteps outside on the landing, and Runt leapt up and went to meet Justice as if he were returning from a long journey. There was much rejoicing.

Justice came in and paused at the sight of Ellen on the floor next to Seth.

"Everything okay?" he asked.

"Did you really jump on a guy who had a gun?" Seth asked him with awe.

"Uh, yeah. Did Ellen tell you about that?" Justice looked at Ellen with a combination of bemusement and approval.

"She did. It's a good story. You should write it down."

"I think Ellen probably wrote it down," Justice said, smiling. He had encouraged Ellen's recording incidents in her notebooks since they'd first met. "Did she tell you how she karate-kicked a crazy guy on a bus after he made it crash?"

"What?" Seth exclaimed, turning to Ellen with expectation.

"Not now," Ellen said. She was glad that Seth had liked her story, but that was more "sharing" than she remembered ever doing, and she felt drained. "I have to go to work." She got to her feet and backed away.

Justice came over and smiled down at Seth. "Do you need to use the bathroom? You've been sleeping all afternoon."

"Ellen took me," Seth said simply.

Ellen saw Justice's jaw twitch, but he didn't look at her. She had the idea that he didn't want to look too amazed. She turned and headed for the hallway. Her chest felt . . . expanded somehow. Like her heart had swelled up. As she went through the door, she glanced back. Justice was watching her with the same look that she had seen on Dory's face when she'd looked at her family around the dinner table. Ellen floated up the stairs to get her bag.

The mood at work was subdued after the excitement of the previous night, but Ellen was curious how things had gone for Jimmy. Knowing that would be tonight's hot topic for the Crows, she decided to find out. Taking a duster, she moved down the rows of aisles until she spotted Kiki and Rosa in canned vegetables. Ellen went down the parallel row until she was level with them, and tuned in.

"So, he has to stay in bed for *three* days?" Kiki was asking. "Because of his *head*?"

"That's what the doctor said." Rosa sighed. "I guess there was some swelling? And they want it to go down."

"That horrible man!" Kiki said. "It *must* have been Eric. Did the police talk to him yet?"

"They want to question him, of course, but they made it pretty clear that without some kind of witness or ID, they wouldn't be able to do much." Rosa was genuinely distressed over this. Ellen reflected that gossiping about your own misfortunes must not be as much fun as talking about other people's, especially if danger was still impending.

"I just can't believe he's going to get away with this!" Kiki fumed, and Ellen could actually hear Kiki's breath streaming through her nostrils, like steam from a teakettle. "It makes my blood boil!"

To Ellen's surprise, she heard a sudden sob. Stooping down, she peered between the stacked gallon cans of tomato sauce. Rosa was slumped on a stool, which she had been using to dust the low shelves, her face in her hands. "I just . . . can't believe it," she sobbed. "What if Jimmy had been killed? And his wife about to have a baby. And Eric is still out there!"

Kiki patted her friend's shoulder with a flat hand. "Come on, don't cry. Jimmy is going to be okay, and we're going to keep an eye on things around here from now on!"

Ellen smiled at that. *From now on.*

Rosa sniffed and blew her nose on a rag. "I'm so afraid he'll come back and hurt someone else. Something is wrong with that man."

"A lot of things are wrong with that man," Kiki agreed fervently. "But now it's best to just stay out of the way and let the police do what they can."

"Which isn't much, apparently," Rosa said with some bitterness. Then she sighed, a long, raggedy sigh. "But I guess we can hope they get him in the end."

Ellen moved on, thinking that sometimes you have to do more than hope. Sometimes you have to give hope a little nudge. Sometimes you have to do something useful.

26

Ellen was so glad to reach the loft in the morning that she almost forgot to check the mailbox just inside the alley door. The postal worker generally came before eight. Ellen assumed it was because the main post office was only a block away. She pulled out the usual assortment of grocery store coupons and pizza delivery ads, a few bills, and a bright pink flyer.

Ellen stopped and stared at the garish paper. It read *Missing, young man, blond, twelve years old, seen in this neighborhood, if spotted, please call*, and then there was a phone number. There was also a photo, but it was muddy on the colored paper and it looked like a school portrait of a much younger Seth.

When she got upstairs, Ellen took it straight to Justice, and he read it out loud to Temerity. Ellen could see from the pillow and blankets folded on the sofa that Justice had spent the night there, Seth having been moved into his bedroom.

He frowned. "At least I doubt anyone would recognize him from this picture. He must be seven or eight here," he explained to Temerity, who was buttering toast.

"And no one will see him for the next few days anyway," Ellen said when he was finished. "Because he's here."

"But the reality is that we have to come up with some kind of plan. Keeping an underage runaway in our home while his guardian is looking for him can't be *completely* legal." He looked down at his watch. "I've got to go. Ellen, you've got tonight off, right?" She confirmed this and he said, "Good. Let's powwow tonight and do some brainstorming. So far, all I can think of is to hire a lawyer and see what they say. I'll be home around five."

When he was gone, Temerity said, "Where's that paper?"

"It's on the table," Ellen told her.

"Well, don't lose it. I have an idea. But we need a co-conspirator."

Ellen just sagged. "Please, no more people, I just can't."

Her friend took a big bite of toast. It made a loud crunch. Temerity chewed thoughtfully and made a sympathetic noise. "I know it's been a tough week for you. Bus crash, meeting the parents, letters, runaways, not to mention all the stuff at work with that Eric guy. Anything new with that anyway?"

Ellen had so much to tell her. As she talked, she felt the screw of guilt in her gut for not being able to report him. She just didn't have that much strength. She finished her recap by explaining that she thought he would be back to try to collect the drugs. This seemed to please Temerity rather than otherwise.

"Interesting. And I'm very proud of you, Ellen. You've been a trouper and I can imagine how stretched you must feel, but you've actually been so brave. You know you're my hero."

"I haven't *done* anything," Ellen moaned.

But Temerity was shaking her head firmly. "Not true. For you to speak up, the way you did for Seth, *and* put yourself in harm's way to stop someone from being assaulted. . . . That's not nothing, that's *amazing*. Amazing Ellen. I think that's what I'm going to start calling you, AE for short." She tested it out, extending the syllables. "*Ayyy-eee*. Okay, maybe not. I sound like a crocodile hunter. But don't worry, I wasn't thinking of asking anyone new into our little bubble. I think, if he's up for it, that Rupert will do very nicely."

Knowing Rupert, Ellen wasn't so sure about that.

"What do you want him to do?" she asked Temerity.

Temerity finished off her toast and wiped the crumbs from her hands. "Oh, just make a phone call. By the way, Beth is going to stop by later to check on Seth, probably around four thirty. She said she and Thelma are going to the Museum of Modern Art this afternoon and they'll come by after. You going to be sleeping?"

"I might be up by then," Ellen said. "Who's watching Seth today?"

Temerity raised a hand. "I am. Nothing gets by me, as you know."

Ellen smiled, but she was a little worried. Even the simple trip to the restroom had been tricky. "What about the, you know, IV and stuff?"

"Oh, Amanda unhooked that last night. I mean, he still has it in his arm, but it's not connected to anything right now. Beth's going to give him another antibiotic dose when she comes later. So he can move around for now, even take a shower if we put plastic over it."

As though on cue, the door to the hallway opened and Seth stuck his head out. He scanned around the loft and spotted the two women at the table.

Temerity had turned to the sound. "Good morning, sleepyhead. How are you feeling?"

A rolling cough answered her, but though it was fruity, it didn't sound as bad as yesterday. "Better," Seth said when he could. "What happened to, uh, that guy?"

"Justice? He went to work," Temerity said. "You want breakfast?"

"Yes, please."

"And then, maybe a shower," Temerity said. "Beth gave me this long plastic-glove thingy and a rubber band so you can wash. Sound good?"

"Could I . . ." Seth's eyes roamed around on the floor, "maybe . . . take a bath instead?"

Ellen smiled. She hadn't been able to resist her huge tub either when she'd first come here.

"I don't see why not. Get it?" Temerity laughed, then explained, "It's funny because I can't see." Seth looked confused, which Temerity couldn't see. "Hey, Ellen, weren't you just going to make some bacon?"

Seth's eyes widened and he proceeded into the room, followed closely by Runt, who had decided having a kid in the house to pet him all day was the Best. Thing. Ever. Seth was wearing Justice's pajama pants and one of his T-shirts. The pants were rolled up at the bottom but still dragging on the floor at his heels. The T-shirt fell past his thighs, and one thin shoulder was escaping through the neck opening.

Ellen fried a whole pack of bacon and scrambled six eggs. She took only three pieces of bacon, plus one for Mouse, and a small portion of eggs for herself. The rest she piled onto a plate with toast that Temerity had made and put it in front of Seth. He ate ravenously, occasionally slipping a treat to Runt, who stayed reverently at his side. "Your appetite is coming back, I see," Temerity said. When Seth raised his head to stare at her after this comment, he found Temerity was pointing to her ear. "You know, you can close your mouth when you chew."

"Mmm, sorry," Seth said, and went back to his meal, taking pains to be more quiet, but he couldn't breathe through his nose with his mouth closed.

Temerity stood up. "Okay, let me know when you're done. I'll show you how to work the tub and where the towels are. Then you can watch TV or read, whatever you want, so long as you stay horizontal. Double doctors' orders! I have to make a phone call. Be right back." Taking her mug, Temerity crossed the room and went into the hall.

Seth watched her go and then turned to Ellen. "How does she do that?"

"Do what?" Ellen asked.

"Walk around like she can see?"

Ellen considered this. "She knows the place really well. It's important not to leave anything lying around. Runt's bad enough, but usually he pants and she can hear him. If she has her stick, she can tell there's something in her path, but she doesn't use it in the house."

"It's so cool," Seth said quietly. "What's wrong with her eyes?"

It had never occurred to Ellen to ask, as she would have considered it an invasion of Temerity's privacy. "She was born that way. I think that's why she's so comfortable with it. It's all she's ever known."

"Yeah." Seth looked down at his plate. "People can get used to all kinds of bad stuff." He yawned, triggering Ellen to do the same.

"I have to get some sleep," Ellen told him. "I just got home from work. You okay?"

Seth shrugged, gestured around him at the expansive loft, and patted his full stomach. "Way better than yesterday." He grinned at her, but immediately a kind of fear spasm flashed across his face before he could stop it. Ellen knew that look.

She sat back and didn't look at him as she spoke. "You know, they won't make you go back to . . . wherever you were, if you're afraid. I'm not sure how they'll help you yet. But I know they will. You might have to help *them* though."

Seth looked at her suspiciously, and Ellen was willing to bet he'd been promised safety before that didn't come. Possibly from the very uncle he was desperate to escape now. "What would they want me to do?" he asked, the distrust apparent in his voice.

Ellen considered this. "When I was in foster care, there were some kids who had to testify against their families when they were in danger. Could you do that?"

Seth's pupils had dilated in fear. "I . . . no," he muttered.

Ellen sighed. "I couldn't either," she admitted. People without a conscience or scruples had controlled Seth's life up to this point. It was those kinds of people who had caused Ellen to start recording life's little misdemeanors, and much worse, in her notebooks, because she'd had no one else to tell. "I think," she said very carefully, "that if you told the truth about why you're here, to the right person, they could help you."

Seth was shaking his head violently. "I don't want to talk about that," he said in a strangled voice.

"I know," Ellen almost whispered. "I don't blame you. There are so many things in my life that were so bad, I don't even remember them, and I've never told anybody." She steadied herself. "So I'm not going to tell you to do what I can't. But you know what? If I'd had a friend like Temerity back then, maybe I would have told her, and my life would have been really different." Ellen sighed again. Seth was staring at her with hopeful confusion. Ellen realized that he was trying to believe she might actually understand.

"Listen," she said, trying to take the pressure off him, "you don't have to do anything right now. Just rest, okay?" She tried to think of something to occupy him. She would have chosen to read. "You want a book, or something?"

"I wish I had a comic book."

Ellen remembered that Amanda had given Justice a collection of some comics for Christmas. It was in a big box on the long bookshelf under the windows. She went and got it, then set it on the table next to him. It was big: three leather-bound volumes nestled together in their own box. Seth squinted at it. "That's not a comic book."

"I know. It's a collection of comics. You can look at it, if you want."

Seth slid one of the volumes out of the linen-covered box and opened it to the first glossy page. He ran his hand over it like it was treasure, reading eagerly. A smile crossed his face, and he turned the page.

Temerity came back out. "Okay, ready for bath time?"

"Okay," Seth said. He carried the book to the sofa and set it carefully on the coffee table to wait for him. He patted it contentedly, then scratched Runt behind the ears, and headed for the bathroom with the dog trotting after him.

"Rupert will be here around two," Temerity called over her shoulder. "In case you're up and you want to come down and say hi."

Ellen was too tired to ask what it was that Temerity had wanted Rupert to do. She went upstairs and stood at her round window for a minute. Ellen felt little bubbles fizzing in her heart, like a soda when you poured it fast.

She had climbed under the covers when she heard a knock at her door. "Yes?" she called.

"Can I come in?" Temerity asked.

"Sure." Ellen sat up. Temerity opened the door, but she didn't come all the way in.

"Remember how that detective, Barclay, said he owed you a favor?" she asked.

Ellen nodded and then remembered to say "Yes."

"Did he give you a number to get in touch with him?"

Ellen's eyes went to her dresser. Barclay's card was still there. "He gave me his card," she said, but suspiciously. "Why?"

"Aha! I knew you were holding out on me. Can I borrow it?" Temerity said. "I think I might have come up with something he can do so he doesn't have to feel indebted anymore."

Ellen came bolt upright. "You can't ask him to find that Frank person," she said in a panic.

Temerity frowned and waved both hands in front of her as though warding off bats. "No, no. It's not that. It has to do with Seth."

"But if you tell him about Seth . . ." Ellen began.

Temerity said impatiently, "Don't you trust me?"

Ellen didn't want to say that yes, she did, kind of, but also . . . not exactly. So instead, she said, "Why won't you talk to the piano guy? He obviously wants to talk to *you*."

Temerity rubbed her fingers together nervously. "Can I be honest?"

Ellen grinned. "No, lie to me."

"Okay. I'm an alien."

Ellen laughed.

"The truth is, *this*"—Temerity pointed to her eyes—"is a pretty big deal. I mean, not for me, but who would choose a blind woman for a girlfriend?"

For the first time Ellen realized that Temerity might need encouragement, too. She was no expert on this, but she knew enough from watching people in romantic and explosive situations to offer at least an observation. "I'm not sure, but it seems to me that nobody knows what will happen with a new person. Not until they get together and try it. I didn't think I'd ever be able to be friends with you," Ellen confessed.

"Well, thanks a lot!" Temerity laughed. "Anyway, it's no big deal. I'm really happy with the way things are." Then before Ellen could comment she said, "Now, quit stalling. Where's the card?" Ellen slipped out of bed and handed it to her. From her pocket, Temerity took a small recorder she sometimes used for this kind of thing and clicked it on. "Read me the number," she said. Ellen did. "Okay, sleep tight!" And with a whistle, the tune of which sounded like mischief to Ellen, her friend went back downstairs.

27

Ellen wasn't sure what woke her up, but she sat up quickly. Distantly, she heard the sound of the door buzzer. She checked the clock. It was almost three. She'd had such a light breakfast, for her, that she felt hungry. Ellen got dressed in sweatpants and a sweater and went down the stairs. As she reached the hallway, she heard a knock at the door.

Ellen hesitated. If it was Rupert, that would be okay, but she wasn't sure she was feeling up to seeing Thelma and Beth. She crept through the dark, windowless hall toward the door to the loft's living area, which was cracked open, but halfway to her vantage point she realized someone else was already there.

It was a man, and she could tell immediately from the silhouette that it was not Justice. Ellen almost cried out, but just then the man moved into the light from the room outside and she saw that it was Detective Barclay. He was so focused on what was going on outside that he hadn't registered her approach at all.

What was going on? Ellen moved against the wall and waited. In a moment, she heard the door to the landing open and then she heard

Rupert's voice, cracking with nervousness, say, "Tony Smith? Come on in."

There was a general shuffling, and then the unmistakably smarmy voice of Seth's uncle said, "Where is he?"

"He's not here, but I'll take you to him as long as you agree to our deal." Rupert's voice was squeaking so badly that he sounded like a teenager whose voice was changing.

"Sure, no problem. Like we said on the phone, you tell me where he is and you get the boy once a week for a month, special rate. How did you know, by the way?"

"He told me," Rupert said, his voice still quavering. "I told him I'd help him, and then I got your flyer. You want to sit down?"

Ellen saw Detective Barclay tense. He pulled something out of his jacket and let it hang in his hand by his side. A gun. Ellen started to back up, and then suddenly the door to Justice's room opened and the hallway was flooded with light as Seth stuck his head out. Barclay spun around and instinctively raised the gun.

Seth registered the gun in the detective's hand and a terrified scream came from his open mouth. Ellen got to him first. She put one hand over his mouth and the other one around his waist, but the boy struggled to get away.

Barclay glanced back over his shoulder, then stepped to one side as the door flew open, concealing him behind it. Ellen had backed into the bedroom, desperately trying to pull Seth with her, but he fought blindly, broke away, and flew across the hall. Ellen fell back and landed hard on the floor of the bedroom. In the doorway stood Seth's uncle. Ellen could see him surveying the boy. He smiled cruelly and advanced on the child. "*There* you are. Did you really think you could hide from me? You'll be sorry you ever ran out on me you ungrateful little—"

He raised his hand to strike the child. Seth whimpered and crouched, covering his head with his hands. Ellen scrambled to get to her feet, but before she could, there was a growl and a blur of fur as Runt passed her and leapt at Smith, locking on to his raised arm. Barclay emerged from behind the door, grabbed the arm from Runt, shouted "Release!" and twisted Smith's arm behind his back. "You're under arrest," pronounced the detective. Runt backed away, but kept up a constant low growl.

Ellen got to Seth and pulled him against her. It was such a strange thing for her to do that she wondered at her own response, but there was so much from which to shield this boy.

Rupert huffed into the open doorway with Temerity behind him. "Did you get him?" she asked breathlessly.

"Oh yeah." The detective had snapped closed the cuffs. "With a little help from my canine friend here."

"Good dog!" Temerity said. Runt whined, his tail wagged once, and then he went back to growling at Smith.

Smith was cursing. "I'll sue you! These people kidnapped my nephew, and I came to get him. How dare you assault me! I'll have that dog put down!"

"You might want to wait till I read you your rights before you say anything else," Barclay said dryly. "Move," he ordered, pushing the protesting man in front of him. He turned and, in a much gentler voice, said to Ellen, "You got him?" meaning Seth.

Ellen nodded, and sank to the floor with her arms around the hyperventilating boy. Temerity waited for the uncle and detective to pass her, and then she came to join them. Leaning down over Seth, she said, "Shh, shhh, it's okay. He's never going to hurt you again. I promise you that!"

"I . . . can't . . . What if he . . ." The boy gasped.

"He won't!" Temerity said. "And you won't have to do anything. I promise you that, too. You don't have to see him, or say anything. Now, come on, let's go in the bedroom and lock the door until they're gone. Good idea?"

Seth scrambled up and shot into Justice's bedroom with Runt at his heels. Temerity went in after them. She found the door, and as she was closing it, she said, "Ellen, let me know when Beth gets here."

"Okay," said Ellen. She was trembling so badly that she had to get to her hands and knees and then use the wall to climb back to her feet. "What just happened?" she whispered to herself.

Ellen went to the living room doorway and slipped in behind it. She watched through the crack between the hinges as Detective Barclay finished reading Smith his rights. The man started trying to wheedle his way out of it. Ellen had known he would. The liar. "Why are you arresting me? You should be arresting *that* guy!" He jerked his head at Rupert. "The pervert called me and wanted me to trade favors from my nephew to get him back."

"Yeah, I know," Barclay said. "But he called me, too, right after, and invited me to stop by and meet you." Barclay sat Smith roughly in a chair and went to the table. He picked up Temerity's tiny recorder and pushed play. Ellen couldn't make out exact words all the way across the room, but she did recognize both Smith's voice and Rupert's, exceedingly nervous, in a conversation. And she could also see Smith's face. It had gone pasty white.

"You're going down," Barclay said simply. He still had his gun in one hand, pointed at the floor. With the other, he pulled out his phone. "Yeah, Barclay here. I need a patrol unit to transfer a suspect." He gave the address.

Rupert was standing as far in the corner of the kitchen as he could squeeze himself, but there was something about the way he was holding his head, and a light in his eyes, that was different. Ellen watched him and realized what it most likely was.

Probably for the first time in his life, this overweight, ultra-shy, gentle artist had taken on the bully.

And won. Ellen knew how much that must have cost him. Warmth spread across her chest.

The uniforms arrived, and Ellen stayed behind the door, watching. Barclay explained that Temerity was with the child, who was traumatized, and she would come downtown later. He did not mention Ellen's presence. They led Smith away in cuffs, he was not talking now. Rupert went with Barclay to give a statement downtown. When they were gone, the door buzzer rang again.

Ellen looked at it. She waited. It buzzed again. Tentatively, she pressed speak. "Hello?"

"Hi, it's Thelma!" called the jaunty voice. Yes, *jaunty*. Ellen pressed the buzzer key, feeling relieved rather than otherwise. Thelma was here, brave Thelma.

She opened the door to the produce manager and the doctor.

"Where is everybody?" Beth asked.

Ellen cleared her throat. As succinctly as she could force herself to bear, she explained what had happened. Both the women's faces hardened into grim frowns, but in Beth's eyes there were also tears.

"Where is he?" Beth demanded.

"Down the hall, last door on the right," Ellen told her.

Both women marched off, and in a second, Ellen heard knocking and then Beth's soft voice calling out, "Seth? It's Beth. Everyone is gone, except Ellen. Can I come in?"

A few minutes later, the five of them emerged. First Thelma, leading the way, then Beth, holding on to Seth, who stared wildly around the room before he seemed convinced that no monsters would leap out at him, then Temerity, who walked slowly, head tilted, listening to the pace of the people in front of her, and last, Runt, tripping up the others in his determination to stay by Seth.

"Let's get you on the sofa," Thelma said, spreading Justice's blanket and fluffing the pillow.

"I'm going to give you something to help you calm down," Beth told him as she helped him onto the sofa. "Thelma, sweetie, can you get my bag?"

Thelma picked it up from where Beth had dropped it. Ellen, without being asked, went and brought the hat rack from Justice's room. When she got back, she had to nudge Runt from his post beside Seth to set it down.

As Beth was reattaching the IV to the line in Seth's arm, Thelma looked down at the book on the coffee table. "Who's reading *Calvin and Hobbes*?" she asked.

Seth, still shell-shocked and wide-eyed, pointed at his chest.

"That is my favorite!" Thelma exclaimed. "I think I've read every one. Do you mind if I look at this?" Seth shook his head, and Thelma picked it up, sat in the chair nearest him, and thumbed through the pages. She paused at one, read it, and then laughed out loud. Seth's head snapped around to look at her.

"Oh, l love this one. Look." She slipped onto the sofa next to Seth and held the book for him to read. Seth looked down at it, and then a smile cracked his face, just a small one, but the trance was broken. Beth continued to work, slipping the blood pressure cuff onto Seth's arm, and then filling a syringe with something clear from a small glass vial.

Ellen shuddered at the sight of the needle and turned away, rubbing the tiny scars on her upper arm, which had been itching since the uniforms had arrived.

Temerity stood by, listening to the activity with a contented smile on her face. When things were settled, she called out, "Beth, can I talk to you for a minute?"

Surprised, Beth looked up from where she'd been repacking her kit. She went to join Temerity and Ellen in the kitchen area.

Temerity was holding something. At first Ellen thought it was Barclay's card, but Temerity corrected that misconception.

"Listen," Temerity said in a low voice so that Seth couldn't hear, although Thelma was laughing with him now, keeping him occupied, while Runt inched his head closer and closer until his curly-haired ears were spread across the boy's chest. "It's only a matter of time until social services shows up. I was hoping you could speak to this woman and help her out. They'll probably need evidence of physical abuse and—"

Beth took the card, which Ellen could now see read SERENA HOFF-MAN. "Of course," Beth agreed. "But social services? Does he not have *anyone* else? No family?"

Temerity sighed. "No. He had a mother, but she relinquished custody, gave it to her brother, that . . . sewer rat who was just arrested. I don't think it's a good idea for Seth to have to testify, so if you could, you know, explain about his injuries, and . . ."

"I can, and I will," Beth said with steel in her voice. She turned and watched Thelma and the boy. "He really needs a home, doesn't he?"

Temerity smiled, and Ellen felt a light go on in her head. *Bingo.* "Yes, he does," Temerity told her. "He's a good kid. I've been amazed at how much he wants to work, and make a better life, in spite of all the horrible stuff he's been through. I'd love to see him find a family that would give him that chance."

Beth was nodding. "Me too," she whispered. Across the room, Thelma raised her head and smiled at Beth. Ellen thought she had never seen two people who appeared to love and respect each other so much, except for maybe Dory and Andy. It made her feel an ache inside, but it was an ache with a glow of joy in it. She knew she would probably never have that kind of connection, but it was enough to know that some people really did.

There was a sudden disturbance as Runt jumped up, scrambled on the rug, and ran to the door. A second later, Ellen heard the key in the lock. Seth cried out and grabbed on to Thelma, who wrapped her arms around him and began to rock him, whispering, "It's okay, buddy, nobody's going to hurt you. No way."

The door opened and Justice came in. He looked around, then said, "Oh, hi. Have a quiet afternoon?"

Temerity feigned a yawn and said, "Boring, really."

But not Seth, he sat bolt upright, so glad to see that it was Justice.

"He came!" he half shouted. "My uncle, he came here and the police, this really cool guy with a leather jacket and a gun, arrested him! And then me and Temerity hid in the bedroom while they took him away, and I hope he never gets out!" There was such intense fury on his face that Justice stopped midway across the room, dumbstruck.

No one spoke for a minute, and then Justice cleared his throat, walked to an armchair, sat down, and sighed. "And I missed it. Well, what a surprise. Tem?"

"Yes, bro?"

"Could you help me out here? I seem to be standing in a thick fog and all you guys are all out in the sun."

"Well, if you'll let me pour a glass of wine first, I'll be glad to bring you into the light," Temerity said. "Of course, it's all midnight for me."

Ellen knew what she meant, but this time it was Temerity who had seen the farthest, and the most clearly.

28

L ater, when Seth was sleeping, and Beth and Thelma had left, reluctantly, promising to return and check on the boy the next day, Temerity and Ellen sat down together at the table. Justice had taken Runt out for a "long walk and a big, juicy congratulations steak."

"What made you think of calling the uncle?" Ellen asked Temerity.

"The flyer. It was fate, really. I didn't want to put Seth through dealing with that horrible man, and I didn't know who or where he was, so our hands were tied, and then the man himself went and gave us his home phone number. Rupert really wanted to help, but I thought he was going to have a heart attack before the call was over." She smiled affectionately. "I was really proud of him."

"It was a good idea," Ellen said.

Temerity said, "But I didn't expect Seth to wake up and come out." She grimaced. "Though, in a way, maybe it was for the best. He saw what happened, instead of us just telling him, so he can trust it more."

"Where were you hiding?" Ellen asked.

Temerity giggled. "Under the counter. I needed to be able to hear the exchange so I could be an *eye*witness!" She threw her head back to laugh with delight, but muted the volume because Seth was still on the sofa.

"So. Anything more happen with the jerko from worko?" she asked.

Ellen explained about Eric being fired and the attack on Rosa's nephew. She told Temerity that the drugs, which she now suspected were possibly the same stuff that Detective Barclay was searching for, were still hidden in the ceiling tile of the men's bathroom.

Temerity listened with her head slowly moving from side to side, as though every sentence was displacing what was in there and sloshing her brain around. When Ellen finished, she said, "So, he'll probably try to go back and get them." She clicked her teeth together twice. "I wish we knew *when*."

Ellen said, "I was worried about Rosa, but she has Saturday nights off, too, so that's good."

"Really?" Temerity perked up. "Would this Eric jerk know that?"

Ellen shrugged. "Sure, I mean, the work assignment list is posted, and he's one of the managers, or was . . . So, yes, he would."

"And it sounds like he's obsessed with revenge as well as his 'gourmet foods.'" Temerity scoffed. "Well, best you can do is keep an eye on Rosa, I suppose. If Eric does come, is there anybody to confront him?"

"There's two new security guards. I don't think they like him very much," Ellen said, remembering the offensive hand gesture Eric had given them on his parting.

"That'll do. Is there any way to make sure one of them is close to where he hid the drugs, so that they're likely to spot him?"

"One of them will be stationed on the dock. They always are for the night shift. They have a booth that's pretty close to the restrooms. And they have walkie-talkie thingies, so they can call each other."

"So all you would need to do is make some noise, you know, knock over some boxes or something, if he comes," Temerity said. "Like you did before, with the car alarm. I wish Rosa knew you were looking out for her."

"I . . . uh, actually talked to her, once," Ellen said.

Temerity slid her hand across the table to find Ellen's. She patted it. "You're coming along quite nicely," she said. "Practically an extrovert."

They both sat for a minute. Ellen was fighting the guilt demon. If only she could speak up, Rosa wouldn't be in jeopardy and Eric might already be in jail. What if he hurt her or someone else? She felt the thrum of her accelerated heartbeat in her jaw and cheeks, which she kept puffing out to try to ease the tension there. Then she said, "There's something else."

Temerity turned attentively toward her. Ellen said, "When I saw Lydia, she told me that her mom had woken up. They're going to see her tomorrow. I didn't want to say anything in front of Justice, you know, until we talked about it."

"Really?" Temerity looked excited. "That's great news. I mean, hopefully she'll recover now."

Ellen wasn't so sure. She'd seen the unnatural angle of Maddy's neck in the bus, and the breathing tubes at the hospital. Sometimes not being able to see protected Temerity as well as hobbled her. "Maybe," was all she said.

"We need to go see her!" Temerity said.

"I'm not sure we can get in." Ellen explained about how she'd been lucky the last time, sneaking in with the linen delivery.

Temerity considered this. "I'll just bet," she said thoughtfully, "that they come every day. I mean, it's a big place, right?" Ellen agreed that it was. "Okay, so they have tons of dirty sheets and scrubs and stuff, every day. We might get lucky again."

Ellen was twitching already. It was one thing for her to move around unseen, but another to trespass into a restricted facility for a second time, with Temerity in tow. But Temerity had her heart set, Ellen could see, and once that huge heart was pulsing forward, there was little or no way to stop it.

To change the subject, Ellen asked, "Do you think Justice will really move out?"

Temerity pursed her lips and sighed. "No," she said. "I mean, he does own this place with me, after all. I think it's more likely that he'd move Amanda in here. For a while anyway."

"Then why didn't you ask him that?"

"Because then he won't think it was his idea," she said.

"Oh," Ellen said, and wondered what that meant.

Seth was feeling well enough to sit at the table for dinner, which Justice fixed when he got back from walking Runt. They ate pasta, and after much prodding, Ellen told the story of the attack on the bus, explaining that was how she had first "met" the detective. Seth listened, rapt, and then exclaimed, "He's so cool."

Ellen smiled crookedly, and surprised herself by saying, "Yes, he is."

"And now," Justice said, as he pushed his plate back, "tonight's movie presentation will begin in just a few minutes. Tem, you get the dishes, Ellen, you man the microwave popcorn, and Seth, come with me."

The movie was an old one, black-and-white. It opened with ships at sea, with the tall masts and billowing white sails. Ellen remembered Seth saying he liked the painting of the tall ships at the library, and knew that was why Justice had rented it. The hues, Ellen decided, all of them silver and gray and rich blacks, made the picture seem much more magical than full color. And this was the kind of story she liked best, filled with action and good deeds and people who did the right thing, because to do otherwise would have made life not worth living. There were storms and battles with pirates and a pretty heroine who could use a sword. Ellen sat near Temerity and whispered the action bits.

Seth fell asleep before the ship sailed off over the horizon, and Justice carried him to bed, with Temerity and Runt trailing behind to tuck him in. Ellen went up to her own cozy room and tried to go to sleep, but images of the ocean, silver and vast, filled with promise and adventure, floated in her mind's eye, and she kept wanting to know what was over that sterling line of the horizon.

The next morning, she and Temerity were in front of the long-term care facility before eight a.m. Ellen had been able to sleep a few hours, which, in addition to the five she'd gotten the day before, seemed to be sufficient. The morning was bitterly cold, and the air stung her nostrils. Ellen didn't have much hope that the linen truck would come this early.

But as it turned out, they didn't need it. Monday, it appeared, was visiting day, and though there was certainly not a stream of people, the occasional individual or family was arriving or leaving. Temerity and Ellen were able to trail in behind a man who stopped to hold the door open for Temerity. He went to the tiny office to sign in, but

Ellen turned aside and directed Temerity down the hall to the stair-well. They made their way to the second floor, and went down the temporarily deserted hallway until Ellen found Maddy's room and listened at the door. There was nothing but the quiet hiss of the ma-chines. They went in.

At first Ellen could see no difference from the last time she had been there. Maddy lay in the bed, her eyes closed and lifeless, and then Ellen realized that the artificial lung machine was gone, and Maddy's chest rose and fell, almost imperceptibly, but on its own.

Temerity felt her way along the bed until she had oriented herself, and then she leaned down and whispered, "Maddy?"

Nothing. She tried it again. "Maddy? Can you hear me?"

The eyelids fluttered, opened a fraction, and closed again. Ellen whispered, "Her eyelids moved."

Temerity smiled and, extending a hand, she found first an arm, then a shoulder, and finally, the woman's cheek. She stroked it gently. "Maddy? Can you hear me?" she said again.

The lids fluttered again, and then opened halfway. The pupils swiveled from side to side, unfocused, slid over Ellen without seeing, then, finally, they settled on Temerity, and the brow tightened. There was an audible rush of air as she opened her mouth, then a single word came out. "Thirsty," she rasped.

Ellen searched around. On the tiny table next to the bed was a plastic pitcher and a Styrofoam cup with a straw. She took hold of it and gave it to Temerity, who explored it, and then held it to Maddy's mouth. The woman sipped, then ran her tongue around her lips.

"Who . . . are you?" she whispered. There was barely any sound.

"My name is Temerity," Temerity said softly. "I'm here with my friend Ellen, who helped Lydia on the bus when it crashed. We've been keeping an eye on her, she's doing great."

Maddy's face contracted. "What's going . . . to . . . happen to . . . her?" she croaked. "Am I . . . going to die?"

"Someday, yes," Temerity said lightly. "But not today, and Lydia is coming to see you."

Maddy's eyes opened fully for the first time at that.

"Has anyone told you where she is?" Temerity asked.

Maddy frowned and then said, "No." Ellen got the impression she had wanted to shake her head but had not been able to do it.

"She's with a wonderful family, they are taking great care of her. But she misses you." Temerity stopped stroking for a moment when a tear touched her finger, then she wiped it away and went on. "She'll be glad you're okay."

"I'm not . . . though," Maddy said. "What will . . . happen to her?"

"That's up to you," Temerity told her. "The reason we came is to tell you that Lydia is doing as well as you could hope. If you get better, she'll be waiting for you, but just in case you don't, well, then you have to do something now, while you can."

Maddy's eyes, though still slightly unfocused, were more alert. She tracked Temerity as best she could without being able to turn her head.

"You need to assign someone to be Lydia's legal guardian. That way they can make decisions for her, and if anything happens to you, they'll be there for her."

"She's all . . . I have," Maddy struggled to say, tears streaming from her eyes.

Ellen felt a surge of something going through her, firming her spine and building pressure in her chest. Suddenly she burst out, "And you'll still have her." Maddy's eyes found and fixed on Ellen now. Ellen went on. "She loves you. I know because she told me. She will want to be with you whenever she can, but she needs someone to take care of her now, and it can't be you. Not for a while anyway." Even without the ability to move anything but her face, Ellen could see that Maddy was feeling the weight of what she had said. "Listen to me," Ellen said, amazing herself at her own forcefulness, "because I don't know much, but I know about this. I think that you are a good mom, and you wouldn't want Lydia to never be sure where she'll be tomorrow, or who will be there for her while you have to stay here." Ellen crossed her fingers tightly and remembered that day, so long ago, when she had been led away by a woman in a uniform into a life without constancy or love. "You don't have to let her go, but you have to let someone else take care of her. That's what I think, anyway."

Maddy wheezed slowly. "I . . . understand."

Spent, Ellen backed away and stood by the door to listen for anyone who might be coming. Temerity took over. "You have been very brave," Temerity told her. "And Lydia has a real friend, a guardian angel in Ellen. I want you to know that, and not be afraid. The people Lydia are staying with are a really good family. Ellen went to make sure, without them knowing it. She thinks you can trust them to do the right thing. And believe me, you can trust *her* to know what the alternative is."

Ellen heard voices outside in the hallway. "Temerity," she hissed in warning. She opened the door a crack and peeked out. The Rushes and Serena Hoffman were coming down the hall with a man in a white jacket. Lydia was in Mr. Rush's arms. Ellen closed the door and looked desperately around the tiny room. The curtain hiding the other bed was pulled closed. "Come on!" She grabbed her friend's arm and pulled her behind it just as the door opened.

"Mama?" Ellen heard Lydia say fearfully.

"Lydia . . . My baby!" Maddy said, and there was both sorrow and ecstasy in the three words.

"Can she give her mom a kiss?" Mrs. Rush asked.

"I think that would be fine," came the unfamiliar voice of the doctor. "Ms. Carson, how are you feeling?" the doctor asked after a moment.

"Hazy," Maddy said. "Thank you for . . . bringing Lydia . . . to see me."

"I knew you would wake up, Mama," Lydia said. "Now you can come home with us. It's warm there!"

"It might be a little while before your mom can go home, sweetie," came Mrs. Rush's voice.

"Listen . . . to me," Maddy forced out in her breathy exhale. There were excruciating pauses as she struggled to fill her lungs with enough air to speak. "I want you . . . to take Lydia . . . for now. If . . . anything happens . . . to me . . . then you can . . . I want . . . legal . . . understand?"

"Ms. Carson? My name is Serena Hoffman, and I'm the social worker on Lydia's case. If you mean that, I can get a verbal agreement from you, with witnesses, saying that you relinquish custody to the Ru—"

She was cut off by Mr. Rush. "No, I think it would be best if we have temporary custody. That way when Madeline gets better, or well enough, she can maybe come stay with us until she can live on her own again. But if she can't make decisions for her daughter, then we should be in a position to do it for her, if she trusts us. And I also think that part of that agreement should be that we will bring Lydia every Monday, more often if she wants, to visit with her mom. Would that be possible?"

There was quiet, and then Serena said, "I don't see why not. Ms. Carson, what do you think?"

"I think . . . yes. Lydia?"

"Yes, Mama?"

"Don't be afraid . . . you have . . . an . . . angel . . . someone to watch . . . out for you."

Ellen could almost hear Lydia smile at the secret, and she felt Temerity squeeze her arm. "I know, Mama. Not everyone can see her. Did you see her?"

"Yes, baby . . . She was . . . here . . . She told me . . . it's okay."

The doctor cleared his throat. "I think that this might be a bit too much excitement for right now. Would it be all right if you all waited outside for a little while? I'd like your mom to rest. Then you can come back and say good-bye for today."

"I think that's a good idea," Mrs. Rush said. There was a rustling of movement and then Mrs. Rush spoke again, her voice thick with emotion. "Thank you for trusting us."

"Thank . . . you."

Serena Hoffman said, "I'm going to prepare this document for you now, just so we have something in outline form, and then we'll have a lawyer write it up and look it over and everyone can witness it. We'll be back in a bit."

There was the shuffling of feet and the sound of a kiss, given with the purity of a child's lips, and then only the sound of the machines.

Ellen peeked out. The room was empty. She and Temerity came out from behind the curtain and went to the bedside.

"Good-bye," Temerity whispered, but Maddy's eyes were closed, though now Ellen could detect life in the woman's sleeping face.

They made their way back out of the building and into the cold air. Neither spoke until they had come to the bus stop. Then Temerity raised her face to the cold wind, breathed deeply, smiled broadly, and said, "She's a good mom, I'm glad."

Ellen was, too. She was busy listening to her heart, which was beating with a steady rhythm. *Lydia CARson, Lydia CARson.* And Ellen knew that Lydia would be loved.

29

"Do you have anything planned for this afternoon?" Justice asked. "Maybe some bull-riding or, I know, we could throw axes at each other."

"You go ahead," Temerity said. "Seth and I are going to help Ellen make bread."

"Oh goody," Justice intoned, "fun with organic chemistry. I wonder if yeast has ever spontaneously exploded."

"Fine," Temerity told him. "You don't get any!"

It was the perfect antidote to too much excitement. Ellen was delighted at the way the yeast foamed in the bowl, and she was surprised to find that the dough didn't feel like wet fabric at all, more like spongy clay. It stuck to her fingers and took patience, but the smell of the bread baking was better than chocolate. Thelma and Beth arrived shortly after it came out of the oven, and Seth served them thick slices with butter and honey, his face glowing with pride as they congratulated him on his culinary expertise. Ellen watched the women closely—both of them looked at Seth in a new way—

and with a surge of pride. Ellen realized that she *recognized* an emotion. They were "coveting," but this time, it was a good thing.

When everyone else had left or gone to bed, Ellen put on her warm jacket and went for a walk. She went to the bakery and watched through the grated door for a long time, not just observing now but absorbing.

She slept most of the day Tuesday, exhausted from the odd hours and the unexpected interactions. When she went to work in the evening, she left especially early, because she wanted to be sure to be there well before Rosa. Ellen might not be able to face up to reporting an attack, but she could darn well try to make sure there wasn't another one.

Ellen checked the work assignment and for a change was pleased that she was working in the same section as Rosa and Kiki. They had auto goods, and she had the parallel aisle. The early evening went smoothly, and when the break came, Ellen went not to the broom closet, but to the women's room on the docks.

She locked herself into a stall with her coffee and a sandwich she'd brought from home. She could hear, through the metal vent high in the wall, the comings and goings of men in their bathroom next door. It was almost time to go back to work when she heard the distinct sound of someone turning the metal trash can upside down.

Ellen crept out of the stall and went to listen at the wall. She heard scraping, rustling, then the door opening. Ellen waited a few seconds, then pushed open her own door to the dock.

She could see the form of a man retreating quickly into the stacked boxes on the dock. He disappeared into the shadows and did not emerge on the other side. Ellen slipped out and found a vantage point of her own. When nothing happened in ten minutes, she decided that maybe she was wrong, and it hadn't been Eric, or, better yet, he'd taken his drugs and left.

Ellen went back to her cart and was cleaning in electronics when Thelma approached Rosa and Kiki. "Ladies, someone decided to bowl a few gallons of strawberry nectar in aisle four. Could you get your mops and join me there?"

Normally this would not have been unusual, but Ellen had just been through that aisle, and it had been fine. Cautiously, she went the opposite way, and doubled back around to where the spill had been reported.

It was a mess. Not just a single plastic jug, but several had burst onto the already cleaned floor. Rosa and Kiki were surveying it with shaking heads. "Looks like somebody overstacked the second shelf," Kiki said, pointing. Ellen followed her finger and saw what she meant. Where there was otherwise a solid three rows of plastic gallon jugs, a gap, ten feet up, showed that a half dozen had fallen.

"We're going to need another bucket," Rosa said. "Ugh, this stuff is so sticky."

"I'll get it. And we'll need the green cleanser, too," Kiki said. "I'll be right back." She spun on her heel, and walked away, erect and disapproving. Rosa sighed and, taking hold of her mop handle, went to work.

Ellen was wondering if she could help without being drawn into any kind of exchange, when a movement arrested her. On the second shelf, just above Rosa, something had moved. Ellen squinted her eyes and stared into the shadows. It was Eric, and he was looking down at Rosa with an evil grin. He turned, and crawled back deeper onto the shelf, and in the next moment, a large crate marked CANNED CORN, 200 COUNT began to slide from the back toward the edge. Ellen started forward, but Rosa had shifted to the far side of the aisle, out of range of the falling objects, and if Ellen shouted, Eric would almost certainly have plenty of time to get away, and he would be back.

In front of Ellen was a set of movable stairs that the floor staff used to access things from the higher shelves. Wishing it weren't so high, Ellen started up. She clambered out onto the shelf through the stacked canned goods until she reached the middle of the shelving where there was a kind of narrow tunnel between the goods. On her hands and knees she began to crawl in Eric's direction. In the twenty seconds it took her to get into position behind him, he had pushed the crate all the way to the edge, and he was crouching, leaning out, peering down, no doubt judging when Rosa would be in his line of fire.

"Hi, there," Ellen said.

Eric spun, lost his balance, scrabbled for a handhold, but found nothing except the slick side of the crate, and toppled out backward. Ellen moved quickly into his place and looked down. Eric was on the floor, stunned, four feet away from a startled Rosa, but pulling himself into a sitting position. Ellen saw Rosa look up, register the heavy groceries he had intended to crush her with, and a howl of rage came from the little woman.

Eric sat fully up, and as he did Rosa's string mop, heavy with sticky syrup, hit him hard in the face. He sputtered and spun onto his hands and knees, slipped in the syrup, and went down again as the mop came down on the back of his head. Rosa was screaming with great force, "You evil, horrible man!" Her shouts had called attention, and Ellen could see Kiki and Thelma running toward the fray. Eric managed to get a hold of the mop when Rosa struck again, and he used it to pull himself up, sending Rosa spinning against the shelf as he yanked it away from her. He wiped the syrup from his eyes and spotted Rosa doubled over. With a look of extreme malice, he grabbed a gallon can from the nearest shelf and raised it over his head.

But he never brought it down. Ellen had only ever seen a little bit of football on TV, but the motion Thelma made now reminded her, forcefully, of the kicker. Without slowing her run, Thelma arrived behind him, swung her right foot up and planted it firmly between Eric's legs from the back.

He rose six inches off the ground, released the can, which hit him in the head, and fell back into the pink ooze, clutching his crotch, with his eyes rolling in his head.

Ignoring Eric, Thelma and Kiki went straight to Rosa and helped her up. Ellen retreated, shuffling herself backward, and her knee landed on something squishy.

She looked down. It was the package from the bathroom. It took Ellen three seconds to realize that meant Eric would not be connected to it. Without thinking, she pushed it to the edge of the shelf with the back of her hand, and let it drop over the edge. It landed on Eric. She ducked back, crawled for all she was worth back to the ladder, and climbed down. Everyone had gone to the opposite aisle to see what the commotion was, and no one had noticed Ellen. She moved down the aisle until she was directly across from the action.

Thelma was limping. "Are you all right?" Kiki asked her.

"I think I broke something," Thelma grunted, hopping on one foot. Other people were running toward them now, including one of the security guards. Rosa shouted, "It's Eric, he tried to push that on me!" She was pointing upward. "But he fell, and—"

"All right, on your feet," the security guard said, leaning over and picking up the package off Eric's chest. "What's this?"

Eric, still writhing on the ground, unable to unclasp his hands from between his legs, registered the package. "It's not mine," he wheezed. The guard opened the top of the envelope and looked in. Then he sniffed at it and recoiled.

"This is meth. Get up," he said, yanking Eric to his feet.

Eric said in a painfully high voice, "It fell off the shelf, anyone could have put it up there! You'll see, check for prints! Mine aren't on it. You can't pin this on me." Doubled over with pain, he groaned. "I just came back to get my jacket and that witch attacked me."

Thelma snorted. "You keep your jacket on a ten-foot-high shelf in canned goods?"

"Let's go," the security guard said. He dragged a limping, sticky Eric away toward the office. There was a moment of quiet, and then Thelma turned to Rosa.

"Nice work!" she exclaimed, raising a hand for a high five, which Rosa performed shyly. "Mop in the face! Excellent. He *so* had that coming."

"But will it be enough?" Kiki asked. She was twisting her hands together. "What if he gets off? I mean, he did try to attack Rosa, but nothing happened, and we can't prove it was him before."

"If that's crystal meth," Thelma pointed out, "which we all knew he was doing and selling, though we couldn't prove it, he won't be bothering anyone for a long time. *Ouch.*" She leaned over and massaged her foot, which she had tested with her weight.

"But what if they can't prove it's his?" Kiki asked, fretting. "You heard him."

Ellen had heard enough. She went quickly back to the locker room, sure that it would be empty, and scribbled a quick note. Then she went to Rosa's locker and slipped the folded paper through the slots at the top. It was a simple note, just a reminder to do something, really. And because it was something totally different, Ellen Homes signed her name.

All the note said was *Change the deodorizer in the dock men's room. Ellen.*

It didn't occur to Ellen to call Detective Barclay until she got home in the morning. After she told the story to Temerity, her friend volunteered to do it. "Oh, he'll love this!" Temerity said. "Gourmet food boxes, you said?"

The detective stopped by that afternoon. He was grateful, but grim. "Unfortunately, this guy has a good lawyer. They are already claiming that he was framed by this Rosa Suerte, and there weren't any of his prints on the package. So it's going to be hard to prove that it was his. It's possible a judge won't even allow it without something else to tie it to him."

Ellen, who was sitting in the armchair away from the detective, cleared her throat. "You'll get proof," she said.

Barclay looked over at her and sighed. "I'm glad you have confidence in me," he said. "Let's hope I deserve it."

"You do," Ellen told him.

And she meant it.

30

The motion-activated wildlife camera with a photo card that held five hundred pictures hidden in the deodorizer and Rosa were soon united. Detective Barclay and a team of detectives, who had descended on Costco after testing the methamphetamine and finding it a match to the batch they had been tracking for months, were stunned to be presented with actual photos of a gloved Eric not only recovering the drugs before his attack on Rosa, but also of him selling them to coworkers in the bathroom, in the days before. The detectives said they would never have expected that kind of tactic from a woman like Rosa, who just blushed and said she'd known he was bad news and she'd been keeping an eye on him.

Rosa was a hero, and Ellen thought that was appropriate. The gossip addict, who was so eager to know everybody's business, had actually produced information that was not only useful, but incriminating.

And there was much rejoicing, though Ellen did not participate in it. She did her work, as usual, but with a lighter heart. She had not found the courage to condemn someone publicly, but she had done it anyway, a different way.

The quiet backbeat had pulsed its way to the front, and Ellen was able to watch, and enjoy, the result of the syncopation.

The next day, however, was anything but relaxing. The loft seemed crowded with people. The first to arrive was Serena Hoffman, who spent a long time sitting with Seth at the table, talking to him about his future. Not long after, Beth and Thelma came in, and the four of them discussed plans as well. Then the three women left together for something called a "home inspection," and Ellen came out of hiding.

Seth was on the sofa with his book of comics, one hand scratching Runt's head in lazy circles. He looked up when Ellen sat down next to him.

"Are you going to live with them?" Ellen asked without preamble.

"I hope so," Seth said. "I mean, I *like* it here." He looked down and blushed.

Ellen's mouth curled up on one side. "I think you got the best of the deal," she told him. "Temerity and Justice will still be around, but you'll have a family of your own. That'll be nice, huh?"

Seth angled his head sideways and said, "Beth says I have to help out at the clinic." His eyes sparkled at that. Then he frowned thoughtfully. "I never thought I'd live with two women."

"Two *kick-ass* women," Ellen added. "Let me tell you a little story about why Thelma has that cast on her foot."

So she told him the story of the night before, leaving out her own part in it, and enjoying his exclamations immensely. When she was done he said, "You should write that down."

Ellen stood up and smiled. "I already did," she said. "What time is it?"

Seth shrugged. "I think it's, like, seven? You going to work?"

"No," Ellen said. "I took the night off. I've been really . . . busy lately, and I just thought I could use a break. Justice and Temerity are staying with you, right?"

"Right." Seth focused hard on Runt for a moment, and the dog's tail thumped the floor as it wagged. "Justice, he's okay, isn't he?" Seth asked.

"Yeah," Ellen agreed. "He's okay. Lots of people are. Not everyone, as we both know, but more than you'd think, I'm finding out." Ellen smiled again and went upstairs to get her coat. She paused in the window to look across the street.

And found someone looking back. The woman raised a hand and waved. With a sense of unreality, Ellen waved back.

When she went back downstairs, Temerity was coming out of the hallway with her violin. "Do you guys mind if I practice a little bit?" she asked.

Seth looked curious, watching the instrument with suspicious, narrowed eyes, but he agreed, "Sure."

"I'm going out," Ellen told her.

"You're going out?" Temerity cocked her head and smiled impishly. "On a Tuesday night? Anywhere in particular?"

"Yes, in fact," Ellen told her, ignoring the flush of heat to her cheeks.

"Uh-huh." Temerity sat down and began to play a few simple notes, then she built on it with harmonies until it was happy and full. *Like me,* thought Ellen, smiling. She opened the door and stood for a moment on the landing.

Temerity stopped playing and tilted her head. She heard it, too. Lush piano music was wafting up the stairwell. It was too clear to be coming from behind the heavy fire doors that sealed off each loft. Ellen went to the railing and peered over it. On the second-floor landing, she could just make out that the door was propped open.

Ellen spun back and walked straight to Temerity. She took her arm and pulled her up off the sofa. "What are you doing?" Temerity asked.

"Making myself useful." Ellen dragged her, violin and all, out the door and onto the landing.

The music was glorious here in the echoing stairwell. They both stood listening as Seth leaned his head around the doorjamb and Runt whined quietly. Seth patted the dog's head and he relaxed into happy panting.

Ellen leaned toward Temerity and whispered, "Do it."

"Do what?" Temerity said.

"Find out. Take the chance. It's for you, and you know it."

With a little tremble of her lips that stretched into a shy smile, Temerity lifted the violin, nestled her chin against it, and drew the bow.

The melody below was joined by a harmony from above. They connected in the middle of this stairwell in a city, sent and received by two like souls making something out of nothing.

Something new, Ellen thought.

Alchemy.

The streets were misty and cold, but the smell of snow was in the air. Ellen walked ten blocks, watching the way people hunkered down away from the cold. *As if they could avoid it,* she thought, amused. At last she came to the place she'd been seeking. She bought a ticket, even making tentative eye contact when the lady in the booth told Ellen to enjoy herself, went through the lobby and into the darkened room. She waited as her eyes adjusted to the dim, shimmering light.

When she found what she was looking for, she went and sat down. Rupert started and turned to see who had chosen the seat right next to him in the almost empty cinema. Ellen smiled shyly and then turned her eyes up to the screen. She watched, enthralled and embraced by the story that unfolded before her in shades of silver light, like rain, like mist, like magic.

And she was content.

Acknowledgments

A million thank-yous to the team at Putnam, especially Nita Taublib, who keeps me on my toes and at my computer, and Meaghan Wagner, who keeps me sane and laughing. To my friends at City of Hope hospital, Dr. Clarke Anderson, the nurses, and the social workers, who make such a difference in the world, I thank the universe you are out there, making life and its trials just a bit easier for the innocents who suffer. As always I am grateful for the constant love and support of my family, Joseph, Creason, and Caleb; how magnificent you are. This book would never have been written if it weren't for Paul Fedorko. I'm the luckiest client in bookdom to have an agent so supportive and kind. And last, I have to acknowledge my author friends who have said such kind things, helped me learn the craft, and been there to answer all my dumb questions. Julie Leto and Julie Kenner, you rock!